THE BELOVÉD VAGABOND

WILLIAM J. LOCKE

CONTENTS

CHAPTER I

THIS is not a story about myself. Like Canning's organ-grinder I have none to tell. It is the story of Paragot, the belovéd vagabond—please pronounce his name French-fashion—and if I obtrude myself on your notice it is because I was so much involved in the medley of farce and tragedy which made up some years of his life, that I don't know how to tell the story otherwise. To Paragot I owe everything. He is at once my benefactor, my venerated master, my beloved friend, my creator. Clay in his hands, he moulded me according to his caprice, and inspired me with the breath of life. My existence is drenched with the colour of Paragot. I lay claim to no personality of my own, and any *obiter dicta* that may fall from my pen in the course of the ensuing narrative are but reflections of Paragot's philosophy. Men have spoken evil of him. He snapped his fingers at calumny, but I winced, never having reached the calm altitudes of scorn wherein his soul has its habitation. I burned to defend him, and I burn now; and that is why I propose to write his *apologia*, his justification.

Why he singled me out for adoption from among the unwashed urchins of London I never could conjecture. Once I asked him.[6]

"Because," said he, "you were ugly, dirty, ricketty, under-sized, underfed and wholly uninteresting. Also because your mother was the very worst washer-woman that ever breathed gin into a shirt-front."

I did not resent these charges, direct and implied, against my mother. She did launder villainously, and she did drink gin, and of the nine uncared-for gutter-snipes she brought into the world, I think I was the most unkempt and neglected. I know that Sunday-school books tell you to love your mother; but if the only maternal caresses you could remember were administered by means of a wet pair of woollen drawers or the edge of a hot flat-iron, you would find filial piety a virtue somewhat abstract. Verily do earwigs care more for their progeny than did my mother. She sold me body and soul to Paragot for half-a-crown.

It fell out thus.

One morning, laden with his—technically speaking—clean linen, I knocked at the door of Paragot's chambers. He called them chambers, for he was nothing if not grandiloquent, but really they consisted in an attic in Tavistock Street, Covent Garden, above the curious club over which he presided. I knocked, then, at the door. A sonorous voice bade me enter. Paragot lay in bed, smoking a huge pipe with a porcelain bowl and reading a book. The fact of one individual having a room all to himself impressed me so greatly with a sense of luxury, refinement and power, that I neglected to observe its pitifulness and squalor. Nor of Paragot's personal appearance was I critical. He had long black hair, and a long black beard, and long black finger-nails. The last were so long and commanding that I thought ashamedly of my own bitten fingertips,[7] and vowed that when I too became a great man, able to smoke a porcelain pipe of mornings in my own room, my nails should equal his in splendour.

"I have brought the washing, Sir," I announced, "and, please, Sir, mother says I'm not to let you have it unless you settle up for the last three weeks."

I had a transient vision of swarthy, hairy legs, as Paragot leaped out of bed. He stood over me, man of all the luxuries that he was, in his nightshirt. Fancy having a shirt for the day and a shirt for the night!

"Do you mean that you will dispute possession of it with me, *vi et armis?*"

"Yes, Sir," said I, confused.

He laughed, clapped me on the shoulder, called me David, Jack the Giant-Killer, and bade me deliver the washing-book. I fumbled in the pocket of my torn jacket and handed him a greasy, dog's-eared mass of paper. As soon as his eyes fell on it, I realised my mistake, and produced the washing book from the other pocket.

"I've given you the wrong one, Sir," said I, reaching for the treasure I had surrendered.

But he threw himself on his bed and dived his legs beneath the clothes.

"Wonderful!" he cried. "He is four foot nothing, he looks like a yard of pack-thread, he would fight me for an ill-washed shirt and a pair of holes with bits of sock round them, and he reads 'Paradise Lost'!"

He made a gesture of throwing the disreputable epic at my head, and I curved my arm in an attitude only too familiarly defensive.[8]

"I found it in a bundle of washing, Sir," I cried apologetically.

At home reading was the unforgivable sin. Had my mother discovered me poring over the half intelligible but wholly fascinating story of Adam and Eve and the Devil, she would have beaten me with the first implement to her hand. I had a moment's terror lest the possession of a work of literature should be so horrible a crime that even Paragot would chastise me.

To my consternation he thrust the tattered thing—it was an antiquated sixpenny edition—under my nose and commanded me to read.

"'Of Man's first disobedience'—Go on. If you can read it intelligently I'll pay your mother. If you can't I'll write to her politely to say that I resent having my washing sent home by persons of no education."

I began in great fear, but having, I suppose, an instinctive appreciation of letters, I mouthed the rolling lines not too brokenly.

"What's a Heavenly Muse?" asked Paragot, as soon as I paused. I had not the faintest idea.

"Do you think it's a Paradisiacal back yard where they keep the Horse of the Apocalypse?"

I caught a twinkle in the blue eyes which he bent fiercely upon me.

"If you please, Sir," said I, "I think it is the Bird of Paradise."

Then we both laughed; and Paragot bidding me sit on the wreck of a cane-bottomed chair, gave me my first lesson in Greek Mythology. He talked for nearly an hour, and I,[9] ragged urchin of the London streets, my wits sharpened by hunger and ill-usage, sat spell-bound on my comfortless perch, while he unfolded the tale of Gods and Goddesses, and unveiled Olympus before my enraptured vision.

"Boy," said he suddenly, "can you cook a herring?"

I came down to earth with a bang. Stunned I stared at him. I distinctly remember wondering where I was.

"Can you cook a herring?" he shouted.

"Yes, Sir," I cried, jumping to my feet.

"Then cook two—one for you and one for me. You'll find them somewhere about the room, also tea and bread and butter and a gas-stove, and when all is ready let me know."

He settled himself comfortably in bed and went on reading his book. It was Hegel's Philosophy of History. I tried to read it afterwards and found that it passed my understanding.

In a confused dream of gods and herrings, I set about my task. Heaven only knows how I managed to succeed. In my childish imagination Jupiter was clothed in the hirsute majesty of Paragot.

And I was to breakfast with him!

The herrings and a half-smoked pipe shared a plate on the top of the ricketty chest of drawers. I had to blow the ash off the fish. A paper of tea and a loaf of bread I found in a higgledy-piggledy mixture of clothes, books and papers. My godlike friend had carelessly put his hair-brush into the butter. The condition of the sole cooking utensil warred even against my sense of the fitness of gridirons, and I cleansed it with his towel.

Since then I have breakfasted in the houses of the wealthy, I have lunched at the Café Anglais, I have dined at the Savoy but never have I eaten, never till they give me a welcoming banquet in the Elysian fields, shall I eat so ambrosial a meal as that first herring with Paragot.

When I had set it on the little deal table, he deigned to remember my existence, and closing his book, rose, donned a pair of trousers and sat down. He gave me my first lesson in table-manners.

"Boy," said he, "if you wish to adorn the high social spheres for which you are destined, you must learn the value of convention. Bread and cheese-straws and asparagus and the leaves of an artichoke are eaten with the fingers; but not herrings or sweetbreads or ice cream. As regards the last you are doubtless in the habit of extracting it from a disappointing wine-glass with your tongue. This in *notre monde* is regarded as bad form. '*Notre Monde*' is French, a language which you will have to learn. Its great use is in talking to English people when you don't want them to understand what you say. They pretend they do, for they are too vain to admit their ignorance. The wise man profits by the vanity of his fellow-creatures. If I were not wise after this manner, should I be here eating herrings in Tavistock Street, Covent Garden?"

I was too full of food and adoration to reply. I gazed at him dumbly worshipping and choked over a cup of tea. When I recovered he questioned me as to my home life, my schooling, my ideas of a future state and my notions of a career in this world. The height of my then ambition was to keep a fried-fish shop. The restaurateur with whom my good mother dealt used to sit for hours in his doorway in Drury Lane reading a book, and I considered this a most dignified and scholarly avocation. When I made this naïve avowal to Paragot, he looked at me with a queer pity in his eyes, and muttered an exclamation in a foreign tongue. I have never met anyone so full of strange oaths as Paragot. As to my religious convictions, they were chiefly limited to a terrifying conception of the hell to which my mother daily consigned me. In devils, fires, chains and pitchforks its establishment was as complete as any *inferno* depicted by Orcagna. I used to wake up of nights in a cold sweat through dreaming of it.

"My son," said Paragot, "the most eminent divines of the Church of England will tell you that a material hell with consuming flames is an exploded fallacy. I can tell you the same without being an eminent divine. The wicked carry their own hell about with them during life—here, somewhere between the gullet and the pit of the stomach, and it prevents their enjoyment of herrings which smell vilely of gas."

"There ain't no devils, then?" I asked.

"*Sacré mille diables*, No!" he shouted. "Haven't I been exhausting myself with telling you so?"

I said little, but to this day I remember the thrilling sense of deliverance from a horror which had gone far to crush the little childish joy allowed me by circumstance. There was no fiery hell, no red-hot pincers, no eternal frizzling and sizzling of the flesh, like unto that of the fish in Mr. Samuel's fish-shop. Paragot had transformed me by a word into a happy young pagan. My eyes swam as I swallowed my last bit of bread and butter.

"What is your name?" asked Paragot.

"Augustus, Sir."

"Augustus, what?"

"Smith," I murmured. "Same as mother's."

"I was forgetting," said he. "Now if there is one name I dislike more than Smith it is Augustus. I have been thinking of a very nice name for you. It is Asticot. It expresses you better than Augustus Smith."

"It is a very good name, Sir," said I politely.

I learned soon after that it is a French word meaning the little grey worms which fishermen call "gentles," and that it was not such a complimentary appellation as I had imagined; but Asticot I became, and Asticot I remained for many a year.

"Wash up the things, my little Asticot," said he, "and afterwards we will discuss future arrangements."

According to his directions I took the tray down to a kind of scullery on the floor below. The wet plates and cups I dried on a greasy rag which I found lying on the sink; and this seemed to me a refinement of luxurious living; for at home, when we did wash plates, we merely held them under the tap till the remains of food ran off, and we never thought of drying them. When I returned to the bedroom Paragot was dressed for the day. His long lean wrists and hands protruded far through the sleeves of an old brown jacket. He wore a grey flannel shirt and an old bit of black ribbon done up in a bow by way of a tie; his slouch hat, once black, was now green with age, and his boots were innocent of blacking. But my eyes were dazzled by a heavy gold watch chain across his waistcoat and I thought him the most glorious of betailored beings.

"My little Asticot," said he, "would you like to forsake your gentle mother's wash-tub and your dreams of a fried-fish shop and enter my service? I, the heir of all the ages, am driven by Destiny to running The Lotus Club downstairs. We call it 'Lotus' because we eat tripe to banish memory. The members meet together in order to eat tripe, drink beer and hear me talk. You can eat tripe and hear me talk too, and that will improve both your mind and your body. While Cherubino, the waiter, teaches you how to be a scullion, I will instruct you in philosophy. The sofa in the Club will make an excellent bed for you, and your wages will be eighteen pence a week."

He thrust his hands in his trouser pockets, and rattling his money looked at me with an enquiring air. I returned his gaze for a while, lost in a delirious wonder. I tried to speak. Something stuck in my throat. I broke into a blubber and dried my eyes with my knuckles.

It was an intoxicated little Asticot that trotted by his side to my mother's residence. There over gin-and-water the bargain was struck. My mother pocketed half-a-crown and with shaky unaccustomed fingers signed her name across a penny-stamp at the foot of a document which Paragot had drawn up. I believe each of them was convinced that they had executed a legal deed. My mother after inspecting me critically for a moment wiped my nose with the piece of sacking that served as her apron and handed me over to Paragot, who marched away with his purchase as proud as if I had been a piece of second-hand furniture picked up cheap.

I may as well remark here that Paragot was not his real name; neither was Josiah Henkendyke by which he was then known to me. He had a harmless mania for names, and I have known him use half a dozen. But that of Paragot which he assumed later as his final alias is the one with which he is most associated in my mind, and to avoid confusion I must call him that from the start. Indeed, looking backward down the years, I wonder how he could ever have been anything else than Paragot. That Phœbus Apollo could once have borne the name of John Jones is unimaginable.

"Boy," said he, as we retraced our steps to Tavistock Street, "you are my thing, my chattel, my *famulus*. No slave of old belonged more completely to a free-born citizen. You will address me as 'master'!"

"Yes, Sir," said I.

"Master!" he shouted. "*Master* or *maître* or *maestro* or *magister* according to the language you are speaking. Now do you understand?"

"Yes, Master," said I.

He nodded approval. At the corner of a by-street he stopped short and held me at arm's length.

"You are a horrible object, my little Asticot," said he. "I must clothe you in a manner befitting the Lotus Club."

He ran me into a slop-dealer's and fitted me out in sundry garments in which, although they were several sizes too large for me, I felt myself clad like Solomon in all his glory. Then we went home. On the way up to his room he paused at the scullery. A dishevelled woman was tidying up.

"Mrs. Housekeeper," said he, "allow me to present you our new scullion pupil. Kindly instruct him in his duties, feed him and wash his head. Also please remember that he answers to the name of Asticot."

He swung on his heel and went downstairs humming a tune. I remained with Mrs. Housekeeper who carried out his instructions zealously. I can feel the soreness on my scalp to this day.

Thus it fell out that I quitted the maternal roof and entered the service of Paragot. I never saw my mother again, as she died soon afterwards; and as my brood of brothers and sisters vanished down the diverse gutters of London, I found myself with Paragot for all my family; and now that I have arrived at an age when a man can look back dispassionately on his past, it is my pride that I can lay my hand on my heart and avow him to be the best family that boy ever had.

CHAPTER II

THE Lotus Club was the oddest society I have met. The premises consisted of one long dingy room with two dingy windows: the furniture of a long table covered with dirty American cloth, a multitude of wooden chairs, an old sofa, two dilapidated dinner-waggons, and a frame against the wall from which, by means of clips, churchwarden pipes depended stem downwards; and by each clip was a label bearing a name. On the table stood an enormous jar of tobacco. A number of ill-washed glasses decorated the dinner-waggons. There was not a curtain, not a blind, not a picture. The further end of the room away from the door contained a huge fireplace, and on the wooden mantelpiece ticked a three-and-sixpenny clock.

During the daytime it was an abode of abominable desolation. No one came near it until nine o'clock in the evening, when one or two members straggled in, took down their long pipes and called for whisky or beer, the only alcoholic beverages the club provided. These were kept in great barrels in the scullery, presided over by Mrs. Housekeeper until it was time to prepare the supper, when Cherubino and I helped ourselves. At eleven the cloth was laid. From then till half past members came in considerable numbers. At half past supper was served. A steaming dish of tripe furnished the head of the table in front of Paragot, and a cut of cold beef the foot.

There were generally from fifteen to thirty present; men of all classes: Journalists, actors, lawyers, out-at-elbows nondescripts. I have seen one of Her Majesty's Judges and a prizefighter exchanging views across the table. A few attended regularly; but the majority seemed to be always new-comers. They supped, talked, smoked, and drank whisky until two or three o'clock in the morning and appeared to enjoy themselves prodigiously. I noticed that on departing they wrung Paragot fervently by the hand and thanked him for their delightful evening. I remembered his telling me that they came to hear him talk. He did talk: sometimes so compellingly that I would stand stock-still rapt in reverential ecstasy: once to the point of letting the potatoes I was handing round roll off the dish on to the floor. I never was so rapt again; for Cherubino picking up the potatoes and following my frightened exit, broke them over my head on the landing, by way of chastisement. The best barbers do not use hot mealy potatoes for the hair.

When the last guest had departed, Paragot mounted to his attic, Mrs. Housekeeper and Cherubino went their several ways—each went several ways, I think, for they had unchecked command during the evening over the whisky and beer barrels—and I, dragging a bundle of bedclothes from beneath the sofa, went to bed amid the fumes of tripe, gas, tobacco, alcohol and humanity, and slept the sleep of perfect happiness.

In the morning, at about eleven, I rose and prepared breakfast for Paragot and myself, which we ate together in his room. For a couple of hours he instructed me in what he was pleased to call the humanities. Then he sent me out into the street for air and exercise, with instructions to walk to Hyde Park, Westminster Abbey, St. Paul's Cathedral, Whiteley's—he always had a fresh objective for me—and to bring him back my views thereon and an account of what I had noticed on the way. When I came home I delivered myself into the hands of Mrs. Housekeeper and turned scullion again. The plates, glasses, knives and forks of the previous evening's orgy were washed and cleaned, the room swept and aired, and a meal cooked for Mrs. Housekeeper and myself which we ate at a corner of the long table. Paragot himself dined out.

On Sunday evenings the Club was shut, and as Mrs. Housekeeper did not make her appearance on the Sabbath, the remains of Saturday night's supper stayed on the table till Monday afternoon. Imagine remains of tripe thirty six hours old!

I mention this, not because it is of any great interest, but because it exhibits a certain side of Paragot's character. In those early days I was not critical. I lived in a maze of delight. Paragot was the Wonder of the Earth, my bedroom a palace chamber, and the abominable Sunday night smell pervaded my senses like the perfumes of all the Arabies.

"My son," said Paragot one morning, in the middle of a French lesson—from the first he was bent on my learning the language—"My son, I wonder whether you are going to turn out a young Caliban, and after I have shewn you the True Divinity of Things, return to your dam's god Setebos?"

He regarded me earnestly with his light blue eyes which looked so odd in his swarthy black-bearded face.

"Is there any hope for the race of Sycorax?"

As we had read "The Tempest" the day before, I understood the allusions.

"I would sooner be Ariel, Master," said I, by way of showing off my learning.

"He was an ungrateful beggar too," said Paragot. He went on talking, but I heard him not; for my childish mind quickly associated him with Prospero, and I wondered where lay his magic staff with which he could split pines and liberate tricksy spirits, and whether he had a beautiful daughter hidden in some bower of Tavistock Street, and whether the cadaverous Cherubino might not be a metamorphosed Ferdinand. He appeared the embodiment of all wisdom and power, and yet he had the air of one cheated of his kingdom. He seemed also to be of reverential age. As a matter of fact he was not yet forty.

My attention was recalled by his rising and walking about the room.

"I am making this experiment on your vile body, my little Asticot," said he, "to prove my Theory of Education. You have had, so far as it goes, what is called

8

an excellent Board School Training. You can read and write and multiply sixty-four by thirty-seven in your head, and you can repeat the Kings of England. If you had been fortunate and gone to a Public school they would have stuffed your brain full of Greek verbs and damned facts about triangles. But of the meaning of life, the value of life, the art of life, you would never have had a glimmering perception. I am going to educate you, my little Asticot, through the imagination. The intellect can look after itself. We will go now to the National Gallery."

He caught up his hat and threw me my cap, and we went out. He had a sudden, breathless way of doing things. I am sure thirty seconds had not elapsed between the idea of the National Gallery entering his head and our finding ourselves on the stairs.

We went to the National Gallery. I came away with a reeling undistinguishable mass of form and colour before my eyes. I felt sick. Only one single picture stood out clear. Paragot talked Italian art to my uncomprehending ears all the way home.

"Now," said he, when he had settled himself comfortably in his old wicker-work chair again, "which of the pictures did you like best?"

Why that particular picture (save that it is the supreme art of a supreme genius) should have alone fixed itself on my mind, I do not know. It has been one of the psychological puzzles of my life.

"A man's head, master," said I; "I can't describe it, but I think I could draw it."

"Draw it?" he echoed incredulously.

"Yes, Master."

He pulled a stump of pencil from his pocket and threw it to me. I felt luminously certain I could draw the head. A curious exaltation filled me as I sat at a corner of the table before a flattened-out piece of paper that had wrapped up tea. Paragot stood over me, as I drew.

"*Nom de Dieu de nom de Dieu!*" cried he. "It is Gian Bellini's Doge Loredano. But what made you remember that picture, and how in the name of Board schools could you manage to draw it?"

He walked swiftly up and down the room.

"*Nom de Dieu de nom de Dieu!*"

"I used to draw horses and men on my slate at school," said I modestly.

Paragot filled his porcelain pipe and walked about strangely excited. Suddenly he stopped.

"My little Asticot," said he, "you had better go down and help Mrs. Housekeeper to wash up the dirty plates and dishes, for your soul's sake."

What my soul had to do with greasy crockery I could not in the least fathom; but the next morning Paragot gave me a drawing lesson. It would be false modesty for me to say that I did not show talent, since the making of pictures is the means whereby I earn my living at the present moment. The gift once discovered, I exercised it in and out of season.

"My son," said Paragot, when I showed him a sketch of Mrs. Housekeeper as she lay on the scullery floor one Saturday night, unable to go any one of her several ways, "I am afraid you are an artist. Do you know what an artist is?"

I didn't. He pronounced the word in tones of such deep melancholy that I felt it must denote something particularly depraved.

"It is the man who has the power of doing up his soul in whitey-brown paper parcels and selling them at three halfpence apiece."

This was at breakfast one morning while he was chipping an egg. Only two eggs furnished forth our repast, and I was already deep in mine. He scooped off the top of the shell, regarded it for a second and then rose with the egg and went to the window.

"Since you have wings you had better fly," said he, and he threw it into the street.

"My little Asticot," he added, resuming his seat. "I myself was once an artist: now I am a philosopher: it is much better."

He cheerfully attacked his bread and butter. Whether it was a sense of his goodness or my own greediness that prompted me I know not, but I pushed my half eaten egg across to him and begged him to finish it. He looked queerly at me for a moment.

"I accept it," said he, "in the spirit in which it is offered."

The great man solemnly ate my egg, and pride so filled my heart that I could scarcely swallow. A smaller man than Paragot would have refused.

From what I gathered from conversations overheard whilst I was serving members with tripe and alcohol, it appeared that my revered master was a mysterious personage. About eight months before, he had entered the then unprosperous Club for the first time as a guest of the founder and proprietor, an old actor who was growing infirm. He talked vehemently. The next night he took the presidential chair which he since occupied, to the Club's greater glory. But whence he came, who and what he was, no one seemed to know. One fat man whose air of portentous wisdom (and insatiable appetite) caused me much annoyance, proclaimed him a Russian Nihilist and asked me whether there were any bombs in his bedroom. Another man declared that he had seen him leading a bear in the streets of Warsaw. His manner offended me.

"Have you ever been to Warsaw, Mr. Ulysses?" asked the fat man. Mr. Ulysses was the traditional title of the head of the Lotus Club.

"This gentleman says he saw you leading a bear there, Master," I piped, wrathfully, in my shrill treble.

There was the sudden silence of consternation. All, some five and twenty, laid down their knives and forks and looked at Paragot, who rose from his seat. Throwing out his right hand he declaimed:

"Ἄνδρα μοι ἔννεπε, Μοῦσα, πολύτροπον, ὃς μάλα πολλὰ πλάγχθη, ἐπεὶ Τροίης ἱερὸν πτολίεθρον ἔπερσεν· πολλῶν δ' ἀνθρώπων ἴδεν ἄστεα καὶ νόον ἔγνω.

"Does anyone know what that is?"

A young fellow at the end of the table said it was the opening lines of the Odyssey.

"You are right, sir," said Paragot, threading his fingers through his long black hair. "They tell of my predecessor in office, the first President of this Club, who was a man of many wanderings and many sufferings and had seen many cities and knew the hearts of men. I, gentlemen, have had my Odyssey, and I have been to Warsaw, and," with a rapier flash of a glance at the gentleman who had accused him of leading bears, "I know the miserable hearts of men." He rapped on the table with his hammer. "Asticot, come here," he shouted.

I obeyed trembling.

"If ever you lift up your voice again in this assembly, I will have you boiled and served up with onion sauce, second-hand tripe that you are, and you shall be eaten underdone. Now go."

I felt shrivelled to the size of a pea. Beneath Paragot's grotesqueness ran an unprecedented severity. I was conscious of the accusing glare of every eye. In my blind bolt to the door I had the good fortune to run headlong into a tray of drinks which Cherubino was carrying.

The disaster saved the situation. Laughter rang out loud and the talk became general. The interlude was forgotten; but the man who said he had seen my master leading bears in Warsaw vanished from the Club for ever after.

The next morning when I entered Paragot's room to wake him I found him reading in bed. He looked up from his book.

"My little Asticot," said he, "leading bears is better than calumny, but indiscretion is worse than both."

And that is all I heard of the matter. I never lifted up my voice in the Club again.

There was a curious black case on the top of a cupboard in his room which for some time aroused my curiosity. It was like no box I had seen before. But one afternoon Paragot took it down and extracted therefrom a violin which after tuning he began to play. Now although fond of music I have never been able to learn any instrument save the tambourine—my highest success otherwise has been to finger out "God save the Queen" and "We won't go home till morning" on the ocarina—and to this day a person able to play the piano or the fiddle seems possessed of an uncanny gift; but in that remote period of my fresh rescue from the gutter, an executant appeared something superhuman. I stared at him with stupid open mouth. He played what I afterwards learned was one of Brahms's Hungarian dances. His lank figure and long hair worked in unison with the music which filled the room with a wild tumult of movement. I had not heard anything like it in my life. It set every nerve of me dancing. I suppose Paragot found his interest in me because I was such an impressionable youngster. When, at the abrupt finale, he asked me what I thought of it, I could scarce stammer a word.

He gave me one of his queer kind looks while he tuned a string.

"I still wonder, my son, whether it would not be better for your soul that you should go on scullioning to the end of time."

"Why, Master?" I asked.

"*Sacré mille diables*," he cried, "do you think I am going to give you a reason for everything? You'll learn fast enough."

He laughed and went on playing, and, as I listened, the more godlike he grew.

"The streets of Paris," said he, returning the fiddle to its case, "are strewn with the wrecked souls of artists."

"And not London?"

"My little Asticot," he replied, "I am a Frenchman, and it is our fondest illusion that no art can possibly exist out of Paris."

I discovered later that he was the son of a Gascon father and an Irish mother, which accounted for his being absolutely bilingual and, indeed, for many oddities of temperament. But now he proclaimed himself a Frenchman, and for a time I was oppressed with a sense of disappointment.

At the Board School I had bolted enough indigestible historical facts to know that the English had always beaten the French, and I had drawn the natural conclusion that the French were a vastly inferior race of beings. It was, I verily believe, the first step in my spiritual education to realise that the god of my idolatry suffered no diminution of grandeur by reason of his nationality. Indeed he gained accession, for after this he talked often to me of France in his magniloquent way, until I began secretly to be ashamed of being English. This had one advantage, in that I set myself with redoubled vigour to learn his language.

So extraordinary was the veneration I had for the man who had transplanted me from the kicks and soapsuds of my former life into this bewildering land of Greek gods and Ariels and pictures and music; for the man who spoke many unknown tongues, wore a gold watch chain, had been to Warsaw and every city mentioned in my school geography, and presided like a king over an assembly of those whom as a gutter urchin I had been wont to designate "toffs"; for the beneficent being who had provided me, Gus Smith alias Asticot, with a nightshirt, condescended to eat half my egg and to allow me to supervise his bedchamber and maintain it in an orderly state of disintegration, hair-brushes from butter and tobacco-ash from fish; for the man who, God knows, was the first of human creatures to awaken the emotion of love within my child's breast—so extraordinary was the veneration I had for him, that although I started out on this narrative by saying it was Paragot's story and not my own I proposed to tell, I hope to be pardoned for a brief egotistical excursion.

Like the gentleman in Chaucer, Paragot had over "his beddes hedde" a shelf of books to which, careless creature that he was, he did not dream of denying me access. In that attic in Tavistock Street I read Smollett and Byron and somehow spelt through "Nana." I also found there the *De Imitatione Christi*, which I read with much the same enjoyment as I did the others. You must not think this priggish of me. The impressionable child of starved imagination will read anything that is printed. In my mother's house I used to purloin the squares of newspaper in which the fried fish from Mr. Samuel'shad been wrapped, and surreptitiously read them. Why not Saint Thomas à Kempis?

I have in my possession now a filthy piece of paper, dropping to bits, on which is copied, in my round Board School boy handwriting, the eleventh chapter of the *De Imitatione*.

It runs:

"My Son, thou hast still many things to learn, which thou hast not well learned yet."

"What are they, Lord?"

"To place thy desire altogether in subjection to my good pleasure and not to be a lover of thyself, but an earnest seeker of my will. Thy desires often excite and urge thee forward: but consider with thyself whether thou art not more moved for thine own objects than for my honour. If it is myself that thou seekest thou shalt be well content with whatsoever I shall ordain; but if any pursuit of thine own lieth hidden within thee, behold it is this which hindreth and weigheth thee down.

"Beware, therefore, lest thou strive too earnestly after some desire which thou hast conceived, without taking counsel of me: lest haply it repent thee afterwards, and that displease thee which before pleased, and for which thou didst long as for a great good. For not every affection which seemeth good is to be forthwith followed: neither is every opposite affection to be immediately avoided. Sometimes it is expedient to use restraint even in good desires and wishes, lest through importunity thou fall into distraction of mind, lest through want of discipline thou become a stumbling-block to others, or lest by the resistance of others thou be suddenly disturbed and brought to confusion.

"*Sometimes indeed it is needful to use violence, and manfully to strive against the sensual appetite, and not to consider what the flesh may or not will; but rather to strive after this, that it may become subject, however unwillingly, to the spirit. And for so long it ought to be chastised and compelled to undergo slavery, even until it be ready for all things; and learn to be contented with little, to be delighted with things simple, and never to murmur at any inconvenience.*"

Let no one be shocked. It was one of the great acts of devotion of my life. I copied this out as a boy, not because it counselled me in my duty towards God, but because it summed up my whole duty to Paragot. Paragot was "Me." I saw the relation between Paragot and myself in every line. Had not I often fallen into distraction of mind over my drawing and books when I ought to have been helping Mrs. Housekeeper downstairs? Was it not want of discipline that made me a stumbling-block that memorable night in the Club? Ought I not to be content with everything Paragot should ordain? And was it not my duty to murmur at no inconvenience?

Years afterwards I showed this paper to Paragot. He wept. Alas! I had not well chosen my opportunity.

I remember, the night after I copied the chapter, Cherubino and I helped Paragot up the stairs and put him to bed. It was the first time I had seen him the worse for liquor. But when one has been accustomed to see one's mother and all her adult acquaintances dead drunk, the spectacle of a god slightly overcome with wine is neither here nor there.

CHAPTER III

THERE was one merit (if merit it was) of my mother's establishment. No skeletons lurked in cupboards. They flaunted their grimness all over the place. Such letters as she received trailed about the kitchen, for all who chose to read, until they were caught up to cleanse a frying-pan. As she possessed no private papers their sanctity was never inculcated; and I could have rummaged, had I so desired, in every drawer or box in the house without fear of correction. When I took up my abode with Paragot, he laid no embargo on any of his belongings. The attic, except for sleeping purposes, was as much mine as his, and it did not occur to me that anything it contained could not be at my disposal.

This must be my apologia for reading, in all innocence, but with much enjoyment, some documents of a private nature which I discovered one day, about a year after I had entered Paragot's service, stuffed by way of keeping them together in an old woollen stocking. They have been put into my possession now for the purpose of writing this narrative, so my original offence having been purged, I need offer no apology for referring to them. There was no sort of order in the bundle of documents; you might as well look for the quality of humour in a dromedary, or of mercy in a pianist, as that of method in Paragot. I managed however to disentangle two main sets, one a series of love letters and the other disconnected notes of travel. In both was I mightily interested.

The love-letters, some of which were written in English and some in French, were addressed to a beautiful lady named Joanna. I knew she was beautiful because Paragot himself said so. "*Pure et ravissante comme une aube d'avril,*" "My dear dream of English loveliness," "the fair flower of my life" and remarks such as these were proof positive. The odd part of it was that they seemed not to have been posted. He wrote: "not till my arms are again around you will your beloved eyes behold these outpourings of my heart." The paper heading bore the word "Paris." Allusions to a great artistic project on which he was working baffled my young and ignorant curiosity. "I have Love, Youth, Genius, Beauty on my side," he wrote, "and I shall conquer. We shall be irresistible. Fame will attend my genius, homage your Beauty; we shall walk on roses and dwell in the Palaces of the Earth." My heart thrilled when I read these lines. *I knew* that Paragot was a great man. Here, again, was proof. I did not reflect that this vision splendid of earth's palaces had faded into the twilight of the Tavistock Street garret. Thank heaven we have had years of remembered life before we learned to reason.

I had many pictures of my hero in those strange letter days, so remote to my childish mind. He crosses the Channel in December, just to skulk for one dark night against the railings of the London Square where she dwelt, in the hope of seeing her shadow on the blind. For some reason which I could not comprehend, the lovers were forbidden to meet. It rains, he sees nothing, but he returns to Paris with contentment in his heart and a terrible cold in his head. But, "I have seen the doorstep," he writes, "*qu'effleurent tous les jours ces petits pieds si adorés.*"

I hate your modern manner of wooing. A few weeks ago a young woman in need of my elderly counsel showed me a letter from her betrothed. He had been educated at Oxford University and possessed a motor-car, and yet he addressed her as "old girl" and alluded to "the regular beanfeast" they would have when they were married; and the damsel not only found nothing wanting in the missive, but treasured it as if it had been an impapyrated kiss. "*Joie de mon âme,*" wrote Paragot, "I have seen the doorstep which your little feet so adored touch lightly every day." I like that better. But this is the opinion of the Asticot of a hundred and fifty. The Asticot of fourteen could not contrast: for him sufficed the Absolute of the romance of Paragot's love-making. Yet I did have a standard of comparison—Ferdinand, whom till then I had regarded as the Prince of Lovers. But he paled into the most prosaic young man before the newly illuminated Paragot, and as for Miranda I sent her packing from her throne in my heart and Joanna reigned in her stead. Little idiot that I was, I set to dreaming of Joanna. You may not like the name, but to me it held and still holds unspeakable music.

The other papers, as I have said, were records of travel, and I instinctively recognized that they referred to subsequent Joanna-less days. They were written on the backs of bills in outlandish languages, leaves torn from greasy note-books, waste stuff exhaling exotic odours, and odds and scraps of paper indescribable. In after years in Paris I besought Paragot, almost on my knees, to write an account of the years of vagabondage to which these papers refer. It would make, I told him, a *picaresque* romance compared with which that of Gil Bias de Santillane were the tale of wanderings round a village pump. Such, said I, is given to few men to produce. But Paragot only smiled, and sipped his absinthe. It was against his principles, he said. The world would be a gentler habitat if there had never been written or graven record of a human action, and he refused to pander to the obscene curiosity of the multitude as to the thoughts and doings of an entire stranger. Besides, literary composition was beset with too many difficulties. One's method of expression had always to be in evening dress which he abhorred, and he could not abide the violet ink and pin-pointed pens supplied in cafés and places where one writes. So the world has lost a new Odyssey.

The notes formed reading as disconnected as a dictionary. They were so abrupt. Incidents were noted which stimulated my young imagination like stinging-nettles; and then nothing more.

"As soon as Hedwige had taught me German, she grew sick and tired of me; and when she wanted to marry an under-officer of cavalry with moustaches reaching to the top of his *Pikelhaube*, who tried to run me through the body when he saw such a scarecrow walking out with her, I left Cassel."

And that was all I learned with regard to Cassel, Hedwige, (save from two other notes) or his learning the German tongue.

The following note is the only one he thought worth while to make of a journey through Russia.

"Novotorshakaya is a beastly hole (*un trou infect*). The bugs are the most companionable creatures in it, and they are the cleanest."

"At Prague," he scribbles on a sheet of paper stained with coffee-cup rings, "I made the acquaintance of a polite burglar, who introduced me to his lady wife, and to other courteous criminals, their spouses and families. My slight knowledge of Czech, which I had by this time acquired, enabled me to take vast pleasure in their society. Granted their sociological premises, based on Proudhon, they are too logical. The lack of imaginative power to break away from convention, *their convention*, is a serious defect in their character. They take their gospel of *tuum est meum* too seriously. I do not inordinately sympathise with people who get themselves hanged for a principle. And that is what my friend Mysdrizin did. An old lady of Prague, obstinate as the old sometimes are, on whom he called professionally, disputed his theories; whereupon, instead of smiling with the indulgence of one who knows the art of living, and letting her have her own way, he convinced her with a life-preserver. His widow, like her predecessor of Ephesus, desiring speedy consolation, I fled the city. My Epicureanism and her iron-bound individualism would have clashed. I had played the Battle of Prague *à quatre mains* sufficiently in my tender childhood. I had no wild yearning to recommence."

Here is another:

"Verona——"

There is no date. None of these jottings bear a date, and when I last saw Paragot he had not the patience to arrange these far off memories. Verona! To me the word recalls immemorable associations—vistas of narrow old streets redolent of the Renaissance, echoing still with brawl and clash of arms, and haunted by the general stock in trade of the artist's historical fancy. But did Verona appeal to Paragot's romantic sense? Not a bit of it.

"At Verona," runs the jotting, "I lodged with the cheeriest little undertaker in the world, who had a capital low-class practice. His wife, four children, and whoever happened to be the lodger, were all pressed into the merry service. We sang *Funiculi funiculà* as we drove in the nails. When I make coffins again I shall sing that refrain. It has an unisonal value that is positively captivating. Had it not been that a diet of spaghetti and anæmic wine, a *tord-boyau*(intestine-twister) of unparalleled virulence undermined my constitution, and that the four children, whose bedroom I shared, all took whooping-cough at once and thus robbed me of sleep, I might have been coffin-making to the tune of *Funiculi, Funiculà* to the present day."

Here and there were jottings of figures. I know now they refer to Paragot's tiny patrimony on which he—and I, in after years—subsisted. It was so small that no wonder he worked now and then for a living wage.

I also see now, as of course I could not be expected to see then, that Paragot, being a creature of extremes, would either have the highest or the lowest. In these travel-sketches, as he cannot go to Grand Hotels, I find him avoiding like lazar-houses the commercial or family hostelries where he will foregather with the half-educated, the half-bred, the half-souled; the offence of them is too rank for his spirit. The pretending simian class, aping the vices of the rich and instinct with the vices of the low, and frank in neither, moves the man's furious scorn. He will have realities at any cost. All said and done, the bugs of Novortovshakaya did not masquerade as hummingbirds, nor merry Giuseppi Sacconi of Verona as a critic of Girolami dai Libri.

"I don't mind," he writes on a loose sheet, apropos of nothing, "the frank dunghill outside a German peasant's kitchen window. It is a matter of family pride. The higher it can be piled the greater his consideration. But what I loathe and abominate is the dungheap hidden beneath Hedwige's draper papa's parlour floor."

When I came to this in my wrongful search through Paragot's papers, I felt greatly relieved. I thought Hedwige had seduced him from his allegiance to Joanna, and that he was sorry she had married the sergeant with moustaches reaching to his *Pikelhaube*, though what part of his person his *Pikelhaube* was, I could not for the life of me imagine. I pictured Hedwige as a gigantic awe-compelling lady. The name somehow conveyed the idea to me. It was peculiarly comforting to learn that she was a horrid girl whose papa had a draper's shop over a dunghill. I no longer bothered my head concerning her, for soon I came across a reference to Joanna.

"I was lounging one day in the Puerta del Sol, that swarming central parallelogram of Madrid, and musing on the possibilities of progress in a nation which contents itself with ox-transport in the heart of its capital, when a carriage drove past me in which I can almost still swear I saw Joanna. It entered the Calle de San Hieronimo. I started in racing pursuit and fell into the arms of a green-gloved soldier. To avoid arrest as a madman or a murderer, for no sane man runs in Spain, I leaped into a fiacre and gave such chase as tomorrow's victim of the bull-ring would allow. We came up with the carriage on the Prado, just in time to see the skirts of a lady vanish through the door of a house. I dismissed my cab and waited. I waited two solid hours. That attracted no attention. Everyone waits in Spain. To stand interminably at a street corner is to take out a patent of respectability. But my confounded heart beat wildly. I had an *agonized desire* to see her again. I addressed the liveried coachman in my best Spanish, taking off my hat and bowing low.

"'Señor, will you have the great goodness to tell me who is that lady?'

"'Señor,' he replied with equal urbanity, 'it is not correct for coachmen to give rapscallions information as to their employers.'

"'When your Señora bids the rapscallion sit beside her in the carriage and orders you to drive, you will regret your insolence,' said I.

"I turned a haughty back on him; but I felt his lackey's eye fixed disapprovingly on my rags.

"'I will hear the sound,' said I to myself, 'of her silvery English voice, or I will die.'

"Then the door opened, and the beautiful lady entered the carriage; *and it was not Joanna.*

"The gods were without bowels of compassion for me that day."

Another scrap contains the following:

"Thus have I come to the end of a five years' vagabondage. I started out as a Pilgrim to the Inner Shrine of Truth which I have sought from St. Petersburg to Lisbon, from Taormina to Christiania. I have lived in a spiritual shadowland, dreaming elusive dreams, my better part stayed by the fitful vision of things unseen. Such an exquisite wild-goose-chase has never man undertaken before or since the dear Knight of La Mancha. And now I come to think of it, I don't know what the deuce I have been after, save that instead of pursuing I have all the time been running away.

"In my next quest I must not proclaim my Dulcinea too loudly. When Hedwige's little sister came to me with a doll into which Hedwige had savagely run hatpins so that the stuffing came out, I consoled the weeping infant with a new doll and the assurance that Hedwige was the spitefullest cat as yet evolved from a feline sex. I had no notion at the time of the reason for Hedwige's viciousness. But now I fancy she must have acted according to mediæval superstition and used the doll as Joanna's hated effigy. I remember that the next time I saw her I criticised her straight Teutonic fringe and fanfaronaded on the captivating frizziness of Joanna's hair. The wonder is that Hedwige did not run hatpins into *me.* The murderer's widow of Prague was built of sterner stuff; she cared not a hempen strand for Joanna, a pale consumptive doxy, according to her picturing, who had jilted me for an eminent swell-mobsman in London."

I spent many happy hours over these scraps, building up the fantastic fairy tale of Paragot's antecedents, and should have gone on reading them for an indefinite time had not Paragot one day discovered me. It was then that I learned the sacrosanctity of private papers.

"I thought, my little Asticot," said he, bending his blue eyes on me, "I thought you were a gentleman."

Only Paragot could have had so crazy a thought. I could not be a gentleman, I reflected, till I had a gold watch-chain. However Paragot expected me to be one without the seal and token of outward adornments, and I promised faithfully to mould myself according to his expectations.

"How much of this nightmare farrago have you read?"

"I know it all by heart, Master," said I.

He took off his old hat and threw it on the bed, and ran his fingers through his hair perplexedly.

"My son," said he at last, "if you were just a common boy I should make you go on your bended knees and lift up your hand and swear that you would not reveal to a living soul the mysteries which these papers contain, and then I should send you to dwell for ever among the tripe-plates. But I see before me a gentleman, a scholar and an artist and I will not submit him to such an indignity."

He put his hand on my head and looked at me in kind irony.

"I will never tell no one, Master," I promised.

"Anyone," he corrected.

"Anyone, Master," I repeated meekly.

"You will wipe it all out of your memory."

I was habitually truthful with Paragot, because he never gave me cause to lie.

"I can't, Master," said I, thinking of my dreams of Joanna.

The seriousness of my tone amused him.

"What has made such an indelible impression on your mind?"

"I can't forget——" I blurted out, moved both by reluctance to yield over my dreams of Joanna and by a desire to show off my familiarity with French, "I can't forget about *ces petits pieds si adorés*."

The smile died from his face, which assumed a queer, scared expression. He went to the window and stood there so long, that I, in my turn grew scared. I realised dimly what I had done, and I could have bitten my tongue out. I drew near him.

"Master," said I timidly.

He did not seem to hear; presently he picked up his hat from the bed and walked out without taking any notice of me.

We did not refer to the papers again until long afterwards, and though they lay unguarded as before in the old stocking, never till this present day have I set my eyes on them.

CHAPTER IV

ONE May morning a year after my surprising of Paragot's secret, I awoke later than usual, the three-and-sixpenny clock on the mantelpiece marking eleven, and huddling on my clothes in alarm I left the foul smelling Club room, and ran upstairs to arouse my master.

To my astonishment he was not alone. A stout florid man, wearing a white waistcoat which bellied out like the sail of a racing yacht, a frock coat and general resplendency of garb, stood planted in the middle of the room, while Paragot still in nightshirt but trousered, sat swinging his leg on a corner of the deal table. I noticed the fiddle which Paragot had evidently been playing before his visitor's arrival, lying on the disordered bed.

"Who the devil is this?" cried the fat man angrily.

"This is Mr. Asticot, my private secretary, who cooks my herrings and attends to my correspondence. Usually he cooks two, but if you will join us at breakfast Mr. Hogson——"

"Pogson," bawled the fat man.

"I beg your pardon," said my master sweetly. "If you will join us at breakfast he will cook three."

"Damn your breakfast," said Mr. Pogson.

"Only two then, Asticot. This gentleman has already breakfasted. You will forgive us for not treating you as a stranger."

Mr. Pogson, who was in a rage, thumped the table with his hand.

"I'll give you to understand Mr. Henkendyke, that I am the proprietor of this club. I have bought it with my money, and I'm not going to see it go to eternal glory as it's doing under your management. I'm not like that old ass Ballantyne. I'm a business man and I'm going to run this club for a profit, and if you continue to be manager you'll jolly well have to turn over a new leaf."

"My good friend," said my master, rising and thrusting his hands in his pockets, "you have told me that about ten times; it is getting monotonous."

"The way this place is run," continued Mr. Pogson, unheeding, "is scandalous. Not a blessed account kept. No check on provisions or drink. Every night your servants are drunk."

"As owls," said Paragot.

"And what the dickens do you do?"

"I give the Lotus Club the prestige of my presidency. I accept a salary and this presidential residence as my remuneration. You do not expect a man like me to keep ledgers and check butcher's bills like a twopennyhalfpenny clerk in the City.

It is you, my dear Mr. Pogson, who have curious ideas of club management. You should put this sort of thing into the hands of some arithmetical hireling. I—" he waved his long fingers tipped with their long nails, magnificently—"am the picturesque, the intellectual, the spiritual guide of the club."

"You are a —— fraud," cried Mr. Pogson, using so dreadful an adjective that I dropped the gridiron. Paragot had trained me to a distaste of foul language. "You are a drunken incompetent thief."

Paragot took his guest's glossy silk hat and gold mounted cane from the table and put them into his hands. He pointed to the door.

"Get out—quickly," said he.

He turned on his heel and sitting on the bed began to play the fiddle. Mr. Pogson instead of getting out stood in front of him quivering like an infuriated jelly, and informed him that it was his blooming club and his blooming room, that he would choose the moment of exit most convenient to his own blooming self; also that Paragot's speedy exit was a matter for his decision. In a dancing fury he heaped abuse on Paragot who played "The Last Rose of Summer," with rather more tremolo than usual. Even I saw that he was dangerous. Mr. Pogson did not heed. Suddenly Paragot sprang to his feet towering over the fat man and swung his fiddle on high like Thor's hammer. With a splitting crash it came down on Mr. Pogson's head. Then Paragot gripped him and running with him to the door, shot him down the stairs.

"That, my little Asticot," said he, "is the present proprietor of the Lotus Club, and this is the late manager."

I ran to the door for the purpose of locking it. Paragot smiled.

"He will not come back. When he has mended what Fluellen calls his 'ploody coxcomb,' he will take out a summons against me for assault."

He threw himself on the bed, while I, in trembling bewilderment, prepared the breakfast. Presently he broke into a loud laugh.

"The fool! The mammonite fool, Asticot! Does he think that Mr. Ulysses-es are picked up by the hundred among the smug young men of the Polytechnic who add up figures, and keep books by double entry? Do you know what double entry is?"

"No, Master," said I from my squatting seat on the floor by the gas stove.

"Thank the gods for your ignorance. It is a nescience whereby human aspirations are cribbed within ruled lines and made to balance on the opposite side. Would you like to see me obey Mr. Mammon's behest and crib my aspirations within ruled lines?"

"No, Master," said I.

"The gods have given you understanding," said he, "which is better than book-keeping by double entry."

At the time I thought my master's attitude magnificent and I despised Mr. Pogson from the bottom of my heart. But since then I have wondered how the deuce the Lotus Club survived a month of Paragot's management. In after years when I questioned him, he said airily that he left all financial questions to Ballantyne, the old actor proprietor, who had grown infirm, and that he was president and not manager. Yet to my certain knowledge he paid wages to Mrs. Housekeeper, Cherubino and myself, and as for tradesmen's bills they were strewn about Paragot's bedchamber like the autumn leaves of Vallombrosa, in greater numbers than the articles of his attire. On the other hand, I have no recollection of moneys coming in. There must have been some loose unbusinesslike arrangement between Ballantyne and himself which most justifiably shocked the business instincts of Mr. Pogson. There I sympathise with the latter. But I must admit that he showed a want of tact in dealing with Paragot.

My master was in gay spirits during breakfast. When he had finished, he declared the meal to be the most enjoyable he had eaten in Tavistock Street. My insensate conceit regarded the statement as a tribute to my culinary skill and I glowed with pride. I informed him that my herring cookery was nothing to what I could do with sprats.

"My little Asticot," said he, filling his porcelain pipe, "I have to offer you my joint congratulation and commiseration. I congratulate you on your being no longer a scullion. I commiserate with you on the loss of your salary of eighteen pence a week. Your sensitive spirit would revolt against taking service under anyone of Mr. Mammon's myrmidons, and even if it didn't, I am sure he would not employ you. Like Caliban no longer will you 'scrape trencher nor wash dish'—at least in the Lotus Club—for from this hour I dismiss you from its service."

He smoked silently in his wicker chair, giving me time to realise the sudden change in my fortunes. Then only did I understand. I saw myself for a desolate moment, cast motherless, rudderless on the wide world where art and scholarship met with contumely and undergrown youth was buffeted and despised. My gorgeous dreams were at an end. The blighting commonplace overspread my soul.

"What would you like to do, my little Asticot?" he asked.

I pulled myself together and looked at him heroically.

"I could be a butcher's boy."

The corners of my mouth twitched. It was a shuddersome avocation, and the prospect of the companionship of other butcher boys who could not draw, did not know French, and had never heard of Joanna filled me with a horrible sense of doom.

Suddenly Paragot leaped up in his wild way to his feet and clapped me so heartily on the shoulder that I staggered.

"My son," cried he, "I have an inspiration. It is spring, and the hedgerows are greener than the pavement, and the high roads of Europe are wider than Tavistock

Street. We will seek them to-day, Asticot *de mon cœur;* I'll be Don Quixote and you'll be my Sancho, and we'll go again in quest of adventures." He laughed aloud, and shook me like a little rat. "*Cela te tape dans l'œil, mon petit Asticot?*"

Without waiting for me to reply, he rushed to the ricketty washstand, poured out water from the broken ewer, and after washing, began to dress in feverish haste, talking all the time. Used as I was to his suddenness my wits could not move fast enough to follow him.

"Then I needn't be a butcher's boy?" I said at last.

He paused in the act of drawing on a boot.

"Butcher's boy? Do you want to be a butcher's boy?"

"No, Master," said I fervently.

"Then what are you talking of?" He had evidently not heard my answer to his question. "I am going to educate you in the High School of the Earth, the University of the Universe, and to-morrow you shall see a cow and a dandelion. And before then you will be disastrously seasick."

"The sea!" I cried in delirious amazement. "We are going on the sea? Where are we going?"

"To France, *petit imbécile*," he cried. "Why are you not getting ready to go there?"

I might have answered that I had no personal preparations to make; but feeling rebuked for idleness while he was so busy, I began to clear away the breakfast things. He stopped me.

"*Nom de Dieu*, we are not going to travel with cups and saucers!"

He dragged from the top of the cupboard an incredibly dirty carpet bag of huge dimensions and decayed antiquity, and bade me pack therein our belongings. The process was not a lengthy one; we had so few. When we had little more than half filled the bag with articles of attire and the toilette stuffed in pell-mell, we looked around for ballast.

"The books, Master," said I.

"We will take the immortal works of Maître François Rabelais, and the dirty little edition of 'David Copperfield.' The remainder of the library we will sell in Holywell Street."

"And the violin?"

He picked up the maimed instrument and, after looking at it critically, threw it into a corner.

"For Pogson," said he.

When we had tied up the books with a piece of stout string providentially lying at the bottom of the cupboard, our preparations were complete. Paragot donned his cap and a storm-stained Inverness cape, grasped the carpet bag and looked round the room.

"*En route*," said he, and I followed with the books. We gained the street and left the Lotus Club behind us for ever.

What Mrs. Housekeeper said, what Cherubino said, what the members said when they found no Mr. Ulysses presiding at the supper table that evening, what Mr. Pogson said when he learned that his assailant had shaken the dust of the Lotus Club from off his feet and strolled into the wide world without giving him the opportunity of serving a summons for assault, I have never been able to discover. Nor have I learned who succeeded Paragot as president and occupied the palatial chamber of all the harmonies that was Paragot's squalid attic. When, in after years, I returned to London the Lotus Club had passed from human memory, and at the present day a perky set of office premises stands on its site. The morality of Paragot's precipitate exodus I am not in a position to discuss. From his point of view the fact of having disliked the new proprietor from their first interview, and broken a fiddle over his head, rendered his position as president untenable. Paragot walked out.

After having sold the books for a few shillings in Holywell Street, we marched up Fleet Street into the City, and entered a stupendous, unimagined building which Paragot informed me was his bank. Elegant gentlemen behind the counter shovelled gold to and fro with the same casual indifference as I had seen grocers' assistants shovel tea. One of them, a gorgeous fellow wearing a white piqué tie and a horse-shoe pin, paid such deference to Paragot that I went out prodigiously impressed by my master's importance. I was convinced that he owned the establishment, and during the next quarter of an hour I could not speak to him for awe.

It was about two o'clock when we reached Victoria Station. There Paragot discovered, for the first time, that there was not a train till nine in the evening. It had not occurred to him that trains did not start for Paris at quarter of an hour intervals during the day.

"My son," said he, "now is the time to make practical use of our philosophy. Instead of heaping vain maledictions on the Railway Company, let us deposit our luggage in the cloak room and take a walk on the Thames Embankment."

We walked thither and sat on a vacant bench beside the Cleopatra's Needle. It was a warm May afternoon. My young mind and body fired by the excitements of the day found rest in the sunny idleness. It was delicious to be here, instead of washing up plates and dishes with Mrs. Housekeeper. Paragot took off his old slouch hat, stretched himself easefully and sighed.

"I am anxious to get to Paris to consult Henri Quatre."

"Who is Henri Quatre, Master?" I asked.

"Henri Quatre is on the Pont Neuf. That is a French saying which means that Queen Anne is dead. He was a great King of France and his statue on horseback is in the middle of a great bridge across the Seine called the Pont Neuf. He is a great friend of mine. I will tell you a story. Once upon a time there lived in Paris a magnificent young man who thought himself a genius. He *was* a genius, my little Asticot. A genius is a man who writes immortal books, paints immortal pictures, rears immortal buildings and commits immortal follies. Don't be a genius, my son, it isn't good for anybody. Well, this young man was clad in purple and fine linen and fared sumptuously every day. He also had valuable furniture. One evening something happened to annoy him."

Paragot paused.

"What annoyed him?" I asked.

"A flaw in what he had conceived to be the scheme of the universe," replied my master. "It annoys many people. The young man being annoyed, cast the fruits of his genius into the fire, tore up his purple and fine linen and smashed his furniture with a Crusader's mace which happened to be hanging by way of an ornament on the wall. It's made of steel with a knob full of spikes, and weighs about nine pounds. I know nothing like it for destroying a Louis Quinze table, or for knocking the works out of a clock. If you're good, my son, you shall have one when you grow up."

I looked gratefully at him. Not content with his kindness to me then, he would be my benefactor still when I reached manhood.

"The young man then packed a valise full of necessaries and went out into the street. It was a rainy November evening. He walked along the quays through the lamp-lit drizzle till he came to the statue of Henri Quatre. The Pont Neuf was alive with traffic and the swiftly passing lights of vehicles threw conflicting gleams over the wet statue. The gas-lamps flickered in the wind." Paragot flickered his long fingers dramatically, to illustrate the gas-lamps. "On all sides rose vague masses of building—the Louvre away beyond the bridge, the frowning mass of the Conciergerie—the towering turrets of Notre Dame—swelling like billows against the sky. Pale reflections came from the river. Do you see the picture, my little Asticot? And the young man clutched the railings that surround the plinth of the statue, and caught sight of the face of Henri Quatre, and Henri Quatre looked at him so kindly that he said: '*Mon bon roi*, you are of the South like myself: I am leaving Paris to go into the wide world, but I don't know where in the wide world to go to.' *And the King nodded his head and pointed to the Gare de Lyon.* And the young man took off his hat and said, '*Mon bon roi*, I thank you!' He went to the Gare de Lyon and found a train just starting for Italy. So he went to Italy. I have a great respect for Henri Quatre."

"And what happened to him then, Master?" I asked, after a breathless pause.

"He became a vagabond philosopher," replied Paragot, refilling his porcelain pipe.

No argument has ever been able to convince Paragot that the statue did not nod its head and point the way to Italy. For some years I myself believed it; but at last it became obvious that the flashing gleams of light over the wet statue had made him the victim of a trick of the eyes. I think the only serious offence I ever gave Paragot was when I presented to him this solution of the mystery.

Varied discourse and a meal in a Strand eating-house filled up the hours till nine o'clock. And then I started for Wonderland with Paragot.

We stayed in Paris but two days. When I asked my master why our sojourn was not longer, he said something about the "bitter-sweet" of it, which I could not understand. I have only two clear memories of Paris. He took me to see Henri Quatre, and explained how the statue nodded and how the hand which held the reins lifted and pointed to the Gare de Lyon. What more conclusive proof of his veracity need I have than actual confrontation with Henri Quatre? The other scene fixed on my mind is a narrow dark street with tall houses on either side; an awning outside a humble café; a little table beneath it at which Paragot and myself were seated. I sipped luxuriously a celestial liquor which I have since learned was grenadine syrup and water; in front of Paragot was a curious opalescent milky fluid of which he drank great quantities during those two days and ever afterwards.

"The time has come," said he, rolling his eyes at me with an awful solemnity and speaking in a thick voice, "the time has come to talk of affairs. First let me impress on you that Henkendyke is an appellation offensive to French ears. Henceforward my name is Pradel—Polydore Pradel. And as it is necessary for you to have an *état civil*, I hereby adopt you as my son. Your name is therefore Asticot Pradel. I hope you like it. You have never known what it is to have a father. Now the possession of a father is a privilege to which every human being has a right. I, Polydore Pradel, confer on you that privilege. My son—"

He raised his glass, clinked it against mine and pledged me.

"Henceforward," said Paragot, "what is good enough for me will I hope not be good enough for you, and what is too bad for me shall never be your portion. I swear it by the devil that dwells in this entrancing but execrated form of alcohol."

He finished his drink and called for another. As soon as the absinthe had curdled with the dropping water, he filled up the glass and drank it off. Then he sat for a long time in bemused silence, while I, perched on my chair, reflected on his great goodness and wondered how I should help him up the darksome stairs of our hotel without the aid of Cherubino.

The next day we started on our pilgrimage. Why we went in one direction more than another, why we went to one place rather than to another, neither he nor I could tell. I never questioned. Sometimes we wandered for days on foot, sleeping in village inns or farm-houses—occasionally under a hedge when the nights were warm. Sometimes we spent two or three days in an old world town, and Paragot would show me cathedrals and churches and lecture me on the history of the place, and set me to sketch bits of the picturesque that took his fancy. In the cool, exquisite cloister of the Chateau of Jacques Cœur at Bourges I learned more of the history of Charles VII than any English boy of my generation. In the Chateau of Blois, the salamanders of François Premier, the statue of Diane de Poictiers, the poison cabinet of Catherine de Medici, the dungeons of the Cardinal de Lorraine, became living testimonies of the past under Paragot's imaginative teaching. He had set his heart on educating me; suddenly as the original impulse had seized him, yet it lasted strong and became the object of his disordered and otherwise aimless life. Books we always had in plenty. Tattered classics are cheap enough in France, and what mattered it if pages were missing? When done with we threw them away. We might have been tracked through the country, like the hares in a paper chase, by the trail of literature we left behind us.

In spite of his unmethodical temperament Paragot made one fixed rule for my habits. In towns and larger villages, I went to bed at nine o'clock. What he did with himself by way of amusement in the evenings I never knew. Nor did it occur to me to conjecture. Healthily tired after a happy day I was only too glad to crawl to whatever queer resting place chance provided, and to sleep the sound sleep of boyhood. To be for ever moving amid a fairyland of novelty, to have no care for the morrow, to have no tasks save those that were a delight, to be under the protecting guidance of a godlike being whose very reproofs were couched in terms of humorous kindness, to eat strange unexpected things, to fraternise in a new tongue, which daily grew more familiar, with any urchin on the high-road or city byway, to pass wondering days among country sights and country sounds—to be in short the perfect vagabond, could boy dream of a more glorious life?

Now and again a whimsy seized my master and he declared that we must work and earn our daily bread by the sweat of our brows. At a farm near Chartres we hired ourselves out to an elderly couple, Monsieur and Madame Dubosc, and spent toilsome but healthy days carting manure. Although Paragot wrought miracles with his pitchfork, I don't think Monsieur Dubosc took him seriously. Peasant shrewdness penetrated to the gentleman beneath Paragot's blouse, and peasant ignorance attributed to him the riches which he did not possess. They became great friends, however, and before we left he succeeded in establishing himself as a kind of oracle by curing a pig of some mysterious disease by means of a remedy which he said he had learned in Dalmatia. Old Madame Dubosc shed tears when we left La Haye.

Sometimes Paragot grew tired of tramping, and we travelled by rail, in the wooden third class compartments of omnibus trains that stopped at every station. Now and then pure chance took us to any particular town. It was at Nancy that Paragot went to the ticket office and said with the utmost politeness:—

"Monsieur, will you have the kindness to give me a ticket?"

"To what destination?" asked the clerk peering through his pigeon hole.

"*Parbleu*," said Paragot, "to any destination you like provided it is not too expensive."

The clerk called him a *farceur* and would have nothing to do with him, but Paragot protested.

"Pardon, Monsieur, I have but one wish, to get away from Nancy. I have seen the Episcopal Palace on the Place Stanislas, the Cathedral, and I have viewed but I have not read the seventy-five thousand volumes in the University Library. You know the places one gets to from Nancy, which I do not. I am a stranger, in your hands. If you could suggest to me a town about 100 kilometres distant——"

"There is Longwy," said the haughty official.

"Then have the kindness to give me two third class tickets to Longwy," said Paragot.

And to Longwy we went. Paragot contemplated the lack of interest in the smug little town.

"To hold out Longwy as a goal to the enthusiastic Pilgrim to the Shrine of Truth," said he, "could only enter the timber-built mind of a French railway official."

The record of our wanderings would mark the stages of my own development, but would be of little count as a history of Paragot. We tramped and trained south through Italy and spent the winter in Rome. Then it entered his head to obtain employment for both of us, as workman and boy, on the excavations of the Forum. We lived in the slums with our brother excavators, and were completely happy. So happy that though we wandered the next year over France and part of Germany the winter again found us working in Rome. In the following Spring we set our faces northward, and in July Destiny overtook us in Savoy.

CHAPTER V

IT was the late afternoon of a sweltering July day. The near hills slumbered in the sunshine. Far away beyond them grey peaks of Alpine spurs, patched with snow, rose in faint outline against the sky. The valley lay in rich idleness, green and gold and fruitful, yielding itself with a maternal largeness to the white fifteenth century château on the hillside. A long white road stretched away to the left following the convolutions of the valley, until it became a thread; on the right it turned sharply by a clump of trees which marked a farm. In the middle of it all, in the grateful shadow cast by a wayside café, sat Paragot and myself, watching with thirsty eyes the buxom but slatternly *patronne* pour out beer from a bottle. A dirty, long-haired mongrel terrier lapped water from an earthenware bowl, at the foot of the wooden table at which we sat. This was Narcisse, a recent member of our vagabond family, whom my master had casually adopted some weeks before and had christened according to some *lucus a non lucendo* principle of his own. I think he was the least beautiful dog I have ever met; but I loved him dearly.

Paragot drained his tumbler, handed it back to be refilled, drained it again and cleared his throat with the contentment of a man whose thirst has been slaked.

"Now one can spit," he exclaimed heartily.

"That is always a comfort to a man," remarked the *patronne*.

"It is the potentiality that is the comfort. Have you apartments for the night, Madame?"

"They are for *des messieurs*—for gentlemen," said the patronne diffidently.

Narcisse having also finished his draught stretched himself out on the ground, his chin on his fore paws, and glanced furtively upwards at the disparaging lady.

"*Tron de l'air!*" cried Paragot, "are we not gentlemen?"

"*Tiens*, you are of the Midi," cried the woman, recognising the expletive—for no one born north of Avignon says "*Tron de l'air*"—"I too am from Marseilles. My husband was a Savoyard. That is why I am here."

"I am a gentleman of Gascony," said my master, "and this is my son Asticot."

"It is a droll name," said the *patronne*.

"We are commercial travellers on our rounds with samples of philosophy."

"It is a droll trade," said the *patronne*.

We were greasy and dirty, sunburnt to the colour of Egyptian felaheen and dressed in the peasant's blue blouse. Creatures more unlike professors of philosophy could not be conceived. But the *patronne* seemed to be impressed—as who was not?—by Paragot.

"The rooms will be three francs, Monsieur," she said after a calculating pause.

"I engage them," said my master. "Asticot, aid Madame to take our luggage up to our bedchambers." I grasped my bundle and handed Paragot's dilapidated canvas gripsack to the *patronne*. He arrested her.

"One moment, Madame. As you see, my portmanteau contains a shirt, a pair of socks, a comb and a toothbrush. Also a copy of the works of the divine vagrant Maître François Villon, which I will take out at once. He was a thief and a reprobate and got nearer hanged than any man who ever lived, and he is the dearest friend I have."

"You have droll friends," remarked the *patronne* continuing her litany.

"And to think that he died four hundred years ago," sighed my master. "Isn't it strange, Madame, that all the bravest men and most beautiful women are those that are dead?"

The landlady laughed. "You talk like a true Gascon, Monsieur. In this country people are so silent that one loses the use of one's tongue."

I departed with her to see after domestic arrangements and when I returned I found Paragot smoking his porcelain pipe, and talking to a dusty child in charge of a goat. Having, at that period, a soul above dusty children in charge of goats. I sprawled on the ground beside Narcisse, and being tired by the day's tramp fell into a doze. The good earth, when you have a casing of it already on clothes and person, is a comfortable couch; but I think you must be in your teens to enjoy it.

I awoke to the sound of Paragot's voice talking to Narcisse. The goat child had slipped away. An ox cart laden with hay lumbered past. The mellowness of late afternoon lay over the land. The shadow cast by the little white café had deepened gradually far beyond the table. From within the house came the faint clatter of footsteps and cooking utensils. Paragot was still smoking. Narcisse sat on his haunches, his ill shaped head to one side and his ears cocked. After making a vicious dig at a flea, he yawned and trotted about after the manner of his kind in search of adventure. Paragot summoned him back.

"My good Narcisse, every spot on the earth has its essential quality which the wise man or dog knows how to enjoy in its entirety. In great cities where life is pulsating around you, you are alert for the unexpected. The underlying principle of a world's backwater like this is restful stagnation. Here you must wallow in the uneventful. In vain you sniff around in quest of the exciting, mistaking like your fellow in the fable the shadow for the substance. The substance here is rest. Here nothing ever happens."

"Pardon, Monsieur," said a voice close upon us. "Is it very far to Chambéry?"

"It does not matter," said a second voice following hard on the first, "for I can go no further."

I jumped to my feet and my master started round in his chair. The first speaker was a girl, the second an old man. She had merely the comeliness of tanned and hair-bleached peasant youth; he was wizened, lined, browned and bent. A cotton umbrella shaded the girl's bare head and she carried in her hand a cane valise covered with grey canvas. The old man was burdened with two ancient shabby cases, one evidently containing a violin and the other some queerly shaped musical instrument. Both the new comers were wayworn and dirty, and my master seeing suffering on the old man's face rose and courteously offered him a chair.

"Sit down and rest," said he, "and Mademoiselle, you are thinking of going to Chambéry? But it is nearly a day's journey on foot."

"We have to play at a wedding tomorrow, Monsieur," said the girl piteously. "It was arranged two months ago, and we must get there in some manner."

"There is a railway station not far off," said I.

"Alas! we have only ten sous in the world, which is not enough to pay for our tickets," she answered. "Imagine, Monsieur, I had a piece of twenty francs in my pocket this morning, and I went to the station to get a ticket, for I had counted on going by railway, as my grandfather is so ill, and when I came to pay, I found I had lost my louis. How, the *bon Dieu* only knows. It is desolating, Monsieur; we had to walk so as to keep our engagement at Chambéry. If we miss it, *nous sommes dans la purée pour tout de bon*."

To be in the *purée* is to be in a very bad mess indeed. The prospect of abject pennilessness filled the damsel's eyes with woe.

"You earn your living by playing at weddings for folks to dance?" asked my master.

"Yes, Monsieur. My grandfather plays the violin and I the zither—we also go to fairs. In the winter we play at cafés in large towns. Life is hard, Monsieur, is it not?"

She closed her umbrella and laid it on the valise. The old man sat by the table, his head resting on his hands, saying nothing.

"When I think of my good louis that is gone!" she added tragically.

The only feature making for charm in a coarse homely face was a set of white even teeth. I found her singularly unattractive. A tear rolled down her cheek and its course was that of a rill in a dusty plain.

"Suppose I lend you the money for the railway tickets?" said my master kindly.

"O Monsieur," she cried, "I should thank you from the depths of my heart. *Grandpère*," she turned to the old man who, ashen faced, was staring in front of him, "Monsieur will lend us enough money to get to Chambéry."

"I can go no further," he murmured.

Then his eyelids quivered, his body moved spasmodically, and he swayed sideways off the chair on to the ground.

We rushed to aid him. The girl put his head on her lap. My master bade me run into the café for brandy. When I returned the old man was dead.

Narcisse sat placidly by, with his tongue out, eyeing his master ironically.

"You are the man," his glance implied, "who said that nothing happens here."

I have known many dogs in my life, but never so mocking and cynical a dog as Narcisse.

It was nearly midnight before my master and I sat down again outside the café. The intervening hours had been spent in journeying to and from the nearest village, and obtaining the necessary services of doctor and curé. My master was smoking his porcelain pipe, as usual, but strangely silent. A faint circle of light came from the open ground-floor window of the café. The white road gleamed dimly, and beyond the hushed valley the hills loomed vague against a black, starlit sky. In the lighted room a few peasants from neighbouring farms drank their sour white wine and discussed the death in low voices. In other circumstances my master would have joined them under pretext of getting nearer the Heart of Life, and would have told them amazing tales of Ekaterinoslav or Valladolid till they reeled home drunk with wine and wonder. And I should have been abed. But to-night Paragot seemed to prefer the silent company of Narcisse and myself.

"What do you think of it all, Asticot?" he asked at length.

"Of what, master?"

"Death."

"It frightens me," was all I could answer.

"What I resent about it," said my master reflectively, "is that one is not able to have any personal concern in the most interesting event in one's career. If you could even follow your own funeral and have a chance of weeping for yourself! You are never so important as when you are a corpse—and you miss it all. I have a good mind not to die. It is either the silliest or the wisest action of one's life; I wonder which."

Presently the girl came down the passage of the café, stood for a moment in the doorway, and seeing Paragot advanced to the table.

"You are very kind, Monsieur," she said, "and for what you have done I thank you from my heart."

"It was very little," said my master. "Asticot, why do you not give Mademoiselle your chair? Your manners are worse than those of Narcisse. Mademoiselle, do me the pleasure of being seated."

She sat down, her feet apart, peasant fashion, her hands in her lap.

"If I had not lost the twenty francs he would not have died," she said dejectedly.

"He would have died if you had brought him here in a carriage. He had aneurism of the heart, the doctor says. He might have died any moment the last ten years. How old was he?"

"Seventy, eighty, ninety—how should I know?"

"But he was your grandfather."

"Ah, no, indeed, Monsieur," she replied in a more animated manner. "He was not a relative. My mother was poor and she sold me to him three years ago."

"Why that is like me, Master!" I cried, vastly interested.

"My son," said he in English, "that is one of the things that must be forgotten. And then, Mademoiselle?" he asked in French.

"Then he taught me to play the zither and to dance. I am sorry he is dead. *Dame, oui, par exemple!* But I do not weep for him as for a grandfather. Oh, no!"

"And your mother?"

"She died last year. So I am all alone."

He asked her what she thought of doing for her livelihood. She shrugged her shoulders with the resignation of her class.

"I can always earn my living. There are brasseries, cafés-concerts in all the towns—I am fairly well known. They will give me an engagement. *Il faut passer par là comme les autres.*"

"You must go through it like the others?" repeated my master. "But you are very young, my poor child."

"I am eighteen, Monsieur, I know I shall not make a fortune. I am not pretty enough even when I paint, and my figure is heavy. That is what Père Paragot used to complain of."

"What was his name?" asked my master, pricking up his ears.

"Berzélius Paragot—and he took the name of Nibbidard, which means 'no luck'—so he loved to call himself Berzélius Nibbidard Paragot."

"Berzélius Nibbidard Paragot," mouthed my master joyously. "I would give anything for a name like that!"

"It is yours if you like to take it," she said quite seriously. "No one will want it any more."

"Little Asticot of my heart," said he, "what do you think of it?"

It struck me as a most aristocratically romantic appellation. I was used to his aliases by this time. He had long ceased to call himself "Pradel," and what was our surname for the moment I am now unable to recollect.

"You look like 'Paragot,' Master," said I, and, in an inexplicable way, he did— as I have before remarked. He called me a psychometrical genius and enquired the name of the young lady.

"Amélie Duprat, Monsieur," she said. "But *pour le métier*—we must have professional names for the cafés—Père Paragot called me 'Blanquette de Veau.'"

"Delicious!" cried he.

"So everyone calls me Blanquette," she explained gravely. There was a silence. Paragot—he really assumed the name from this moment—refilled his pipe. The belated peasants, having finished their wine, clattered out of the café, and took off their hats as they passed us.

"Life is very hard, is it not, Messieurs?" remarked Blanquette. It seemed to be her favourite philosophic proposition. She sighed. "If Père Paragot had only lived to play at the wedding tomorrow!"

"What then?"

"I should have had ten francs."

"Ah!" said my master.

"First I lose my louis, and now I lose my ten francs! ah! *Sainte Vierge de Miséricorde!*"

It was heart-rending. Sometimes they received more than the stipulated fee at these village weddings. They passed the hat round. If the guests were mellow with good wine, which makes folks generous, they often earned double the amount. And they always had as much as they liked to eat, and could take away scraps in a handkerchief.

"And good wholesome nourishment, Monsieur. Once it was half a goose."

And now there was nothing, nothing. Blanquette did not believe in the *bon Dieu* any longer. She buried her face in her arms and wept. Paragot smoked helplessly for a few moments. I, unused to women's tears, felt the desolation of the race of Blanquette de Veau overspread me. But that I considered it to be beneath my dignity as a man, I should have wept too.

Suddenly Paragot brought his fist down on the table and started to his feet. Blanquette lifted a scared wet face, dimly seen in the half light.

"*Tonnerre de Dieu!*" cried he, "If you hold so much to your ten francs and half a goose, I myself will come with you to Chambéry tomorrow and fiddle at the wedding."

"You, Monsieur?" she gasped.

"Yes, I. Why not? Do you think I can't scrape catgut as well as Père Paragot?"

He walked to and fro declaring his musical powers in his boastful way. If he chose he could rip out the hearts of a dead Municipal Council with a violin, and could set a hospital for paralytics a-dancing. He would have fiddled the children of Hamelin away from the Pied Piper. Didn't Blanquette believe him?

"But yes, Monsieur," she said fervently.

"Ask Asticot."

My faith in him was absolute. To my mind he had even understated his abilities. The experience of the disillusioning years has since caused me to modify my opinions; but Paragot's boastfulness has not lessened him in my eyes. And this leads to a curious reflection. When a Gascon boasts, you love him for it; when a Prussian does it, your toes tingle to kick him to Berlin. His very whimsical braggadocio made Paragot adorable, and I am at a loss to think what he would have been without it.

"Of course," said he, "if you are proud, if you don't want to be seen in the company of a scarecrow like me, there is nothing more to be said."

Blanquette humbly repudiated the charge of pride. Her soul was set on her ten francs and she didn't care how she got them. She accepted Monsieur's generous offer out of a full heart.

"That's sense," said my master. "We shall rehearse at daybreak."

CHAPTER VI

Dawn found us all in a field some distance from the café—Paragot, Blanquette, Narcisse, the zither, the fiddle and I, and while the two musicians rehearsed the jingly waltzes and polkas that made up the old man's répertoire, I tried to explain the situation to Narcisse who sat with his ears cocked wondering what the deuce all the noise was about.

"Ah, Monsieur," said Blanquette, during a pause, "you play like a great artist."

"Didn't I tell you so?" he cried triumphantly.

"You must have studied much."

"Prodigiously," said he.

"Père Paragot had played the violin for sixty years, but he could not make it sing like that."

"You would not compare Père Paragot with my master?" I exclaimed by way of rebuke.

Blanquette acquiesced humbly.

"When one hears Monsieur, one has the devil in one's body."

"Listen to this," said the delighted Paragot jumping on to his feet and tucking the fiddle beneath his chin.

And there in the pure dawn with nothing but God's sky and green fields around us, he played Gounod's "Ave Maria," putting into his execution all his imaginative fervour, and accentuating the tremolo passages in a vibrating ecstasy which to Blanquette's uncultured soul was the very passion of music. I have since learned that the greatest violinists do not overemphasise the tremolo.

"Ah Dieu! it is beautiful," she murmured.

"Isn't it?" cried Paragot. "And it touches your heart, my little Blanquette, eh? We are all artists together."

"I, Monsieur?"

She laughed and ran her hands over the zither strings.

"I ought to be at work in the fields. So Père Paragot used to say. I make no progress—I am as stupid as a goose."

Two hours afterwards we started for Chambéry, as odd a procession as ever gave food for a high-road's gaiety. From the old grey valise carried the previous day by Blanquette she had produced much property finery. A black velveteen jacket resplendent with pearl-buttons, velveteen knee-breeches tied with ribbons at the knees, and a rakish Alpine hat with a feather adorned my master's person.

His own disreputable heavy boots and a pair of grey worsted stockings may not have formed a fastidious finish to the costume; but in my eyes he looked magnificent. Towards the transfiguration of Blanquette a Pandora box could not have effected more. She was attired in a short skirt, a white *fichu* moderately fresh, a kind of Italian head-dress and scarlet stockings. Enormous gilt ear-rings swung from her ears; a cable of blue beads encircled her neck; her lips were dyed pomegranate, her eyes darkened and her cheeks touched with rouge. A pair of substantial gilt shoes slung over her shoulders clinked their heels together as she walked. Narcisse barked his ecstatic admiration around this beauteous creature, and had I been a dog I should have barked mine too. My dignity as a man only allowed me to cast sidelong glances at her and hope that she would soon put on the gilt shoes. As for my master, on beholding her, he doffed his hat and saluted her with a fantastic compliment, whereat the girl blushed brick-red and turned her head away.

"Motley's the only wear, my son," he cried gaily. "In this cap and bells, I see life under a different aspect. Never has it appeared to me sweeter and more irresponsible. Don't you feel it? But I forgot. You haven't any motley. I apologise for my want of tact. Blanquette," he added in French, "why haven't you found a costume for Asticot?"

Blanquette replied in her matter-of-fact way that she hadn't any. They walked on together, and I dropped behind suddenly realising my pariahdom. I wondered whether these magnificent beings would be ashamed of my company when we arrived at Chambéry. I pictured myself sitting lonesome with Narcisse in the market-place while they revelled in their splendour, and the self-pity of the child overcame me.

"Master," said I dismally, "what shall Narcisse and I do while you are at the wedding?"

He wheeled round and regarded me, and I knew by the light in his eyes that an inspiration was taking shape behind them.

"I'll buy you a red shirt and pomade your hair, and you shall be one of us, my son, and go round with the hat."

I exulted obviously.

"Now the dog will feel out of it," said he, perplexed. "I will consult Blanquette. Do you think we could shave Narcisse and make him think he's a poodle?"

"That would be impossible, Monsieur," replied Blanquette gravely.

As Narcisse was enjoying himself to his heart's content, darting from side to side of the road and sniffing for the smells his soul delighted in, I did not concern myself about his feelings.

For Paragot's suggestion which I knew was ironically directed against myself, I did not care. So long as I was to be with my companions and of them, irony did not matter. I caught the twinkle in his eye and laughed. He was as joyous as Narcisse. The gladness of the July morning danced in his veins. He pulled the violin and bow out of the old baize bag and fiddled as we walked. It must have been an amazing procession.

And the old man whose clothes and functions we had assumed lay cold and stiff in the little lonely room with candles at his head and his feet. During our railway journey to Chambéry Blanquette told us in her artless way what she knew of his history. In the flesh he had been a crabbed and crotchety ancient addicted to drink. He had passed some years of his middle life in prison for petty thefts. In his youth—Blanquette's mind could not grasp the idea of Père Paragot having once been young—he must have been an astonishing blackguard. He had been wont to beat Blanquette, until one day realising her young strength she held him firm in her grip and threatened to throw him into a pond if he persisted in his attempted chastisement. Since then he had respected her person, but to the day of his death he had cursed her for anserine stupidity. An unlovely, loveless and unloved old man. Why should Blanquette have wept over him? She had not the Parisian's highly strung temperament and capacity for facile emotion. She was peasant to the core, slow to rejoice, and slow to grieve, and she had the peasant's remorseless logic in envisaging the elemental facts of existence. Père Paragot was wicked. He was dead. *Tant mieux.*

Blanquette had not the divine sense of humour which rainbows the tears of the world. That was my dear master's possession. But at the obvious she could laugh like any child of unsophistication. In the long shaded avenue of Chambéry, with its crowded market-stalls on either side—stalls where you saw displayed for sale rolls of calico and boots and gauffrettes and rusty locks and melons and rosaries and flyblown books—Paragot bought me my red shirt (which—*mirabile dictu!*—had tasselled cords to tie the collar) and pomade for my hair. He also purchased a yard of blue chiffon which he tied in an artistic bow round Narcisse's neck, whereat Blanquette laughed heartily; and when Narcisse bolted beneath a flower-stall and growling dispossessed himself of the adornment, and set to with tooth and claw to rend it into fragments, she threw herself on a bench convulsed with mirth. As Paragot had spent fifty centimes on the chiffon I thought this hilarity exceedingly ill-natured; but when another and a larger dog came up to see what Narcisse was doing and in half a minute was whirling about with Narcisse in a death grapple, and Blanquette sprang forward, separated the two dogs at some risk and took our bleeding mongrel to her bosom, consoling him with womanly words of pity, I saw there was something tender in Blanquette which mitigated my resentment.

The Restaurant du Soleil, where the marriage feast was held, was an earwiggy hostelry on the outskirts of the town, sheltered from the prying roadway by a screen of green lattice and a series of *tonnelles*, the dusty arbours, each furnished with table and chairs, beloved of French revellers. Above the entrance gate stretched the semi-circular sign-board bearing in addition to the name, the legend "Jardin. Noces. Fêtes." Within, a few lime-trees closely planted threw deep shadow over the grassless garden; shrubs and flowers wilted in a neglected bed.

Usually the forlorn demesne was supervised by a mangy waiter brooding over mangy tables and by a mangier cat who kept a furtive eye on the placarded list of each day's *plat du jour* and wondered when her turn would come for Thursday's *Sauté de lapin*. But tables, cat and waiter cast manginess aside when *we*(the pride of that day still remains and makes me italicise the word) came down to play at the wedding of Adolphe Querlat and Léontine Bringuet.

"*Tiens!* where is Père Paragot?" asked fat Madame Bringuet—perspiring in unaccustomed corset and black bombazine.

"Alas! he is no longer, Madame," explained Blanquette. "He had a seizure yesterday. He fell off his chair, and we picked him up stone dead."

"*Tiens, tiens*, but it is sad."

"But no. It does not matter. This gentleman will make you dance much better than Père Paragot," and she whispered encomiums into Madame's ear.

"Enchanted, Monsieur. And your name?"

My master swept a courtly bow with his feathered hat—no one ever bowed so magnificently as he.

"Berzélius Nibbidard Paragot, *cadet*, at your service."

"You must be hungry, Monsieur Paragot—and Mademoiselle and this little monsieur," said Madame Bringuet hospitably. "We are at table in the *salle à manger*. You will join us."

We entered the long narrow room and sat down to the banquet. Heavens! what a feast! There were omelettes and geese and eels and duck and tripe and onion soup and sausages and succulences inconceivable. Accustomed to the Spartan fare of vagabondage I plunged into the dishes head foremost like a hungry puppy. Should I eat such a meal as that to-day it would be my death. Hey for the light heart and elastic stomach of youth! Some fifty persons, the*ban and arrière ban* of the relations of the young couple, guzzled in a wedged and weltering mass. Wizened grandfathers and stolid large-eyed children ate and panted in the suffocating heat, and gorged again. Not till half way through the repast did tongues begin to wag freely. At last the tisane of champagne—syrupy paradise to my uncultivated palate—was handed round and the toasts were drunk. The bride's garter was secured amid boisterous shouts and innuendos, and then we left the stifling room and entered the garden, the elders to smoke and drink and gossip at the little tables beneath the verandah, the younger folk to dance on the uneven gravel. Young as I was, I felt grateful that no physical exercise was required of me for some hours to come. Even Narcisse and the cat (which followed him) waddled heavily to the verandah where we were to play.

The signal to start was soon given. Paragot tucked his violin under his chin, tuned up, waved one, two, three with his bow; Blanquette struck a cord on her zither and the dance began. At first all was desperately correct. The men in their ill-fitting broadcloth and white ties and enormous wedding favours, the women in their tight and decent finery, gyrated with solemn circumspection. But by degrees the music and the good Savoy wines and the abominable cognac flushed faces and set heads a-swimming. The sweltering heat caused a gradual discarding of garments. Arms took a closer grip of waists. Loud laughter and free jests replaced formal conversation; steps were performed of Southern fantasy; the dust rose in clouds; throats were choked though countenances streamed; the consumption of wine was Rabelaisian. And all through the orgy Paragot fiddled with strenuous light-heartedness, and Blanquette thrummed her zither with the awful earnestness of a woman on whose efforts ten francs and perhaps half a goose depended. But it was Paragot who made the people dance. To me, sitting in red shirt and pomaded hair at his feet, it seemed as if he were a magician. He threw his bow across the strings and compelled them to do his bidding. He was the great, the omnipotent personage of the feast. I sunned myself in his glory.

Indeed, he had the incommunicable gift of setting his soul a-dancing as he played, of putting the devil into the feet of those who danced. The wedding party were enraptured. If he had consumed all the bumpers he was offered, he would have been as drunk as a fiddler at an Irish wake. During a much needed interval in the dancing he advanced to the edge of the verandah and as a solo played Stephen Heller's "Tarantella," which crowned his triumph. With his unkempt beard and swarthy face and ridiculous pearl-buttoned velveteens, there was an air of rakish picturesqueness about Paragot, and he retained, what indeed he never quite lost, a certain aristocracy of demeanour. Wild cries of "*Bis!*" saluted him when he stopped. Men clapped each other on the shoulder uttering clumsy oaths, women smiled at him largely. Madame Bringuet, reeking in her tight gown, held up to him a brimming glass of champagne; the bride threw him a rose. He kissed the flower, put it in his button-hole and after bowing low drank to her health. I recalled my childish ambition to keep a fried fish shop and despised it heartily. If I only could play the violin like Paragot, thought I, and win the plaudits of the multitude, what greater glory could the earth hold? The practical Blanquette woke me from my dreams. Now was the moment, said she, to go round with the hat. I swung myself down from the verandah, the traditional shell (in lieu of a hat) in my hand, and went my round. Money was poured into it. Time after time I emptied it into my bulging pockets. When I returned to the verandah, Blanquette's eyes distended strangely. She glanced at Paragot, who smiled at her in an absent manner. For the moment the artist in him was predominant. He was the centre of his little world, and its adulation was as breath to his nostrils.

This is what I, the mature man, know to be the case. To me, then, he was but the King receiving tribute from his subjects. When Paragot with a flourish of his bow responded to the encore, I found my hand slip into Blanquette's and there it remained in a tight grip till flushed and triumphant he again acknowledged the applause. Nothing was said between Blanquette and myself, but she became my sworn sister from that moment. And Narcisse sat at our feet looking down on the crowd, his tongue lolling out mockingly and a satiric leer on his face.

"My children," said Paragot, on our return journey in the close, ill-lighted, wooden-seated third-class compartment, "we have had a glorious day. One of those sun-kissed, snow-capped peaks that rise here and there in the monotonous range of life. It fills the soul with poetry and makes one talk in metaphor. In such moments as these we are all metaphors, my son. We are illuminated expressions of the divine standing for the commonplace things of yesterday and tomorrow. We have accomplished what millions and millions are striving and struggling and failing to do at this very hour. We have achieved *success!* We have left on human souls the impress of our mastery! We are also all of us dog-tired and, I perceive, disinclined to listen to transcendental conversation."

"I'm not tired, master," I declared as stoutly as the effort of keeping open two leaden eyelids would allow.

"And you?" he asked turning to Blanquette by his side—I occupied the opposite corner.

She confessed. A very little. But she had listened to all Monsieur had said, and if he continued to talk she would not think of going to sleep. Whereupon she closed her eyes, and when I opened mine I saw that her head had slipped along the smooth wooden back of the carriage and rested on Paragot's shoulder. Through sheer kindliness and pity he had put his arm around her so as to settle her comfortably as she slept. I envied her.

When she awoke at the first stoppage of the train, she started away from him with a little gasp.

"O Monsieur! I did not know. You should have told me."

"I am only Père Paragot," said he. "You must often have had your head against this mountebank jacket of mine."

She misunderstood him. Her eyes flashed.

"It is the first time in my life—I swear it." She held up her two forefingers crossed and kissed them. "Père Paragot! *ah non!* neither he nor another. I am an honest girl, though you may not think so."

"My good Blanquette," said he kindly, taking her scarred coarse hand in his, "you are as honest a girl as ever breathed, and if Père Paragot didn't let you put your sleepy little head on his shoulder he must have been a stonier hearted old curmudgeon than you have given one to believe."

So he soothed her and explained, while our two fellow passengers, a wizened old peasant and his wife, regarded them stolidly.

"*Mon Dieu*, it is hot," said Blanquette. "Don't you think so, Asticot? I wish I had a fan."

"I will make you one out of the paper the fowl is wrapped in," said Paragot.

Not half a goose, but a cold fowl minus half a wing had been our supplementary guerdon. Decently enveloped in a sheet of newspaper it lay on her lap. When he had divested it of its covering, which he proceeded to twist into a fan, it still lay on her lap, looking astonishingly naked.

At the next station the old peasant and his wife got out and we had the compartment to ourselves. Blanquette produced from her pocket a handkerchief knotted over an enormous lump.

"These are the takings, Monsieur. It looks small; but they changed the coppers into silver at the restaurant for me."

"It's a fortune," laughed my master.

"It is much," she replied gravely, and undoing the knot she offered him with both hands the glittering treasure. "I hope you will be a little generous, Monsieur—I know it was you who gained the *quête*."

"My good child!" cried he, interrupting her and pushing back her hands, "what lunacy are you uttering? Do you imagine that I go about fiddling for pence at village weddings?"

"But Monsieur—"

"But little imbecile, I did it to help you, to enable you to get your ten francs and half a goose. Asticot too. Haven't you been enchanted all day to be of service to Mademoiselle? Do you want to be paid for wearing a red shirt with a tasselled collar and pommade in your hair? Aren't we going about the world like Don Quixote and Sancho Panza rescuing damsels in distress? Isn't that the lodestar of our wanderings?"

"Yes, master," said I.

Blanquette looked open-mouthed from him to me, from me to him, scarce able to grasp such magnanimity. To the peasant, money is a commodity to be struggled for, fought for, grasped, prized; to be doled out like the drops of a priceless Elixir Vitæ. Paragot had the aristocratic, artistic scorn of it; and I, as I have said before, was the pale reflexion of Paragot.

"It is yours," I explained, as might a great prince's chamberlain, "the master gained it for you."

The tears came into her eyes. The corners of her lips went down. Paragot turned half round in his seat and put his hands on her shoulders.

"If you spill tears on the fowl you will make it too salt, and I shall throw it out of the window."

Paragot paid the modest funeral expenses of the worn-out fiddler. Asked why he did not leave the matter in the hands of the communal authorities he replied that he could not take a man's name without paying for it. Such an appellation as Berzélius Nibbidard Paragot was worth a deal coffin and a mass or two. This fine sense of integrity was above Blanquette's comprehension. She thought the funeral was a waste of money.

"It should go to benefit the living and not the dead," she argued.

"Wait till you are dead yourself," he replied, "and see how you would like to be robbed of your name. There are many things for you to learn, my child."

"*Il n'y a pas beaucoup*—not many," she said with a sigh. "We who are poor and live on the high-roads learn very quickly. If you are hungry and have two sous you can buy bread. If you only have two sous and you throw them to a dog who doesn't need them, you have nothing to buy bread with, and you starve. And it is not so easy to gain two sous."

Paragot sucked reflectively at his porcelain pipe.

"Asticot," said he, "the *argumentum ad ventrem* is irrefutable."

"Now I must go and make my *malle*" she said. "I return to Chambéry to try to earn my two sous."

"Won't you stay here over the night? You must be very tired."

"One must work for one's living, Monsieur," she said moving away.

It was afternoon. We had trudged the three dusty miles back from the tiny churchyard where we had left the old man's unlamented grave, and Paragot, as usual, was washing his throat with beer. It must be noted, not to his glorification, that about this time a chronic dryness began to be the maincharacteristic of Paragot's throat, and the only humectant that seemed to be of no avail was water.

The sun still blazed and the hush of the July afternoon lay over the valley. Paragot watched the thickset form of Blanquette disappear into the café; he poured out another bottle of beer and addressed Narcisse who was blinking idly up at him.

"If she had a pair of decent stays, my dog, or no stays at all, she might have something of a figure. What do you think? On the whole—no."

Narcisse stood on his hind legs, his forepaws on his master's arm, and uttered little plaintive whines. Paragot patted him on the head.

As I was engaged a yard or two away, elbows on knees, in what Paragot was pleased to call my studies—Thierry's "Récits des Temps Mérovingiens," a tattered, flyblown copy of which he had bought at Chambéry—he was careful not to interrupt me; he talked to the dog. Paragot had to talk to something. If he were alone he would have talked to his shadow; in his coffin he would have apostrophised the worms.

"Yes, my dog," said he, after a draught of beer. "We have passed through more than we wotted of these two days. We have held a human being by the hand and have faced with her the eternal verities. Now she is going to earn her two sous in the whirlpool, and the whirlpool will suck her down, and as she has not claims to beauty, Narcisse, of any kind whatsoever, either of face or figure, hers will be a shuddersome career and end. Say you are sorry for poor Blanquette de Veau."

Narcisse sniffed at the table, but finding it bare of everything but beer, in which he took no interest, dropped on his four legs and curled himself up in dudgeon.

"You damned cynical sensualist," cried my master. "I have wasted the breath of my sentiment upon you." And he called out for the landlady and more beer.

Presently Blanquette emerged laden with zither case and fiddle and little grey valise and the pearl-buttoned suit which was slung over one arm.

"Monsieur," she said, putting down her impedimenta, "the *patronne* has told me that you have paid for my lodging and my nourishment. I am very grateful, Monsieur. And if you will accept this costume it will be a way of repaying your kindness."

Paragot rose, took the suit and laid it on his chair.

"I accept it loyally," said he, with a bow, as if Blanquette had been a duchess.

"*Adieu, Monsieur, et merci*," she said holding out her hand.

Paragot stuck both his hands in his trousers pockets.

"My good child," said he, "you are bound straight for the most cheerless hell that was ever inhabited by unamusing devils."

Blanquette shrugged her shoulders and spoke in her dull fatalistic way.

"*Que voulez-vous?* I know it is not gay. But it is in the *métier*. When Père Paragot was alive it was different. He had his good qualities, Père Paragot. He was like a watch-dog. If any man came near me he was fierce. I did not amuse myself, it is true, but I remained an honest girl. Now it is changed. I am alone. I go into a brasserie to play and dance. I can get an engagement at the Café Brasserie Tissot," and then after a pause, turning her head away, she added the fatalistic words she had used before: "*If faut passer par là, comme les autres.*"

"I forbid you!" cried my master, striding up and down in front of her and ejaculating horrible oaths. He invoked the sacred name of pigs and of all kinds of other things. My attention had long since been diverted from the learned

Monsieur Thierry, and I wondered what she had to pass through like the others. It must be something dreadful, or my master would not be raving so profanely. I learned in after years. Of all mutilated lives there are few more ghastly than those of the *fille de brasserie* in a small French provincial town. And here was Blanquette about to abandon herself to it with stolid, hopeless resignation. There was no question of vicious instinct. What semblance of glamour the life presented did not attract her in the least. A sweated alien faces rabbit-pulling in the East End with more pleasurable anticipation.

"I am not going to allow you to take an engagement in a brasserie!" shouted my master. "Do you hear? I forbid you!"

"But Monsieur——" began Blanquette piteously.

Then Paragot had one of his sudden inspirations. He crashed his fist on the little table so that the glass and bottles leaped and Narcisse darted for shelter into the café.

"*Tron de l'air!*" he cried. "I have it. It is an illumination. Asticot—here! Leave your book. I shall be Paragot in character as well as name. We shall fiddle with Blanquette as we fiddled yesterday—and I shall be a watch-dog like Père Paragot and keep her an honest girl. We'll make it a firm, Paragot and Company, and there will always be two sous for bread and two to throw to a dog. I like throwing sous to dogs. It is my nature. Now I know why I was sent into the world. It was to play the fiddle up and down the sunny land of France. My little Asticot, why haven't we thought of it before? You shall learn to play the trumpet, Asticot, and Narcisse shall walk on his hind legs and collect the money. It will be magnificent!"

"Are you serious, Monsieur?" asked Blanquette, trembling.

"Serious? Over an inspiration that came straight from the *bon Dieu?* But yes, I am serious. *Et toi?*" he added sharply using for the first time the familiar pronoun, "are you afraid I will beat you like Père Paragot?"

"You can if you like," she said huskily; and I wondered why on earth she should have turned the colour of cream cheese.

CHAPTER VII

NOT being content with having attached to his person a stray dog and a mongrel boy and rendering himself responsible for their destinies, Paragot must now saddle himself with a young woman. Had she been a beautiful gipsy, holding fascinating allurements in lustrous eyes and pomegranate lips, and witchery in a supple figure, the act would have been a commonplace of human weakness. But in the case of poor Blanquette, squat and coarse, her heavy features only redeemed from ugliness by youth, honesty and clean teeth, the eternal attraction of sex was absent.

From the decorative point of view she was as unlovely as Narcisse or myself. She was dull, unimaginative, ignorant, as far removed from Paragot as Narcisse from a greyhound. Why then, in the name of men and angels, should Paragot have taken her under his protection? My only answer to the question is that he was Paragot. Judge other men by whatever standard you have to hand; it will serve its purpose in a rough and ready manner; but Paragot—unless with me idolatry has obscured reason—Paragot can only be measured by that absolute standard which lies awful and unerring on the knees of the high gods.

Of course he saved the girl from a hideous doom. Thousands of kindly, earnest men have done the same in one way or another. But Paragot's way was different from anyone else's. Its glorious lunacy lifted it above ordinary human methods.

So many of your wildly impulsive people repent them of their generosities as soon as the magnanimous fervour has cooled. The grandeur of Paragot lay in the fact that he never repented. He was fantastic, self-indulgent, wastrel, braggart, what you will; but he had an exaggerated notion of the value of every human soul save his own. The destiny of poor Blanquette was to him of infinitely more importance than that of the wayward genius that was Paragot. The pathos of his point of view had struck me, even as a child, when he discoursed on my prospects.

"I am Paragot, my son," he would say, "a film full of wind and wonder, fantasy and folly, driven like thistledown about the world. I do not count. But you, my little Asticot, have the Great Responsibility before you. It is for you to uplift a corner of the veil of Life and show joy to men and women where they would not have sought it. Work now and gather wisdom, my son, so that when the Great Day comes you may not miss your destiny." And once, he added wistfully—"as I have missed mine."

As Paragot decided that we should not start off then and there into the unknown but remain at the café until we had laid our plan of campaign, Blanquette took her valise into the house, and, for the rest of the day, busied herself in the kitchen with the *patronne;* Paragot drank with the villagers in the café; and I, when Thierry and Narcisse had given me all the companionship they had to offer, curled myself up on the mattress spread in a corner of the tiny *salle à manger* and went to sleep.

The next morning Paragot awakened with an Idea. He would go to Aix-les-Bains which was close by, and would return in the evening. The nature of his errand he would not tell me. Who was I, little grey worm that I was, to question his outgoings and his incomings? The little grey worm would stay with Blanquette and Narcisse and see to it that they did not bite each other. I humbly accepted the rebuke and obeyed the behest. The afternoon found the three of us in a field under a tree; Blanquette embracing her knees, and the dog asleep with his throat across her feet. She was wearing her old cotton dress, and as she had been helping the *patronne* all the morning, her sleeves were rolled up to her elbows displaying stout, stubby arms. The top button of her bodice was open; she was bare-headed, but her hair, little deeper in shade than her tanned face and neck, was coiled neatly. Had it not been for the hard grip of the day before I should have jealously resented her admission into our vagabond fraternity. As it was, from the height of my sixteen-year-old masculinity I somewhat looked down upon her: not as poor Blanquette, the zither-playing vagrant; but as a girl. Could we, creation's lords, do with a creature of an inferior sex in our wanderings? Could she perform our feats of endurance? I questioned her anxiously.

"*Moi?*" she laughed, "I am as strong as any man. You will see."

She leaped to her feet and, before I could protest, had picked me off the ground like a kitten and was tossing me in her arms.

"*Voilà!*" she said, depositing me tenderly on the grass; and having collected the dislodged Narcisse she embraced her knees and laughed again. It was a kind honest laugh; a good-natured, big boy's laugh, coming full out of her eyes and shewing her strong white teeth. I lost the sense of insult in admiration of her strength.

"You should have been a boy, Blanquette," said I.

She assented, acknowledging at once her inferiority and thus restoring my self respect.

"You are lucky, you, to be one. In this world the egg is for the men and the shell is for the women."

"Why don't you cut off your hair and put on boy's clothes?" I asked. "Then you would get the egg. No one could tell the difference."

"You don't think I look like a woman? I? *Mon Dieu!* Where are your eyes?"

She was actually indignant with me who had thought to please her: my first encounter with the bewildering paradox of woman.

"*Ah! mais non*," she panted. "I may be strong like a man, but *grâce à Dieu*, I don't resemble one. Look."

And she sat bolt upright, her hands at her waist developing her bust to its full extent. She was not *jolie, jolie*, she explained, but she was as solidly built as another; I was to examine myself and see how like I was to the flattest of boards. Routed I chewed blades of grass in silence until she spoke again.

"Tell me of the *patron*."

"The *patron?*" I asked, puzzled.

"Yes—Monsieur—your master."

"You must call him *maître*," said I, "not *patron*." For the *patron* was any peddling "boss," the leader of a troupe of performing dogs or the miserable landlord of a village inn, Paragot a *patron!*

"I meant no harm. I have too much respect for him," said Blanquette, humbly.

Again reinstated in my position of superiority I explained the Master to her feminine intelligence.

"He has been to every place in the world and knows everything that is to be known, and speaks every language that is spoken under the sun, and has read every book that ever was written, and I have seen him break a violin over a man's head."

"*Tiens!*" said Blanquette.

"In the Forum at Rome last winter he had an argument with the most learned professor in Europe who is making the excavations, and proved him to be wrong."

"*Tiens!*" repeated Blanquette, much impressed, though of Forum or excavations she had no more notion than Narcisse.

"If he wanted to be a king tomorrow, he would only have to go up to a throne and sit upon it."

"But no," said Blanquette. "To be a king one must be a king's son."

"How do you know that he isn't?" I asked with a could-and if-I-would expression of mystery.

"King's sons don't go about the high roads with little *gamins* like you," replied the practical Blanquette.

"How do you know that I am not a king's son too?" I asked, less with the idea of self-aggrandisement than that of vindication of Paragot.

"Because you yourself said that your mother sold you as my mother sold me to Père Paragot."

Whereupon it suddenly occurred to me that as far as retentiveness of memory was concerned, Blanquette was not such a fool as in my arrogance I had set her down to be. I was going to retort that his magnificence in purchasing me proved him a personage of high order, but as I quickly reflected that the same argument might apply to the rank of the contemned Père Paragot, I refrained. A silence ensuing, I uncomfortably resolved to study my master with a view to acquiring his skill in repartee.

"But what does he do, the Master?" enquired Blanquette.

"Do? What do you mean?"

"How does he earn his living?"

"That shows you know nothing about him," I cried triumphantly. "King's sons do not earn their living. They have got it already. Haven't you ever read that in books?"

"I can read and write, but I don't read books," sighed Blanquette. "I am not clever. You will have to teach me."

"This is the book I am reading," said I, taking the "Récits des Temps Mérovingiens" from my pocket.

Again Blanquette sighed. "You must be very clever, Asticot."

"Not at all," said I modestly, but I felt that it was nice of Blanquette to realise the intellectual gulf between us. "It is the Master who has taught me all I know." I spoke, God wot, as if my knowledge would have burst through the covers of an Encyclopædia—"Three years ago I could not speak a word of French. Fancy. And now——"

"You still talk like an Englishman," said Blanquette.

Looking back now on those absurd far-off days, I wonder whether after all I did not learn as much that was vital from Blanquette as from Paragot. Her downright, direct, unimaginative common-sense amounted to genius. At the time I preferred genius in the fantastic form which inflated my bubbles of self-conceit, instead of bursting them; but in after life one has a high appreciation of the burster.

In the moment's mortification, however, I recriminated.

"You make worse mistakes than I do. You say '*j'allons faire*,' when you ought to say '*je vais faire*' and I heard you talk about *une chien*."

"That is because I have no education," replied Blanquette, with her grave humility. "I speak like the peasants; not like instructed people—not like the Master, for instance."

"No one could speak like the Master," said I.

There was a long silence. Blanquette hugged her knees and Narcisse snored at her feet, accepting her as vagabond comrade. I lay on my back and forgot Blanquette; and out of the intricacies of myriad leaf and branch against the sky wove pictures of Merovingian women. There where the black branches cut a lozenge of blue was the pale Queen Galeswinthe lying on her bed. Through yon dark cluster of under-leaves one could discern the strangler sent by King Hilperic to murder her. And in that radiant patch silhouetted clear and cold and fierce in loveliness was Frédégonde waiting for the King. She was a glittering sword of a woman whose slayings fascinated me. I much preferred her to the gentler Brunehilde whose form I saw outlined in a soft shadow of green. I tried to find frames in my aerial gallery for Brunehilde's two daughters, Ingonde and Chlodoswinde, especially the latter whose name appealed to my acquired taste for odd nomenclature, and the conscious effort brought me back to the modern world, and the sound of Blanquette's voice.

"*Tu sais*, Asticot, I can wash the Master's shirts and mend his clothes. I can also make his coffee in the morning."

Her eyes had a far-away look. She was living in the land of day dreams even as I had been.

"I always prepare the Master's breakfast," said I jealously.

"It is the woman's duty."

"I don't care," I retorted.

She unclasped her hands, and coming forward on to her knees and bending over me, brushed a strand of hair from my forehead.

"I will prepare yours too, Asticot," she said gently, "and you will see how nice that will be. Men can't do these things where there is a woman to look after them. It is not proper."

So, flattered in my masculinity, being ranked with Paragot as a "man," I took a sultanesque view of the situation and graciously consented to her proposed ministrations.

Paragot came back triumphant from Aix-les-Bains. Hadn't he told me he had been inspired to go there? The man who played the violin at the open-air Restaurant by the Lac de Bourget had just that day fallen ill. The result, a week's engagement for Blanquette and himself.

"But, my child," said he, "you will have to suffer an inharmonious son of Satan who makes a discordant Hades out of an execrable piano. He had the impudence to tell me that he came from the Conservatoire. He, with as much ear for music as an organ-grinder's monkey! He said to me—Paragot—that I played the violin not too badly! I foresee a hideous doom overhanging that young man, my children. Before the week is out I will throw him into the maw of his soul-devouring piano. Ha! my children, give me to drink, for I am thirsty."

Mindful of my dignity as a man, I glanced at Blanquette, who went into the café obediently, while I stayed with my master. It was a sweet moment. Paragot gripped me by the shoulder.

"My son, while Blanquette and I work, which Carlyle says is the noblest function of man, but concerning which I have my own ideas, you cannot live in red-shirted, pomaded and otherwise picturesque and studious laziness. Look," he cried, pointing to a round, flat object wrapped in paper which he had brought with him. "Do you know what that is?"

"That," said I, "is a cake."

"It is a tambourine," said my master.

The next day found us in the garden of the little lake-side restaurant at Aix-les-Bains playing at lunch time. The young man at the piano whom I had expected to see a fiend in human shape was a harmless consumptive fellow who played with the sweet patience of a musical box. He shook hands with me and called me "*cher collègue*," and before nightfall told me of a disastrous love-story in consequence of which, were it not for his mother, he would drown himself in the lake. He effaced himself before Paragot much as the bellows-blower does before the organist. His politeness to Blanquette would have put to the blush any young man at the Bon Marché or the Louvre. His name was Laripet.

I was ordered to make modest use of my tambourine until sufficient instruction from Paragot should authorise him to let me loose with it; I was merely to add to the picturesqueness of the group on the platform, and at intervals to go the round of the guests collecting money. I liked this, for I could then jingle the tambourine without fear of reproof. You have no idea what an ordeal it is for a boy to have a tambourine which he must not jingle. But the shady charm of the garden compensated for the repression of noisy instincts. After months of tramping in the broiling sun, free and perfect as it was, the easy loafing life seemed sweet. We went little into the gay town itself. For my part I did not like it. Aix-les-Bains consisted of a vast Enchanted Garden set in a valley, great mountains hemming it round. Skirting the Enchanted Garden were shady streets and mysterious palaces, some having gardens of their own of a secondary enchantment, and shops where jewels and perfumes and white ties and flowers and other objects of strange luxury were exhibited in the windows. But these took the humble place of mere accessories to the Enchanted Garden, jealously guarded against Asticot by great high gilded railings and by blue-coated, silver-buttoned functionaries at the gates. Within rose two Wonder Houses gorgeous with dome and pinnacle, bewildering with gold and snow, displaying before the aching sight the long cool stretch of verandahs, and offering the baffling glimpse of vast interiors whence floated the dim sound of music and laughter; and bright, happy beings, in wondrous raiment, wandered in and out unchallenged, unconcerned, as if the Wonder Houses were their birthright.

I, a shabby, penniless little Peri, stood at the gilded gates disconsolate. I didn't like it. The mystery of the unknown beatitude within the Wonder Houses oppressed me to faintness. *It was unimaginable.* Through the leaves of a tree I could see the pale Queen Galeswinthe; but through those gay enchanting walls I could see nothing. They baulked my soul. When I tried to explain my feelings to Paragot he looked at me in his kind, sad way and shook his head.

"My wonder-headed little Asticot," said he, "within those gewgaw Wonder Houses——" Then he stopped abruptly and waved me away, "No. It's a devilish good thing for you to have something your imagination boggles at. Stick to the Ideal, my son, and hug the Unexplained. The people who have solved the Riddle of the Universe at fifteen are bowled over by the Enigma of their cook at fifty. Plug your life as full as it can hold with fantasy and fairy-tale, and thank God that your soul is baulked by the Mysteries of the Casinos of Aix-les-Bains."

"But what do they do there, Master?" I persisted.

"The men worship strange goddesses and the women run after false gods, and all practice fascinating idolatries."

I did not in the least know what he meant, which was what he intended. When I consulted Blanquette one morning, as she and I alone were sauntering down the long shady avenue which connects the town with the little-port of the lake, she said that people went into the Cercle and the Villa des Fleurs, the two Wonder Houses aforesaid, merely to gamble. I pooh-poohed the notion.

"The Master says they are Temples of great strange gods, where people worship."

"Gods! What an idea! *Il n'y a que le bon Dieu*," quoth Blanquette.

"You have evidently not heard of the gods of Greece and Rome, Jupiter and Apollo and Venus and Bacchus."

"*Ah, tiens*," said Blanquette. "I have heard Italians swear 'Corpo di Bacco.' That is why?"

"Of course," said I in my grandest manner, "and there are heaps of other gods besides."

"All the same," she objected, "I always thought the Italians were good Catholics."

"So they may be," said I, "but that doesn't prove that there are not beautiful gods and goddesses and idols and shrines in the Cercle and the Villa des Fleurs."

As this was unanswerable Blanquette diverted the conversation to the less transcendental topic of the premature baldness of Monsieur Laripet.

If the doings of the bright happy beings were hidden from me while they worshipped in the Casinos, I at least met them at close quarters in the garden of the Restaurant du Lac. In some respects this garden resembled that of the Restaurant du Soleil at Chambéry. There was a verandah round the restaurant itself, there were trees in joyous leafage, there were little tables, and there were waiters hurrying to and fro with napkins under their arms. But that was all the resemblance. Our little platform stood against the railings separating the garden from the quay. Behind us shimmered the blue lake, great mountains rising behind; away on the right, embosomed in the green mountainside, flashed the white Château de Hautecombe. Always in mid-lake a tiny paddle-steamer churned up a wake of white foam. On the quay itself stood an enchanting little box—a *camera obscura*—to which I as a fellow artist was given the *entrée* by the proprietor, and in which one could see heavenly pictures of the surrounding landscape; there were also idle cabs with white awnings, and fezzed Turks perspiring under furs and rugs which they hawked for sale. In front of us, within the garden, a joyous crowd of the radiantly raimented laughed over dainty food set on snowy cloths. Here and there a lobster struck a note of colour, or a ray of sunlight striking through the red or gold translucencies of wine in a glass: which distracted my attention from my orchestral duties and caused an absent-minded jingle of my tambourine.

What I loved most was to make my round among the tables and mingle closely with the worshippers. Of the men, clean and correct in their perfectly fitting flannels, sometimes stern, sometimes mocking, sometimes pettishly cross, I was rather shy; but I was quite at my ease with the women, even with those whose many rings and jewels, violent perfumes and daring effects of dress made me instinctively differentiate from their quieter and less bejewelled sisters. Blanquette laughingly called me a "*petit polisson*" and said that I made soft eyes at them. Perhaps I did. When one is a hundred and fifty it is hard to realise that one's little scarecrow boy's eyes may have touched the hearts of women. But the appeal of the outstretched tambourine was rarely refused.

"Get out of this," the man would say.

"But no. Remain. *Il a l'air si drôle*—what is your name?"

"*Je m'appelle Asticot, Madame, à votre service.*"

This always amused the lady. She would search through an invariably empty purse.

"Give him fifty centimes."

And the man would throw a silver piece into the tambourine.

Once I was in luck. The lady found a ten-franc piece in her purse.

"That is all I have."

"I have no change," growled the man.

"If I give you this," said the lady, "what would you do with it?"

"If Madame would tell me where to get it, I would buy a photograph of Madame," said I, with one of Paragot's "inspirations"; for she was very pretty.

"*Voilà*," she laughed putting the gold into my hand. "*Tu me fais la cour, maintenant.* Come and see me at the Villa Marcelle and I will give you a photograph gratis."

But Paragot when I repeated the conversation to him called the lady shocking names, and forbade me to go within a mile of the Villa Marcelle. So I did not get the photograph.

The next best thing I loved was to see Blanquette's eyes glitter when I returned to the platform and poured silver and copper into her lap. She uttered strange little exclamations under her breath, and her fingers played caressingly with the coins.

"We gain more here in a day than Père Paragot did in a week. It is wonderful. *N'est-ce pas, Maître?*" she said one morning.

Paragot tuned his violin and looked down on her.

"Money pleases you, Blanquette?"

"Of course."

She counted the takings sou by sou.

"Yet you did not want to accept your just share."

"What you make me take is not just, Master," she said, simply.

Much as she loved money, her sense of justice rebelled against Paragot's division of the takings—a third for Laripet, a third for Blanquette and a third for himself which he generously shared with me. Père Paragot used to sweep into his pockets every sou and Blanquette had to subsist on whatever he chose to allow for joint expenses. Her new position of independence was a subject for much inward pride, mingled however with a consciousness of her own unworthiness. Monsieur Laripet, yes; she would grant that he was entitled to the same as the Master; but herself—no. Was not the Master the great artist, and she but the clumsy strummer? Was he not also a man, with more requirements than she—tobacco, absinthe, brandy and the like?

"A third is too much," she added.

"If you argue," said he, "I will divide it in halves for Laripet and yourself, and I won't touch a penny."

"That would be idiotic," said Blanquette.

"It would be in keeping with life generally," he answered. "In a comic opera one thing is not more idiotic than another. Yes, Monsieur Laripet, we will give them *Funiculi, Funiculà.* I once drove in coffin nails to that tune in Verona. Now we will set people eating to it in Aix-les-Bains—we, Monsieur Laripet, you and I, who ought to be the petted minions of great capitals! It is a comic opera."

"One has to get bread or one would starve," said Blanquette pursuing her argument. "And to get bread one must have money. If I had all the money you would not eat bread."

"I should eat *brioches*," laughed Paragot quoting Marie Antoinette.

"You always laugh at me, Master," said Blanquette wistfully.

Paragot drew his bow across the strings.

"There is nothing in this comical universe I don't laugh at, my little Blanquette," said he. "I am like good old Montaigne—I rather laugh than weep, because to laugh is the more dignified."

Laripet struck a chord on the piano. Paragot joined in and played three bars. Then he stopped short. There was not the vestige of a laugh on his face. It was deadly white, and his eyes were those of a man who sees a ghost.

The four bright happy beings, two ladies and two men who had just entered the garden and at whom his stare was directed, took no notice, but followed a bowing maître d'hôtel to a table that had been reserved for them.

I sprang to the platform, on the edge of which I had been squatting at Blanquette's feet.

"Are you ill, Master?"

He started. "Ill? Of course not. Pardon, Monsieur Laripet. *Recommençons.*"

He plunged into the merry tune and fiddled with all his might, as if nothing had happened. But I saw his nostrils quivering and the sweat running down his face into his beard.

CHAPTER VIII

WHEN *Funiculi Funiculà* was over he sat on the wooden chair provided for him and wiped his face. His hands shook. He beckoned me to come near.

"Do I look too grotesque a mountebank Tomfool?" he asked in English.

He was wearing the pearl-buttoned velveteen suit whose magnificence he had enhanced by newly purchased steel-buckled shoes and black stockings, and to a less bigoted worshipper than me I suppose he must have looked a mountebank Tomfool; but I only gaped at his question.

"Do I?" he repeated almost fiercely.

"You look beautiful, Master," said I.

He passed his lean fingers wearily over his eyes. "Pardon, my little Asticot. There are things in Heaven and Earth etc. Myriads of Mysteries. As many in the heart of man as in your Wonder Houses yonder. Get me some brandy. Three *petits verres* poured into a tumbler."

I went off to the restaurant and obtained the drink. When I returned they were playing the mocking chorus that runs through "Orphée aux Enfers."

The number over, Paragot drained the glass at one gulp. The company broke into unusual applause. Some one shouted "*Bis!*"

"Get me some more," said he. "Do you know why I chose that tune?"

"No, Master."

"Because twenty devils entered into me and played leapfrog over one another."

"I am very fond of that little tune. It is so gay," said Blanquette, as if she were introducing a fresh topic of conversation.

"I detest it," said my master.

The maître d'hôtel came up and asked that the chorus should be played again as an encore. I fetched Paragot's drink and having set it down beside him on the platform, went round with my tambourine. When I reached the table at which the four new comers were seated I found that they spoke English. They were a young man in a straw hat, a young girl, a forbidding looking man of forty with a beaky nose, and the loveliest lady I have ever seen in my life. She had the complexion of a sea-shell. Her eyes were the blue of glaciers, and they shone cold and steadfast; but her lips were kind. Her black hair under the large white tulle hat had the rare bluish tinge, looking as if cigarette smoke had been blown through it. Small and exquisitely made she sat the princess of my boyish dreams.

"I call it a ripping tune," cried the young girl.

"I hate it more than any other tune in the world," said the lovely lady with a shiver.

Her voice was like a peal of bells or running water or whatever silvery sounding things you will.

"It is very absurd to have such prejudices," said the beaky-nosed man of forty. He spoke like a Frenchman, and like a very disagreeable Frenchman. How dared he address my princess in that tone?

I extended my tambourine.

"*Qu'est-ce que vous désirez?*" asked the straw-hatted young man in an accent as Britannic as the main deck of the Bellerophon.

"Anything that the ladies will kindly give me, Sir," I replied in our native tongue.

"Hullo! English? What are you knocking about France for?"

I glanced at the lovely lady. She was crumbling bread and not taking the least notice of me. I was piqued.

"My Master thinks it the best way to teach me philosophy, Sir," said I politely. If I had not learned much philosophy from him I had at least learned politeness. The lady looked up with a smile. The young girl exclaimed that either my remark or myself—I forget which—was ripping. I paid little heed to her. I have always disregarded the people of one adjective; they seem poverty-stricken to one who has sunned himself in the wealth of Paragot's epithets.

"Your master is the gentleman in the pearl buttons?" enquired the young man.

"Yes, Sir."

"What's his name?"

"Berzélius Nibbidard Paragot, Sir," said I so proudly that the lovely princess laughed.

"I must look at him," she said turning round in her chair.

I too glanced at the familiar group on the platform: Laripet with his back to us, working his arms and shoulders at the piano; Blanquette seated on the other side, thrumming away at the zither on her lap; Narcisse lolling his tongue in that cynical grin of his; and Paragot fiddling in front, like a fiddler possessed, his clear eyes fixed on the lady in a most uncanny stare.

When she turned again, she shivered once more. She did not look up but went on crumbling bread. It shocked me to notice that the pink of her sea-shell face had gone and that her fingers trembled. Then a wild conjecture danced through my brain and I forgot my tambourine.

"You still here?" laughed the young man. "What are you waiting for?"

I started. "I beg your pardon, Sir," said I moving away. He laughed and called me back.

"Here are two francs to buy a philosophy book."

"And here are five sous not to come and worry us again," said the older man in French. While I was wondering why they tolerated such a disagreeable man in the party my beautiful lady's fingers flew to the gilt chain purse by her side. "And here are five francs because you are English!" she exclaimed; and as she held me for a second with her eyes I saw in them infinite depths of sadness and longing.

When I returned to the platform the piece had just been brought to an end. Paragot poured his second brandy down his throat and sat with his head in his hands. I shed, as usual, my takings into Blanquette's lap. On seeing the five-franc piece her eyes equalled it in size.

"*Tiens! Cent sous!* who gave it you?"

I explained. The most beautiful lady in the world. Paragot raised his head and looked at me haggardly.

"Why did she give you five francs?"

"Because I was English, she said."

"Did she talk to you?"

"Yes, Master, and I have never heard anyone speak so beautifully."

Paragot made no answer, but began to tune his violin.

During the next interval my quartette left the restaurant. I ran to the gate, and bowed as they passed by.

The young fellow gave me a friendly nod, but the lovely lady swept out cold-eyed, looking neither to right nor left. A large two-horsed cab with a gay awning awaited them on the quay. As my lady entered, her skirt uplifted ever so little disclosed the most delicately shaped, tiny foot that has ever been attached to woman, and then I felt sure.

"Those little feet so adored." The haunting phrase leaped to my brain and I stood staring at the departing carriage athrill with excitement.

It was Joanna—lovelier than I had pictured her in my Lotus Club dreams, more gracious than Ingonde or Chlodoswinde or any of the *belles dames du temps jadis* whose ballade by Maître François Villon my master had but lately made me learn by heart and whose names were so many "sweet symphonies." It was Joanna, "pure and ravishing as an April dawn"; Joanna beloved of Paragot in those elusive days when I could not picture him, before he smashed his furniture with a crusader's mace and started on his wanderings under the guidance of Henri Quatre. It was Joanna whom he had an agonized desire to see in Madrid and whose silvery English voice he had longed to hear. And I, Asticot, had seen her and had heard her silvery voice. Among boys assuredly I was the most blessed.

But Paragot seemed that day of all men the most miserable, and I more dog-like than Narcisse in my sympathy with his moods, almost lifted up my nose and whined for woe. All my thrill died away. I felt guilty, oddly ashamed of myself. I took a pessimistic view of life. What, thought I, are Joannas sent into the world for, save to play havoc with men's happiness? Maître François Villon was quite right. Samson, Sardanapalus, David, Maître François himself, all came to grief over Joannas. *"Bien heureux qui rien n'y a."* Happy is he who has nothing to do with 'em.

As soon as we were free Paragot left us, and went off by himself; whereupon I, mimetic as an ape, rejected the humble Blanquette's invitation to take a walk with her, and strolled moodily into the town with Narcisse at my heels. A dog fight or two and a Byronic talk with a little towheaded flower-seller who gave me a dusty bunch of cyclamen—as a *porte-bonheur* she said prettily—whiled away the time until the people began to drift out of the Wonder Houses to dress for dinner. I lingered at the gates, going from one to the other, in the unavowed hope, little idiot that I was, of seeing Joanna. At last, at the main entrance to the Villa des Fleurs I caught sight of Paragot. He had changed from the velveteens into his vagabond clothes, and was evidently on the same errand as myself. I did not venture near, respecting his desire for solitude, but lounged at the corner of the main street and the road leading down to the Villa, playing with Narcisse and longing for something to happen. You see it is not given every day to an impressionable youngster, his brain stuffed with poetry, pictures, and such like delusive visionary things, to tumble head first into the romance of the actual world. For the moment the romance was at a standstill. I longed for a further chapter. It was a pity, I reflected, that we did not live in Merovingian times. Then Paragot and I could have lain in wait with our horses—everyone had horses in knightly days—and when Joanna came near, we should have killed the beaky-nosed man, and Paragot would have swung her on his saddlebow and we should have galloped away to his castle in the next kingdom, where Paragot, and Joanna and I, with Blanquette to be tirewoman to our princess, would have lived happy ever after. What I expected to get for myself, heaven knows: it did not strike me that perennial contemplation of another's bliss might wear out the stoutest altruism.

Then suddenly out of the door of the Villa came two ladies, one of whom I recognised as Joanna and the other as the young girl of the luncheon party. The façade of the villa stretches across the road and is about a hundred yards from the corner. I saw Paragot stand rigid, and make no sign of recognition as she passed him by, with her head up, like a proud queen. I felt an odd pain at my heart. Why was she so cruel? Her eyes were of the blue of glaciers, but all the rest of her face had seemed tender and kind. I was aware, in a general way, that radiantly attired ladies do not shake hands with ragamuffins in public places, but you must please to remember that I no more considered Paragot a ragamuffin than I thought Blanquette the equal of Joanna. Paragot to me was the peer of kings.

I turned away sorrowing and sauntered up the little street that leads to the Etablissement des Bains. I was disappointed in Joanna and did not want to see her again. She should be punished for her cruelty. I sat down on one of the benches on the Place, and looking at the Mairie clock stolidly thought of supper. They made famous onion soup at the little auberge where we lodged, and Paragot, himself a connoisseur, had pronounced their *tripes à la mode de Caen* superior to anything that Mrs. Housekeeper had executed for the Lotus Club. Besides I was getting hungry. With youth a full heart rarely compensates an empty stomach, and now even my heart was growing empty.

Presently who should emerge into the Place but the two ladies. I sat on my bench and watched them cross. They were evidently going up the hill to one of the hotels behind the Etablissement. In her white dress and white tulle hat coloured by three great roses, with her beautiful hair and sea-shell face and swaying supple figure, she looked the incarnation of all that was worshipful in woman. I could have knelt and prayed to her. Why was she so cruel to my master? I regarded her with mingled reproach and adoration. But the mixed feeling gave place to one of amazement when I saw her separate from her companion, who continued her way up the hill, and strike straight across the Place in my direction.

She was coming to me.

I rose, took off my ragged hat and twirled it in my fingers, which was the way that Paragot had taught me to be polite in France.

"I want to speak to you," she said quickly. "You are the boy with the tambourine, aren't you?"

"Yes, Mademoiselle."

Paragot had threatened to shoot me if I called any young lady "Miss."

"What is the name of the—the gentleman who played the violin?"

"Berzélius Nibbidard Paragot."

"That is not his real name?"

"No, Mademoiselle," said I.

"What is it?"

"I don't know," said I. "This is a new name; he has only had it a week."

"How long have you known him?"

"A long, long time, Mademoiselle. He adopted me when I was quite small."

"You are not very big now," she said with a smile.

"I am nearly sixteen," said I proudly.

To herself she murmured, "I don't think I can be mistaken."

In a different tone she continued, "You spoke some nonsense about his being your master and teaching you philosophy."

61

"It wasn't nonsense," I replied stoutly. "He teaches me everything. He teaches me history and Shakespeare and François Villon, and painting and Schopenhauer and the tambourine."

Her pretty lips pouted in a little gasp of astonishment as she leaned on her long parasol and looked at me.

"You are the oddest little freak I have come across for a long time."

I smiled happily. She could have called me anything opprobrious in that silvery voice of hers and I should have smiled. Now I come to think of it "smile" is the wrong word. The man smiles, the boy grins. I grinned happily.

"Has your master always played the violin in orchestras like this?"

"Oh, no, Mademoiselle," said I. "Of course not. He only began four days ago."

"What was his employment till then?"

"Why, none," said I.

It seemed absurd for Paragot to have employment like a man behind a shop-counter. I remembered acquaintances of my mother's who were "out of employment" and their unspeakable vileness. Then, echo of Paragot (for what else could I be?), I added: "We just walk about Europe for the sake of my education. My master said I was to learn Life from the Book of the Universe."

The lovely lady sat down.

"I believe you are nothing more nor less than an amazing little parrot. I'm sure you speak exactly like your master."

"Oh, no, Mademoiselle," said I modestly, "I wish I could. There is no one who can talk like him in all the world."

She gave me a long, steady, half-frightened look out of her blue eyes. I know now that I had struck a chord of memory; that I had established beyond question in her mind Paragot's identity with the man who had loved her in days past; that old things sweet and terrifying surged within her heart. Even then, holding their secret, I saw that she had recognised Paragot.

"You must think me a very inquisitive lady," she said, with a forced smile; "but you must forgive me. What you said this morning about your master teaching you philosophy interested me greatly. One thing I should like to know," and she dug at the gravel with the point of her parasol, "and that I hardly like to ask. Is he—are you—very poor?"

"Poor?" It was a totally new idea. "Why, no, Mademoiselle; he has a great bank in London which sends him bank-notes whenever he wants them. I once went with him. He has heaps of money."

The lady rose. "So this going about as a mountebank is only a masquerade," she said, with a touch of scorn.

"He did it to help Blanquette," said I.

"Blanquette?"

"The girl who plays the zither. My master has adopted her too."

"Oh, has he?" said the lady, the blue of her eyes becoming frosty again. I dimly perceived that in mentioning Blanquette I had been indiscreet. In what respect, I know not. I had intended my remark to be a tribute to Paragot's wide-heartedness. She took it as if I had told her of a crime. Women, even the loveliest of dream Joannas, are a mystifying race. "*Bien heureux qui rien n'y a.*"

"Goodbye," she said.

"Goodbye, Mademoiselle."

She must have read mortification in my face, for she turned after a step or two, and said more kindly.

"You're not responsible, anyway." Then she paused, as if hesitating, while I stood hat in hand, as I had done during our conversation.

"I wonder if I can trust you."

She took her purse from the bag hanging at her waist and drew out a gold piece.

"I will give you this if you promise not to tell your Master that you have spoken to me this afternoon."

I shrank back. Remember I had been for three years in the hourly companionship of a man of lofty soul for all his waywardness, and he had modelled me like wax to his liking. The gold piece was tempting. I had never owned a gold piece in my life—and all the frost had melted from Joanna's eyes. But I felt I should be dishonored in taking money.

"I promise without that," I said.

She put the coin back in her purse and held out her delicately gloved hand.

"Promise with this, then," she said.

And then I knew for the first time what an exquisite sensitive thing is a sweet, high-bred lady. Only such a one could have performed that act of grace. She converted me into a besotted little imbecile weltering in bliss. I would have pledged my soul's welfare to execute any phantasmagoric behest she had chosen to ordain.

"I am leaving Aix tomorrow morning—but if you are ever in any trouble—by the way what is your name?"

"Asticot Pradel," said I, reflecting for the first time that though Polydore Pradel had perished and Berzélius Nibbidard Paragot reigned in his stead, my own borrowed or invented name remained unaltered. Augustus Smith lingered in my memory as a vague, mythical creature of no account.

Joanna smiled. "You are a little masquerader too. Well—if you are ever in any trouble, and I can help you—remember the Comtesse de Verneuil, 7 Avenue de Messine, Paris."

This offer of friendship took my breath away. I grinned stupidly at her. I was also puzzled.

"What is the matter?" she laughed.

"The Comtesse de Verneuil?—but you are English," I stammered.

"Yes. But my husband is French. He is the Comte de Verneuil. Remember 7 Avenue de Messine."

She nodded graciously and turned away leaving a stupefied Asticot twirling his hat. Her husband! And I had been calling her Mademoiselle all the time! And I had been weaving fairy tales of our riding off with her to Paragot's castle! She was married. Her husband was the Comte de Verneuil! Worse than that. Her husband was the disagreeable beaky-nosed man who gave me five sous to go away.

A sense of desolation, disaster, disillusionment overwhelmed me. I sat on the bench and burst out crying and Narcisse jumped up and licked my face.

CHAPTER IX

IT was nearly midnight when Paragot returned to our inn on the outskirts of the town. He reeled up to the doorstep where I sat in the moonlight awaiting his return.

"Why aren't you in bed?"

"It was too hot and I couldn't sleep, Master," said I. As a matter of fact I had been dismally failing to compose a poem on Joanna after the style of Maître François Villon. Just as youthful dramatists begin with a five act tragedy, so do youthful poets begin with a double ballade. In order to eke out the slender stock of rhymes to Joanna, I had to drag in Indianna which somehow didn't fit. I remember also that she showered her favours like manna, which was not very original.

Paragot seated himself heavily by my side.

"The moon has a baleful influence, my son," said he in a thick voice. "And you'll come under it if you sit too long beneath its effulgence. That's what has happened to me. It makes one talk unmentionable imbecility."

He just missed concertina-ing the last two words, and looked at me with an air of solemn triumph.

"It isn't the Man in the Moon's fault, my little Asticot," he continued. "I've been having a very interesting conversation with him. He is a most polite fellow. He said if I would go up and join him he would make room for me. It's all a lie, you know, about his having been sent there for gathering sticks on a Sunday. He went of his own accord, because it was the only place where he could be four thousand miles away from any woman. Think of it, little Asticot of my heart. There are lots of lies told about the moon, he says. He looks down on the earth and sees all of us little worms wriggling in and out and over one another and thinking ourselves so important and he cracks his sides with laughing; and your bald-headed idiots with spyglasses take the cracks for mountain ranges and volcanoes. I'm going to live in the moon, away from female feminine women, and if you are good my son, you shall come too."

I explained to him as delicately as I could that I should regard such a change rather as a punishment than as a reward. He broke into a laugh.

"You too—with the milk of the feeding-bottle still wet on your lips? The trail of the petticoat's over us all! What has been putting the sex feminine into your little turnip-head? Have you fallen in love with Blanquette?"

"No, Master," said I. "When I fall in love it will be with a very beautiful lady."

Paragot pointed upwards. "I see another crack in my friend's sides. We all fall in love with beautiful ladies, my poor Asticot, one after the other, plunging into destruction with the comic sheep-headedness of the muttons of Panurge. Another woolly one over? Ho! ho! laughs the man in the moon, and crack go his sides."

The door opened behind us and the proprietor of the auberge appeared on the threshold.

"Give me half a litre of red wine, Monsieur Bonnivard," cried Paragot. "I am the descendant of Maître Jehan Cotard whose throat was so dry that in this world he was never known to spit."

"Bien, Monsieur," said the *patron*.

Paragot filled his porcelain pipe and lit it with clumsy fingers, and did not speak till his wine was brought.

"My son, we are leaving Aix the first thing in the morning."

I started up in alarm. We had not finished our engagement at the Restaurant du Lac.

"I care no more for the Restaurant du Lac than for the rest of the idiot universe," he declared.

"But Blanquette—it would break her heart."

"All women's hearts can be mended for twopence."

"And men's?"

"They have to go about with them broken, my son, and the pieces clank and jangle and chink and jingle inside like a crate of broken crockery. We leave Aix tomorrow."

"But Master," I cried, "there is no necessity."

"What do you mean?"

"She is leaving Aix herself tomorrow."

"She!" he shouted, quite sober for the moment. "Who the devil do you mean by 'she'?"

I upbraided myself for a vain idiot. Here was I on the point of breaking my oath sworn on Joanna's hand. I felt ashamed and frightened. He grasped my shoulder roughly.

"Who do you mean by 'she'? Tell me."

"The Lady of the Lake, Master," said I.

He looked at me for a moment keenly, then relaxed his grip and shrugged his shoulders with the ghost of a laugh.

"If you see holes in ladders in this perspicacious fashion you'll have to forsake the paths of art for the higher walks of the Prefecture of Police."

He puffed silently at his pipe for a few moments and then turning his head away asked me in a low voice:

"How can you know that she is leaving tomorrow?"

I lied for the first time to Paragot.

"I overheard her say so while I was waiting with the tambourine."

"Sure?"

"Quite sure."

This seemed to satisfy him, to my great relief. How my poor little oath would have fared under cross examination I don't know. At any rate honour was saved. Paragot laid aside his pipe and looked wistfully into the past over his wine bowl.

"The Lady of the Lake," he murmured. "I have called her many things good and bad in my time, but never that. You are a genius, my little Asticot."

He finished his wine slowly, holding the bowl in both hands. The moon smiled at us in a friendly way, sailing high over the mountains. There entered my head the novel reflection that he was smiling on all men alike, the good and the bad, the just and the unjust. He was smiling just the same on Joanna's beaky-nosed husband.

Her husband! Something caught at my heart. Did Paragot know? I debated anxiously in my mind whether I should impart the disastrous information. If he knew that she was a married woman he would put foolish thoughts out of his head, for it was only in Merovingian and such like romantic epochs that men loved other men's wives. I touched him timidly on the arm.

"Master,—I overheard something else."

"Did you?"

"She is married, and that is her husband."

"Did he take off his hat?"

"No, Master."

"He is a scaly-headed vulture," said Paragot dreamily.

"He only gave me five sous," said I, relieved and yet disappointed at finding that my disclosure produced no agitation.

Paragot fumbled in his pocket. "We will not batten on his charity," said he, and he cast three or four coppers into the silent street. They crashed, rolled and fell over with little chinks. Narcisse who had hitherto been asleep trotted out and sniffed at them. Paragot laughed; then checked himself, and holding up a long-nailed forefinger looked at me with an air of awful solemnity.

"Listen to the wisdom of Paragot. There is not a woman worth a clean man that does not marry a scaly-headed vulture."

He murmured an incoherence or two, and there was then a long silence. Presently his head knocked sharply against the lintel. I roused him.

"Master, it won't be good for us to sit any longer in the moonshine."

He turned a glazed look on me. "Minerva's Owl," said he, "I am quite aware of it."

He rose and lumbered into the inn, and I, having guided him up the narrow staircase to his room, descended to my bunk in a corner of the tiny salon. My sleeping arrangements were always sketchy.

In the morning when I questioned him as to our departure from Aix, he affected not to understand, and told me that I had been dreaming and that the moonshine had affected my brain.

"Consider, my son," said he, "that when I returned last night, I found you fast asleep on the doorstep, and you never woke up till this morning."

From this I gathered that for the second time he had dosed the book of his life to my prying though innocent eyes. I also learned the peculiar difference between Philip drunk and Philip sober.

When our engagement at Aix was at an end, the proprietor of the restaurant desired to renew it, but Paragot declined. The sick violinist whom we had replaced had recovered and Paragot had seen him on the quay looking through the railings with the hungry eyes of a sort of musical Enoch Arden. Blanquette had some little difficulty in preventing him from rushing out there and then and delivering his fiddle into the other's hands. It was necessary to be reasonable, she said.

"*Nom de Dieu!*" he cried, "if I were reasonable I should be lost. Reason would set me down in Paris with gloves and an umbrella. Reason would implant a sunny smile on my face above the red ribbon of the Legion of Honour. It would marry me to the daughter of one of my *confrères* at the Académie des Beaux Arts. It would make me procreate my species, *cré nom de Dieu!* It would make me send you and Asticot and Narcisse to the devil. If I were reasonable I should not be Paragot. The man who lives according to reason has the heart of a sewing-machine."

But out of regard for Blanquette he served his time faithfully at the Restaurant du Lac, and reconciled his conscience with reason by giving the hungry violinist his own share of the takings. It was only when Blanquette suggested the further exploitation of Aix that he showed his Gascon obduracy. If there was one place in the world where the soul sickened and festered it was Aix-les-Bains. Mammon was King thereof and Astarte Queen. He was going to fiddle no more for sons of Belial and daughters of Aholah. He had set out to travel to the Heart of Truth, and the way thither did not lead through the Inner Shrine of Dagon and Astaroth. Blanquette did not in the least know what he was talking about, and I only had a vague glimmer of his meaning. But I see now that his sensitive nature chafed at the false position. Among the simple village folk he was a personality, compelling awe and admiration. Among the idlers of Aix, whom in his loftiness he despised, he was but the fiddling mountebank to whom any greasy wallower in riches could cast a disdainful franc.

So once more we took to the high road, and Paragot threw off the depressing burden of Mammon (Joanna) and became his irresponsible self again.

I have but confused memories of our fantastic journeyings. Stretches of long white road and blazing sun. Laughing valleys and corn fields and white farmsteads among the trees. Now and then a village fête or wedding at which we played to the enthusiasm of the sober vested peasantry. Nights passed in barns, deserted byres, on the floor of cottages and infinitesimal cafés. Hours of idleness by the wayside after the midday meal, when the four of us sat round the fare provided by Blanquette, black bread, cheese, charcuterie and the eternal bottle of thin wine. It was rough, but there was plenty. Paragot saw to that, in spite of Blanquette's economical endeavours. Sometimes he would sleep while she and I chatted in low voices so as not to wake him. She told me of her wanderings with the old man, the hardness of her former life. Often she had cried herself to sleep for hunger, shivering in wet rags the long night through. Now it was all changed: she ate too much and was getting as fat as a pig. Did I not think so? *Voilà!* In her artless way she guided my finger into her waistband and then swelled herself out like the frog in the fable to prove the increase in her girth. She spoke in awestricken whispers of the Master himself. Save that he was utterly kind, impulsive, generous, boastful, and according to her untrained ear a violinist of the first quality, she knew not what manner of man he was. She had enough imagination to feel vaguely that he had dropped from vast spaces into her narrow world. But he was a mystery.

Once, the previous summer, as she was resting by the roadside with the old man, even as we were doing then, an amiable person, she told me, with easel and stool and paint-box, came along and requested their permission to make an oil sketch of them. While he painted he conversed, telling them of Sicily whither he was going and of Paris whence he came. In a dim way she associated him with Paragot. The two had the same trick of voice and manner, and held unusual views as to the value of five francs. But the amiable painter had been a gentleman elegantly dressed, such as she saw in the large towns driving in cabs and consuming drinks in expensive cafés, whereas the Master was attired like a peasant and slept in barns and did everything that the elegantly dressed gentlemen in cafés did not do. At all events she was penetrated with the consciousness of a loftier mind and spirit, and she contented herself even as I did with being his devoted slave.

Often too she spoke of her own ambitions. If she were rich she would have a little house of her own. Perhaps for company she would like someone to stay with her. She would keep it so clean, and would mend all the linen, and do the cooking, and save to go to market, would never leave it from one year's end to the other. A good sleek cat to curl up by the fireside would complete her felicity.

"But Blanquette!" I would cry. "The sun and the stars and the high road and the smell of spring and the fields and the freedom of this life—you would miss them."

"*J'aime le ménage, moi,*" she would reply, shaking her head.

Of all persons I have ever met the least imbued with the vagabond instinct was the professional vagabond Blanquette de Veau.

Sometimes, instead of sleeping, Paragot would talk to us from the curious store of his learning, always bent on my education and desirous too of improving the mind of Blanquette. Sometimes it was Blanquette who slept, Narcisse huddled up against her, while Paragot and I read our tattered books, or sketched, or discussed the theme which I had written overnight as my evening task. It was an odd school; but though I could not have passed any examination held by the sons of men, I verily believe I had a wider culture, in the truest sense of the word, than most youths of my age. I craved it, it is true, and I drank from an inexhaustible source; but few men have the power of directing that source so as to supply the soul's need of a boy of sixteen.

Well, well—I suppose Allah Paragot is great and Mahomet Asticot is his prophet.

We wandered and fiddled and zithered and tambourined through France till the chills and rains of autumn rendered our vagabondage less merry. The end of October found us fulfilling a week's engagement at a brasserie on the outskirts of Tours. Two rooms over a stable and a manger in an empty stall below were assigned to us; and every night we crept to our resting places wearied to death by the evening's work.

I have always found performance on a musical instrument exhausting in itself: the tambourine, for instance, calls for considerable physical energy; but when the instrument, tambourine, violin or zither, is practised for several hours in a little stuffy room filled with three or four dozen obviously unwashed humans, reeking with bad tobacco and worse absinthe, and pervaded by the ghosts of inferior meals, it becomes more penitential than the treadmill. A dog's life, said Paragot. Whereat Narcisse sniffed. It was not at all the life for a philosopher's dog, said he.

On the morning of the last day of our engagement, Blanquette entered Paragot's bedchamber as usual, with the bowls of coffee and hunks of coarse bread that formed our early meal. I had risen from my manger and crept into Paragot's room for warmth, and while he slept I sat on the floor by the window reading a book. As for Blanquette she had dressed and eaten long before and had helped the servant of the café to sweep and wash the tables and make the coffee for the household. It was not in her peasant's nature to be abed, which, now I come to think of it, must be a characteristic of the artistic temperament. Paragot loved it. He only woke when Blanquette brought him his coffee. Ordinarily he would remonstrate with picturesque oaths at being aroused from his slumbers, and having taken the coffee from her hands, would dismiss her with a laugh. He observed the most rigid propriety in his relations with Blanquette. But this morning he directed her to remain.

"Sit down, my child; I have to speak to you."

As there was no chair or stool in the uncomfortable room—it had lean-to walls and bare dirty boards and contained only the bed and a table—she sat obediently at the foot of the bed next to Narcisse and folded her hands in her lap. Paragot broke his bread into his coffee and fed himself with the sops by means of a battered table-spoon. When he had swallowed two or three mouthfuls he addressed her.

"My good Blanquette, I have been wandering through the world for many years in search of the springs of Life. I do not find them by scraping catgut in the Café Brasserie Dubois."

"It would be better to go to Orléans," said Blanquette. "We were at the Café de la Couronne there last winter and I danced."

"Not even your dancing at Orléans would help me in my quest," said he.

"I don't understand," murmured Blanquette looking at him helplessly.

"Have the kindness," said he, pointing to the table, "to smash that confounded violin into a thousand pieces."

"*Mon Dieu!* What is the matter?" cried Blanquette.

"It does not please me."

"I know it is not a good one," said Blanquette. "We will save money until we can buy a better."

"I would execrate it were it a Stradivarius," said he, his mouth full of sop. "Asticot," he called, "don't you loathe your tambourine?"

"Yes, Master," I replied from the floor.

"Do you love playing the zither?"

"But no, Maître," said Blanquette.

"Why then," said my master, "should we pursue a career which is equally abominable to the three of us? We are not slaves, *nom d'un chien!*"

"We must work," said Blanquette, "or what would become of us?"

Paragot finished his coffee and bread and handed the bowl to Blanquette who nursed it in her lap, while he settled himself snugly beneath the bedclothes. The autumn rain beat against the dirty little window and the wind howled through chinks and crevices, filling the room with cold damp air. I drew the old blanket which I had brought from my manger-bed closer round my shoulders. Blanquette with her peasant's indifference to change of temperature sat unconcerned in her thin cotton dress.

"But what will become of us?" she repeated.

"I shall continue to exist," said he.

"But I, what shall I do?"

"You can fill my porcelain pipe, and let me think," replied Paragot.

She rose in her calm obedient way and, having carried out his orders, reseated herself at the foot of the bed.

"You are the most patient creature alive," said he, "otherwise you would not be contented to go on playing the zither, which is not a very exhilarating instrument, my little Blanquette. I am not patient, and I am not going to play the violin again for a million years after tonight, and the violin is superior to the zither."

Blanquette regarded him uncomprehending.

"If I were a king I would live in a palace and you should be my housekeeper. But as I am a ragged vagabond too idle to work, I am puzzled as to the disposal of you."

She grew very white and rose to her feet.

"I understand. You are driving me away. If it is your desire I will earn my living alone. *Je ne vous serai pas sur le dos.*"

For all her vulgar asseveration that she would not be on his back, her manner held a dignity which touched him. He held out his hand.

"But I don't drive you away, little idiot," he laughed. "On the contrary. You are like Asticot and Narcisse. You belong to me. But Asticot is going to learn how to become an artist, and Narcisse when he is bored can hunt for fleas. You are a young woman; things must arrange themselves differently. But how? *Voilà tout!*"

"It is very simple," said Blanquette.

"How, simple?"

"*Dame!* I can work for you and Asticot."

"The devil!" cried Paragot.

"But yes," she went on earnestly. "I know that men are men, and sometimes they do not like to work. It happens very often. *Tiens! mon maître*, I am alone, all that is most alone. You are the only friends I have in the world, you and Asticot. You have been kinder to me than any one I have ever met. I put you in my prayers every night. It is a very little thing that I should work for you, if it fatigues you to scrape the fiddle in these holes of cabarets. It is true. True as the *bon Dieu.* I would tear myself into four pieces for you. *Je suis brave fille*, and I can work. But no!" she cried, looking deep into his eyes. "You can't refuse. It is not possible."

"Yes, I refuse," said Paragot.

He had turned on his side, face on palm, elbow on pillow, had regarded her sternly as she spoke. I saw that he was very angry.

"For what do you take me, little imbecile? Do you know that you insult me? I to be supported by a woman? *Nom de Dieu de Dieu!*"

His ire blazed up suddenly. He cursed, scolded, boasted all in a breath. Blanquette looked at him terrified. She could not understand. Great tears rolled down her cheeks.

"But I have made you angry," she wailed.

The scornful spurning of her devotion hurt her less than the sense of having caused his wrath. The primitive savage feminine is not complicated by over-subtlety of feeling. As soon as she could speak she broke into repentant protestation. She had not meant to anger him. She had spoken from her heart. She was so ignorant. She would tear herself into four pieces for him. She was *brave fille*. She was alone and he was her only friend. He must forgive her.

I, feeling monstrously tearful, jumped to my feet.

"Yes, Master, forgive her."

He burst out laughing. "Oh what three beautiful fools we are! Blanquette to think of supporting two hulking men, I to be angry, and Asticot to plead tragically as if I were a tyrant about to cut off her head. My little Blanquette, you have touched my heart, and who touches the heart of Paragot can eat Paragot's legs and liver if he is hungry and drink his blood if he is thirsty. I will remember it all my life, and if you will bring me my déjeuner I will stay in bed till this afternoon."

"Then I am not to leave you?" she asked, somewhat bewildered.

"Good heavens no!" he cried. "Because I am sick of fiddling do you suppose I am going to send you adrift? We shall settle down for the winter. Some capital. Which one would you like, Asticot?"

"Buda-Pesth," said I at random.

"Very well," said Paragot, "the day after tomorrow we start for Buda-Pesth. Now let me go to sleep."

We took exactly two months getting to Buda-Pesth. The only incident of our journey which I clearly remember is a week's sojourn at the farm of La Haye near Chartres where we had carted manure, and where we renewed our acquaintance with Monsieur and Madame Dubosc.

CHAPTER X

In Buda-Pesth three things happened.

First, Paragot slipped in the street and broke his ankle bone, so that he lay seven weeks in hospital, during which time Blanquette and I and Narcisse lived like sparrows on the housetops, dazed by the incomprehensibilities of the strange city.

Secondly, Paragot's aunt, his mother's sister, died intestate leaving a small sum of money which he inherited as her nearest surviving relative.

Thirdly, Paragot fell into the arms of Theodor Izelin the painter, an old friend of Paris student days.

The consequences of the first accident, though not immediate, were lasting. Paragot walked for ever afterwards with a slight limp, and his tramps along the high-roads of Europe had to be abandoned.

The consequence of the second was that Paragot went to London. Some legal formality, the establishment of identity or what not, necessitated his presence. I daresay he could have arranged matters through consuls and lawyers and such-like folk, but Paragot who was childishly simple in business matters obeyed the summons to London without question.

As a consequence of the third I became an inmate of the house of Theodor Izelin.

It was all very bewildering.

It was arranged that during Paragot's absence in England I should board with Izelin, Blanquette with Izelin's elderly model, a lady of unimpeachable respectability and a rough and ready acquaintance with the French language, and that Narcisse should alternate between the two establishments. Paragot's business concluded, he would return to Buda-Pesth, collect us and go whither the wind might drift him. I was provided with a respectable outfit and with detailed instructions as to correct behaviour in a lady's house. Theodor Izelin's wife was a charming woman.

Everything was arranged; but who could reckon on Paragot?

On the night before his departure—indeed it must have been two or three in the morning—Paragot burst into my little attic bedroom, candle in hand, and before I had time to rub my startled eyes, sat down on the bed and began to speak.

"My son," said he, "I have had an inspiration!"

Who but Paragot would have awakened a boy at two or three in the morning to announce an inspiration? And who but Paragot would alter the course of human lives on the flash of an impulse?

"It came," he cried, "while I was supping with Izelin. I told him. I worked it all out. He agreed. So it is settled."

"What, Master?" I asked, sitting up. His slouch felt hat and his swarthy bearded face, his glittering eyes and the candle on his knees gave him the air of an excited Guy Fawkes.

"Your career, my son. The money I am going to collect in London shall be devoted to your education. You shall learn to paint, infant Raphael and Izelin shall teach you. And you shall learn the manners of a gentleman, and Madame Izelin shall teach you. And you shall learn what it is to have a heart, and if you care a hang for Paragot two years' separation shall teach you."

"Two years!" I cried aghast. "But master I can't live two years here without you!"

"We find we can live without a devil of a lot of things when we have to, my son. When I smashed my furniture with the crusader's mace I thought I could not live anywhere without—something. But here I am as alive as a dragon-fly."

He went on talking. It was for my good. His broken ankle bone had compelled him to resign his peripatetic tutorship in the University of the Universe. In a narrower Academy he would be but a poor instructor. If he had taught me to speak the truth and despise lies and shams, and to love pictures and music and cathedrals and books and trees and all beautiful things, *nom de Dieu!* he had accomplished his mission. It was time for other influences. When an inspiration such as tonight's came to him he took it as a command from a Higher Power (I am convinced that he believed it), against which he was powerless.

"Providence ordains that you stay here with the Izelins. Afterwards you shall go to Janot's studio in Paris. In the meantime you can attend classes in the humanities at Buda-Pesth."

"I can't understand the beastly language!" I grumbled.

"You will learn it, my son."

"No one ever speaks it out of Hungary," I contended.

"My son," said he, "the value of a man is often measured by his useless and fantastic attainments."

Then the candle end sputtered out and we were in darkness. Paragot bade me good night, and left me to a mingled sense of burned candle grease and desolation.

He departed the next day. Blanquette and I with a dejected Narcisse at our heels, walked back from the railway station to the hotel, where losing all sense of manly dignity I broke down crying and Blanquette put her arm round my neck and comforted me motherwise.

Two months afterwards Paragot wrote to Blanquette to join him in Paris, and when the flutter of her wet handkerchief from the railway carriage window became no longer visible, then indeed I felt myself to be a stranger in a strange land.

Two years! I can remember even now their endless heartache. The Izelins were kind; Madame Izelin, a refined Hungarian lady, became my staunch friend as well as my instructress in manners; my life teemed with interests, and I worked like a little maniac; but all the time I longed for Paragot. Had it not been for his letters I should have scented my way back to him like a dog, across Europe. Ah those letters of Paragot—I have them still—what a treasury they are of grotesque fantasy and philosophic wisdom! They gave me but little news of his doings. He had settled down in Paris with Blanquette as his housekeeper. His floridly anathematised ankle kept him hobbling about the streets while his heart was chasing butterflies over the fields. He had founded a coenaculum for the cultivation of the Higher Conversation at the Café Delphine. He had taken up Persian and was saturating himself with Hafiz and Firdusi. His health was good. Indeed he was a man of iron constitution.

Blanquette now and then supplemented these meagre details of objective life. The master had taken a *bel appartement*. There were curtains to his bed. Food was dear in Paris. They had been to Fontainebleau. Narcisse had stolen the sausages of the concierge. The Master was always talking of me and of the great future for which I was destined. But when I became famous I was not to forget my little Blanquette. I see the sprawling mis-spelt words now: "*Il ne fot jamés oublié ta petite Blanquette.*"

As if I could ever forget her!

I arrived in Paris one evening a day or two earlier than I was expected. It had been ordained by Paragot that I should break my journey at Berlin, in order to visit that capital, but affection tugged at my heart-strings and compelled me to travel straight through from Buda-Pesth. It was Paragot and Blanquette and Narcisse that I wanted to see and not Berlin.

Yet when I stepped out of the train on to the Paris platform, I was conscious for the first time of development. I was decently attired. I had a bag filled with the garments of respectability. I had money in my pocket, also a packet of cigarettes. A porter took my luggage and enquired in the third person whether Monsieur desired a cab. The temptation was too great for eighteen. I took the cab in a lordly way and drove to No. 11 Rue des Saladiers where Paragot had his "bel appartement." And with the anticipatory throb of joy at beholding my beloved Master was mingled a thrill of vain-glorious happiness. Asticot in a cab! It was absurd, and yet it seemed to fall within the divine fitness of things.

The cab stopped in a narrow street. I had an impression of tall houses looking fantastically dilapidated in the dim gas-light, of little shops on the ground floor, and of little murky gateways leading to the habitations above. Beside the gateway of No. 11 was a small workman's drinking shop, sometimes called in Paris a *zinc* on account of the polished zinc bar which is its principal feature. Untidy, slouching people filled the street.

Directed by the concierge to the *cinquième à gauche,* I mounted narrow, evil smelling, badly lighted stairs, and rang at the designated door. It opened; Blanquette appeared with a lamp in her hand.

"*Monsieur désire?*"

"*Mais c'est moi, Blanquette.*"

In another minute she had ushered me in, set down the lamp and was hugging me in her strong young arms.

"But my little Asticot, I did not know you. You have changed. You are no longer the same. *Tu es tout à fait monsieur!* How proud the Master will be."

"Where is he?"

Alas, the Master did not expect me to-day and was at the Café Delphine. She would go straightway and tell him. I must be tired and hungry. She would get me something to eat. But who would have thought I should have come back a *monsieur!* How I had grown! I must see the *appartement.* This was the salon.

I looked around me for the first time. Nothing in it save the rickettiness of a faded rep suite arranged primly around the walls, and a few bookshelves stuffed with tattered volumes suggested Paragot. The round centre table, covered with American cloth, and the polished floor were spotless. Cheap print curtains adorned the windows and a cage containing a canary hung between them. Three or four oleographs—one a portrait of Garibaldi—in gilt frames formed the artistic decoration.

"It was I who chose the pictures," said Blanquette proudly.

She opened a door and disclosed the sleeping chamber of the Master, very bare, but very clean. Another door led into the kitchen—a slip of a place but glistening like the machine room of a man-of-war.

"I have a bedroom upstairs, and there is one also for you which the Master has taken. Come and I will show you."

We mounted to the attics and I was duly installed.

"I would have put some flowers if I had known you were coming," said Blanquette.

We went down again and she prepared food for me, her plain face beaming as she talked. She was entirely happy. No one so perfect as the Master had ever been the head of a household. Of course he was untidy. But such was the nature of men. If he did not make stains on the floor with muddy boots and lumps of meat thrown to Narcisse, and litter the rooms with clothes and tobacco and books, what occupation would there be for a housekeeper? As it was she worked from morning to night. And the result; was it not neat and clean and beautiful? Ah! she was happy not to be playing the zither in *brasseries*. All her dreams were realised. She had a *ménage*. And she had the Master to serve. Now would she fetch him from the Café Delphine.

Half an hour afterwards he strode into the room, followed by Blanquette and Narcisse. He spoke in French and embraced me French fashion. Then he cried out in English and wrung me by the hand. He was almost as excited as Narcisse who leaped and barked frantically.

"It is good to have him back, eh Blanquette?"

"*Oui, Maître.* He does not know how sad it has been without him."

Blanquette smiled, wept and removed the remains of my supper. Then she set on the table glasses and a bottle of *tisane* they had bought on the way home. We drank the sour sweet champagne as if it were liquid gold and clinked glasses, and with Narcisse all talked and barked together. It was a glad home-coming.

Paragot had changed very little. The hair on his temple was beginning to turn grey and his sallow cheeks were thinner. But he was the same hairy unkempt creature of prodigious finger nails and disreputable garments, still full of strange oaths and picturesque fancy, and still smoking his pipe with the porcelain bowl.

Presently Blanquette retired to bed and Paragot and I talked far into the night. Before we separated, with a comprehensive wave of the hand he indicated the primly set furniture and polished floor.

"Did you ever behold such exquisite discomfort?"

Poor Blanquette!

CHAPTER XI

How far away it all seems; Paris; the Rue des Saladiers: the *atelier* Janot where the illustrious painter called us his children and handed us the sacred torch of his art for us to transmit, could we but keep it aflame, to succeeding generations; the Café Delphine, with Madame Boin, fat, pink, urbane, her hair a miracle of perrukery, enthroned behind the counter; my dear Master, Paragot, himself! How far away! It is not good to live to a hundred and fifty. The backward vista down the years is too frighteningly long.

I found Paragot established as the Dictator of the Café Delphine. No one seemed to question his position. He ruled there autocratically, having instituted sundry ordinances disobedience to which had exile as its penalty. The most generous of creatures, he had nevertheless ordained that as Dictator he should go scot-free. To have declined to pay for his absinthe or *choucroute* would have closed the Café Delphine in a student's face. He had a prescriptive right to the table under the lee of Madame Boin's counter, and the peg behind him was sacred to his green hat. To the students he was a mystery. No one knew where he lived, how he subsisted, what he had been. Various rumours filled the *Quartier*. According to one he was a Russian Nihilist escaped from Siberia. Another, and one nearer the mark, credited him with being a kind of Rip van Winkle revisiting old student scenes after a twenty years' slumber. He seemed to pass his life between the Luxembourg Gardens, the Pont Neuf and the Café Delphine. "Paris," he used to say, "it is the Boul' Mich'!" Although he would turn to the absolute stranger who had been brought as a privilege to his table and say, using the familiar second person singular, "Buy me an evening paper," or addressing the company at large, "Somebody is going to offer me an absinthe," and promptly order it, he was never known to borrow money.

This eccentricity vexed the soul of the *Quartier*, where the chief use of money is to be borrowed. To me the idea of Paragot asking needy youngsters for the loan of five francs was exquisitely ludicrous; I am only setting down the impression of the *Quartier* regarding him. Not only did he never borrow but sometimes gave whole francs in charity. One evening an unseemly quarrel having arisen between two law-students from Auvergne (the Bœotia of France) and the waiter as to an alleged overcharge of two sous, Paragot arose in wrath, and dashing a louis on the table with a "*Hercule paie-toi*," stalked majestically out of the Café. A deputation waited on him next day with the object of refunding the twenty francs. He refused (naturally) to take a penny. It would be a lesson to them, said he, and they meekly accepted the rebuke.

"But what did you study here, before you went to sleep?" an impudent believer in the Rip van Winkle theory once asked him.

"The lost arts of discretion and good manners, *mon petit*," retorted Paragot, with a flash of his blue eyes which scorched the offender.

The students paid his score willingly, for in his talk they had full value for their money. I found the Café Delphine a Lotus Club, with a difference. Instead of being the scullion I was a member, and took my seat with the rest, and, though none suspected it, paid for Paragot's drinks with Paragot's money. Our real relations were never divulged. It would affect both our positions, said he. To explain our friendship, it was only necessary to say that we had met at Buda-Pesth where I had been sent to study with the famous Izelin, who was a friend of Paragot's.

"My son," said he, "the fact of your being an Englishman who has studied in Buda-Pesth and speaks French like a Frenchman will entitle you to respect in the *Quartier*. Your previous acquaintance with me, on which you need not insist too much, will bring you distinction."

And so it turned out. I felt that around me also hung a little air of mystery, which was by no means unprofitable or unpleasant. To avoid complications, however, and also in order that I should have the freedom befitting my man's estate and my true education in the *Quartier*, Paragot threw me out of the nest in the Rue des Saladiers, and assigning to me a fixed allowance bade me seek my own shelter and make my way in the world.

I made it as best I could, and the months went on.

Why I should have been dreaming outside the Hôtel Bristol that afternoon, I cannot remember. If to Paragot Paris was the Boulevard Saint-Michel, to me it spread itself a vaster fairyland through which I loved to wander, and before whose magnificences I loved to dream. Why not dream therefore in the Place Vendôme? Surely my aspirations in those days soared as high as the Column, and surely the student's garb (beloved and ordained by Paragot)—the mushroom-shaped cap, the tight ankled, tight throated velveteens—rendered any eccentricity a commonplace. Early Spring too was in the air, which encourages the young visionary. Spruce young men and tripping *modistes* with bandboxes under their arms and the sun glinting over their trim bare heads hurried along through the traffic across the Place and landed on the pavement by my side. I must own to have been not unaffected by the tripping milliners. Why should they not weave themselves too into a painter lad's spring visions?

Suddenly a lady—of so radiant a loveliness as to send *modistes* packing from my head—emerged from the Hôtel Bristol and crossed the broad pavement to a waiting victoria. She had eyes like the blue of glaciers and the tenderest mouth in the world. She glanced at me. A floppy picturesque Paris student, lounging springlike in the Place Vendôme, is worth a fair lady's glance of curiosity. I raised my cap. She glanced at me again, haughtily; then again, puzzled; then stopped.

"If I don't know you, you are a very ill-bred young man to have saluted me," she said in French. "But I think I have seen you before."

"If I had not met you before I should not have bowed. You are the Comtesse de Verneuil," said I in English, very boyishly and eagerly. The spring and the sight of Joanna had sent the blood into my pasty cheeks.

"I once played the tambourine at Aix," I added.

She grew suddenly pale, put her hand to her heart and clutched at a bunch of Parma violets she was wearing. They fell to the ground.

"No, no, it is nothing," she said, as I stepped forward. "Only a slight shock. I remember you perfectly. You said your name was Asticot. I asked you to come and see me. Why haven't you?"

"You said I might come if I were in want. But thanks to my dear Master I am not." I picked up the violets.

"Your master?" She looked relieved, and thanked me with a smile for the flowers. "He is well? He is with you in Paris? Is he still playing the violin?"

"He is well," said I. "He is in Paris, but he only plays the violin at home when, as he says, he wants to have a conversation with his soul."

The frost melted from her eyes and they smiled at me.

"You have caught his trick of talking."

"You once called me an amazing parrot, Madame," said I. "It is quite true."

"In the meantime," said she, "we can't stand in the Place Vendôme for ever. Come for a drive and we can talk in the carriage."

"In the——" I gasped stupefied, pointing to the victoria.

"Why not?" she laughed. "Do you think it's dangerous?"

"No," said I, "but——"

But she was already in the carriage; and as I stepped in beside her I noted the tips of her little feet so adored by Paragot.

"I'm glad you're English," she remarked, arranging the rug. "A young Frenchman would have replied with the obvious gallantry. I think the young Englishman rather despises that kind of obviousness."

The coachman turned on his seat and asked whither he should drive Madame la Comtesse.

"Anywhere. I don't know"—then desperately, "Drive to the fortifications. Where the fortifications are I haven't the remotest idea. I believe they are a kind of pleasure resort for people who want to get murdered. You hear of them in the papers. We'll cross the river," she said to the coachman.

We started, drove down the Rue Castiglione, along the Rue de Rivoli, struck off by the Louvre and over the Pont Neuf. Standing in conversation with Joanna,

I had the gutter urchin's confidence of the pavement, the impudence of the street. Seated beside Madame la Comtesse de Verneuil in an elegant victoria I was as dumb as a fish, until her graciousness set me more at my ease. As we passed through the *Quartier* I trembled lest any of my fellow students should see me. "*Asticot avec une femme du monde chic! Il court les bonnes fortunes ce sacré petit diable. Ou l'as-tu pêchée?*" I shivered at their imagined ribaldries. And all the time I was athrill with pride and joy—suffused therewith into imbecility. Verily I must be a *monsieur* to drive with Countesses! And verily it must be fairyland for Asticot to be driving in Joanna's carriage.

"That is Henri Quatre," said she pointing to the statue as we crossed the bridge.

"It was the first thing my Master brought me to see in Paris—years ago," I said, with the very young's curious mis-realisation of time. "He is very fond of Henri Quatre."

"Why?" she asked.

I told her vaguely the story of the crusader's mace. She listened with a somewhat startled interest.

"I believe your Master is mad," she remarked. "Indeed," she added after a pause, "I believe everyone is mad. I'm mad. You're mad."

"Oh, I am not," I cried warmly.

"You must be to set up a human god and worship him as you do your Master. You are the maddest of all of us, Mr. Asticot."

A touch of light scorn in her tone nettled me. Even Joanna should not speak of him irreverently.

"If he had bought you from your mother for half-a-crown," said I, "and made you into a student at Janot's, you would worship him too, Madame."

"I have been wondering whether you kept your promise to me," she said—I wish women were not so disconcertingly irrelevant—"but now I am quite sure."

"Of course I didn't tell my master," I declared stoutly.

"Good. And this little drive must be a secret too."

"If you wish," I said. "But I don't like to have secrets from him."

"Give me his address," she said after a pause, and I noticed she spoke with some effort. "Does he still go by that absurd name? What was it?"

"His name is Berzélius Paragot, and he lives at No. 11 Rue des Saladiers."

"Do you know his real name?"

"Yes, Madame," said I. "It is Gaston de Nérac. I only learned it lately through Monsieur Izelin."

"Do you know Izelin, too?" she asked.

I explained my stay in Buda-Pesth. I also mentioned Monsieur Izelin's reticence in speaking of Paragot's early days.

I think he was cautioned by my Master.

"And who do you think I am?" The sudden question startled me.

"You," said I, "are Joanna."

"Indeed? How long have you known that, pray?"

"When I came to you with the tambourine at Aix-les-Bains."

"I don't understand," she said, the frozen blue coming into her eyes. "Did he tell you then—a child like you?"

"He has never mentioned your name to me, Madame," I said eagerly, for I saw her resentment.

"Then how did you know?"

I recounted the history of the old stocking. I also mentioned Paragot's appeal to me as a scholar and a gentleman.

A wan smile played about her lips.

"Was that soon after he bought you for half-a-crown?"

"Yes, Madame," said I.

"And an old stocking?"

"Yes, Madame. And since then we have never spoken of the papers."

"But how did you know I was the—the Joanna of the papers?"

"I guessed," said I. I could not tell her of the *petits pieds si adorés*.

"You are an odd boy," she said. "Tell me all about yourself."

Unversed in woman's wiles I flushed with pleasure at her flattering interest. I did not perceive that it was an invitation to tell her all about Paragot. I related, however, artlessly the story of my life from the morning when I delivered my tattered copy of "Paradise Lost" to Paragot instead of the greasy washing book: and if my narrative glowed rosier with poetic illusion than the pages on which it has been set down, pray forgive nineteen for seeing things in a different light and perspective from a hundred and fifty. In my description of the Lotus Club, for instance, I felt instinctively that Madame de Verneuil would wince at the sound of tripe; I conveyed to her my own childish impression of the magnificence of Paragot's bedchamber, and the story of our wanderings became an Idyll of No Man's Land.

"And what is he doing now?" We had grown so confidential that we exchanged smiles.

"He is cultivating philosophy," said I.

Perhaps it was a sign of my development that I could detect a little spot of clay in my idol.

We had gone south, past the Observatoire to Montrouge, and had turned back before I realised that we were in the Boulevard Saint-Michel again near the prearranged end of my drive.

"Do you know why I am so glad to have met you to-day?" she asked. "I think—indeed I know I can trust you. I am in great trouble and I have an idea that your Master can help me."

She looked at me so earnestly, so wistfully, her face seemed to grow of a sudden so young and helpless, that all my boy's fantastic chivalry was roused.

"My Master would lay down his life for you, Madame," I cried. "And so would I."

"Even if I never, never, in this world forgave him?"

"You would forgive him in the next, Madame," I answered, scarce knowing what I said, "and he would be contented."

The carriage stopped at the appointed place. I felt as if I were about to descend from the side of an Olympian goddess to sordid humanity, to step from the Land East of the Sun and West of the Moon on to the common earth. It was I who looked wistful.

"May I come to see you, Madame?"

The quick fear came into her eyes.

"Not as yet, Mr. Asticot," she said holding out her hand. "My husband is queer tempered at times. I will write to you."

The carriage drove off. For the second time she had left me with her husband on her lips. I had forgotten him completely. I stamped my foot on the pavement.

"He is a scaly vulture," said I, echoing Paragot. Gods! How I hated the poor man.

One evening, about a week after this, some seven or eight of us were gathered around Paragot's table at the Café Delphine. Two were *rapins*—we have no word for the embryo painter—my companions in Janot's *atelier*. Of the rest I only remember one—poor Cazalet. He wore a self-tailored grotesque attire, a brown stuff tunic girt at the waist by a leathern belt, shapeless trousers of the same material, and sandals. He had long yellow hair and untrimmed chicken fluff grew casually about his face. A sombre genius, he used to paint dark writhing horrors of souls in pain, and in his hours of relaxation to drink litres of anisette. At first he disliked and scoffed at me because I was an Englishman, which grieved me sorely, for I regarded him as the greatest genius, save Paragot, of my acquaintance. I found him ten years afterwards a *sous-chef de gare* on the Belgian frontier.

It was about half past eleven. Our table gleamed a motley wilderness of glasses and saucers. Only two other tables were occupied: at the one two men and a woman played *manille*, on the other a pair of players rattled dominoes, Madame Boin, sunk into her rolls of fat, drowsed on her throne behind thecounter. Hercule stood by, his dirty napkin tucked under his arm, listening to Paragot's discourse. Through the glass side of the café one could see the moving, flaring lights of the Boulevard Saint-Michel. Paragot sipped absinthe and smoked his eternal pipe with the porcelain bowl, and talked.

"The *Quartier Latin!* Do you call this bourgeois-stricken aceldama the *Quartier Latin?* Do you miserable little white mice in clean shirts call this the*Vie de Bohème?* Is there a devil of a fellow among you, save Cazalet whose chilblains make him indecent, who doesn't wear socks? Haven't you all dress suits? Aren't you all suffocating with virtue? Would any Marcel of you lie naked in bed for two days so that Rodolfe could pawn your clothes for the wherewithal to nurse Mimi in sickness? Is there a Mimi in the whole etiolated *Quartier?*"

"But yes, *mon vieux*," said my friend Bringard who prided himself on his intimacy with life. "There are even a great many."

Paragot swept his skinny fingers in a circular gesture.

"Where are they? Here? You see not. It is a stunted generation, my gentle little lambs. Why *sacré nom de Saint-Antoine!*" he cried, with one of his apposite oaths, "the very pigs in the good days could teach you lessons in the romantic. Vices you have—but the noble passions? No! Did you ever hear of the Café du Cochon Fidèle? Of course not. What do you know? It was situated in the Rue des Cordiers. Mimi la Blonde was the *demoiselle du comptoir*. Ah *bigre!* There are no such *demoiselles du comptoir* now. Exquisite. Ah!" He blew a kiss from the tips of his long nails.

"You are very impolite, Monsieur Paragot," cried Madame Boin from her throne.

"Listen, Madame," said he, "to the story of the pig and you shall judge. The whole quartier was mad for Mimi, including a pig. Yes, a great fat clean pig with sentimental eyes. He belonged to the *charcutier* opposite. I am telling you the authentic history of the *Quartier*. Every day the devoted animal would stand at the door and gaze at Mimi with adoration—ah! but such an adoration, my children, an adoration, respectful, passionate, without hope. Only now and then his poor sensitive snout quivered his despair. Sometimes happier rivals, with two legs, *mais pour ça pas moins cochons que lui*, admitted him into the café. He would sit before the counter, his little tail well arranged behind him, his ears cocked up politely, his eyes full of tears—he wept like a cow this poor Népomucène—they called him Népomucène—and when Mimi looked at him he would utter little cries of the heart like a strangulated troubadour. Ah, it was hopeless this passion; but for one long year he never wavered. The *Quartier* respected him. Of him it was said: "Love is given to us as a measure to gauge our power of suffering." Suddenly Mimi disappeared. She married a certain Godiveau, a charcoal merchant in the vicinity. Népomucène stood all day by the door with haggard eyes. Then knowing she would return no more, he walked with a determined air to the roadway of the Boul' Mich' and cast himself beneath the wheels of an omnibus. He committed suicide."

Paragot stopped abruptly and finished his absinthe. There was vociferous applause. I have never met anyone with his gift of magical narration. Hercule was summoned amid a confused hubbub and received orders for eight or nine different kinds of drink. We were fantastic in our potations in those days.

"Ah!" said Paragot, excited as usual by his success, "*ou sont les neiges d'antan?* Where is the good Père Cordier of the Café Cordier? He would play billiards with his nose, and a little pug nose at that, my children. When it grew greasy he would chalk it deliberately. Once he made a break of two hundred and forty-five. A champion! The Café Cordier itself? Swept long ago into the limbo of dear immemorable dissolute things. Then there was the Café du Bas-Rhin on the Boul' Mich' where Marie la Démocrate drank fifty-five bocks in an evening against Hélène la Sévère who drank fifty-three. Where are such women now, O generation of slow worms? Where is——"

He stopped. His jaw dropped. "My God!" he exclaimed in English, rising from his chair. We followed his gaze. Astounded, I too sprang up.

It was the Comtesse de Verneuil standing in the doorway and looking in her frightened way into the café: Joanna in dark fitting toque and loose jacket beneath which one saw a gleaming high evening dress. I noted swiftly that she had violets in her toque. Her beauty, her rare daintiness compelled a stupefied silence. I sped towards the door and went with her into the street. A closed carriage stood by the kerb.

She took me by the front of my loose jacket and twisted it nervously.

"Get him out, Mr. Asticot. Tell him I must see him."

"But how did you come here?" I asked.

"I went first to the Rue des Saladiers. The servant told me I should find him at the Café Delphine."

I left her outside, and re-entering, met him in the middle of the Café, grasping his green hat in one hand and the pipe with the porcelain bowl in the other. All eyes were turned anxiously towards us.

"She has come for you, Master," I whispered. "She needs you. Come."

"What does she want with me? It was all over and done with thirteen years ago." His voice shook.

"She is waiting," said I.

I drew him to the door and he obeyed me with strange docility. He drew a deep breath as soon as we emerged on to the wind-swept pavement.

"Gaston."

"Yes," said he.

They remained looking at each other for several seconds, agitated, neither able to speak.

"You were very cruel to me long ago," she said at last.

My Master remained silent; the wooden stem of the pipe snapped between his fingers and the porcelain bowl fell with a crash to the pavement.

"Very cruel, Gaston. But you can make a little reparation now, if you like."

"I repair my cruelty to you?" He laughed as men laugh in great pain. "Very well. It will be a fitting end to a topsy-turvy farce. What can I do for Madame la Comtesse?"

"My husband is ill. Come to him. My carriage is here. Oh, put on your hat and don't stand there French fashion, bareheaded. We are English."

"We are what you will," said my Master putting on his hat. "At present however I am mystified by your lighting on me in the dustbin of Paris. You must have done much sifting."

"I will tell you as we drive," she said.

I walked with them across the pavement and opened the carriage door.

"Goodnight, Mr. Asticot," said Madame la Comtesse holding out her hand.

Paragot looked from me to her, shrugged his shoulders and followed her into the carriage. My master had many English attributes, but in the shrug, the pantomime of Kismet, he was exclusively French.

CHAPTER XII

"*Mais dis donc, Asticot*," said Blanquette holding a half egg-shell in each hand while the yolk and white fell into the bowl, "who was the lady that came last night and wanted to see the Master?"

"You had better ask him," said I.

"I have done so, but he will not tell me."

"What did he say?"

"He told me to ask the serpent. I don't know what he meant," said Blanquette.

I explained the allusion to the curiosity of Eve.

"But," objected the literal Blanquette, "there is no serpent in the Rue des Saladiers—unless it is you."

"You have beaten those eggs enough," I remarked.

"You can teach me many things, but how to make omelettes—ah no!"

"All right," said I, "when your inordinate curiosity has spoiled the thing, don't blame me."

"She is very pretty," said Blanquette.

"Pretty? She is entirely adorable."

Blanquette sighed. "She must have a great many lovers."

"Blanquette!" cried I scandalised, "she is married."

"Naturally. If she weren't she could not have lovers. I wish I were only half as beautiful."

The lump of butter cast into the frying-pan sizzled, and Blanquette sighed again. I must explain that I had come, as I often did, to share Paragot's midday meal, but as he was still abed, Blanquette had enticed me into her tiny kitchen. The omelette being for my sole consumption I may be pardoned for my interest in its concoction.

"So that you could be married and have lovers?" I asked in a superior way.

"Too many lovers make life unhappy," she replied sagely. "If I were pretty I should only want one—one to love me for myself."

"And for what are you loved now?"

"For my omelettes," she said with a deft turn of the frying-pan.

"Blanquette," said I, "*je t'adore*."

She laughed with an "*es-tu bête!*" and ministered to my wants as I sat down to my meal at a corner of the kitchen table. She loved this. Great as was her pride in the speckless and orderly salon, she never felt at her ease there. In the kitchen she was herself, at home, and could do the honours as hostess.

"Do you think the beautiful lady is in love with the Master?"

"You have been reading the *feuilletons* of the *Petit Journal* and your head is full of sentimental nonsense," I cried.

"It is not nonsense for a woman to love the Master."

"Oho!" I exclaimed teasingly, "perhaps you are in love with him too."

She turned her back on me and began to clean a spotless casserole.

"*Mange ton omelette*," she said.

My meal over, I went to Paragot's room. I found him in bed, not as usual pipe in mouth and a tattered volume in his hand, but lying on his back, his arms crossed beneath his head, staring into the white curtains of which Blanquette was so proud.

"My son," said he, after he had enquired after my welfare and my lunch and advised me as to cooling medicaments wherewith to mitigate a certain pimplous condition of cheek, "My son, I want you to make me a promise. Swear that if a hitch occurs in your scheme of the cosmos, you will not break up your furniture with a crusader's mace. Such a proceeding has infinite consequences of effraction. It disrupts your existence and ends with the irreparable smash of your porcelain pipe." Whereupon he asked me for a cigarette and began to smoke reflectively.

"One ought to order one's scheme so that no hitch can occur," said I.

"As far as I can gather from the theologians that is beyond the power even of the Almighty," said Paragot.

Blanquette appeared with the morning absinthe.

"The hitch, my son, in my case was beyond mortal control," he said looking up at the bed-curtains. "You may think that I caused it in the first place. You heard me last night accused of cruelty. You, discreet little image that you are, know more about things than I thought. And yet you must wonder, now that you are nearly a man, what can be, what can have been between this disreputable hairy scallywag who is eating the bread of idleness and," with a sip of his absinthe, "drinking the waters of destruction, and that fair creature of dainty life. Don't judge anyone, my little Asticot '*Hi sumus, qui omnibus veris falsa quædam esse dicamus, tanta similitudine, ut in iis nulla insit certe judicandi et assentiendi nota.*' That is Cicero, an author to whom I regret I have not been able to introduce you, and it means that the false is so mingled with the true and looks so like it, that there is no sure mark whereby we may distinguish one from the other. It is a damned fool of a world."

In this chastened mood I left him.

I learned later in the day that the appearance of the Comtesse in the Café Delphine and the exodus of Paragot had caused no small sensation. Cazalet had peeped through the glass door.

"*Cré nom de nom*, she is driving him off in her own carriage!"

He returned to the table and drank a glass of anisette to steady his nerves. Who was the lady? Evidently Paragot was leading a double life. Madame Boin nodded her head mysteriously as though possessed of secrets she would not divulge. They spent the evening in profitless conjecture. The fact remained that Paragot, the hairy disreputable scallywag, had relations with a high born and beautiful woman. It was stupefying. *C'était abracadabrant!* That was the final word. When the Quartier Latin calls a thing *abracadabrant* there is no more to be said.

The Café Delphine was far from being the school of discretion and good manners that Paragot frequented in his youth, but such was his personal influence that when he reappeared in his usual place no one dared allude to the disconcerting incident. Paragot had recovered from the chastened mood and was gay, Rabelaisian, and with great gestures talked of all subjects under heaven. One of the International Exhibitions was in prospect and many architects' offices were busy with projects for the new buildings. A discussion on these having arisen— two of our company were architectural students—Paragot declared that the Exhibition would be incomplete without a Palais de Dipsomanie. Indeed it should be the central feature.

"*Tiens!*" he cried, "I have an inspiration! Some one give me a soft black pencil. Hercule, clear the table."

He caught the napkin from beneath Hercule's arm and as soon as the glasses were removed, he dried the marble top, and holding the pencil draughtsman's fashion, a couple of inches from the point, began to draw with feverish haste. His long fingers worked magically. We bent over him, holding our breath, as gradually emerged the most marvellous, weird, riotous dream of drunken architecture the world could ever behold. There were columns admirably indicated, upside down. The domes looked like tops of half inflated balloons. Enormous buttresses supporting nothing leaned incapable against the building. Bottles and wine cups formed part of the mad construction. Satyrs' heads leered instead of windows. The whole palace looked reeling drunk. It was a tremendous feat of imagination and skill. The hour that he spent in elaborating it passed like five minutes. When he had finished he threw down his pencil.

"*Voilà!*"

Then he called for his drink and emptied the glass at a gulp. We all clamoured our admiration.

"But Paragot," cried one of the architectural students in considerable excitement, "you are a trained architect, and a great architect! It is the work of a genius. Garnier himself could not have done it."

Paragot whipped up the napkin from the seat and, before we could protest, rubbed the drawing into a black smudge.

"I am a poet, painter, architect, musician and philosopher, *mon petit* Bibi," said he, "and my name is Berzélius Nibbidard Paragot."

It was growing late and we all rose in a body—except Paragot, who made a point of remaining after everyone had gone. He caught me by the sleeve.

"Stay a bit to-night, my little Asticot," said he.

Usually he would not allow me to remain late at the Café. It was bad for my health; and indeed I was not supposed to waste my time thus more than two evenings a week. Paragot did not include my seeing him make a Helot of himself as part of my education. This was the theory at the back of his mind. In practice it had occurred at intervals since the days (or nights) of the Lotus Club.

Paragot ordered another drink. It was astonishing, said he, how provocative of thirst was any diversion from the ordinary course of life.

"If the pig of the Café Cordier had been human," he remarked, "he would have sat down and consumed intoxicating liquors instead of throwing himself under the wheels of an omnibus. My son," he said with solemn eyes, "reverence that pig. It is few of us who have his courage and single-heartedness."

He went on talking for some time in a semi-coherent strain, clouding over with dim allusions the vital idea which, I verily believe, had I been a kind woman of the world instead of a raw youth of nineteen, he would have crystallised with flaming speech. I could only listen to him dumbly, vaguely divinatory through my love for him and I suppose through a certain temperamental sensitiveness, but alas! uncomprehending by reason of my inexperience in the deeps of life.

Presently he announced that he was ready to start. He walked somewhat unsteadily to the door, his hand on my shoulder.

"My little son Asticot," said he on the threshold, "I am so far on my road to immortality that I ought to have vine-leaves in my hair; instead of which I have wormwood in my heart. Will you kindly take me to the Pont Neuf."

"But dear Master," said I, "what on earth are you going to do there?"

"I have something important to say to Henri Quatre."

"You can say it better," I urged, "in the Rue des Saladiers."

"To the Pont Neuf," said he brusquely, pushing me away.

I had to humour him. We started up the Boulevard Saint-Michel. It was drizzling with rain.

"Master, we had better go home."

He did not reply, but strode on. I have a catlike dislike of rain. I bear it philosophically, but that is all. To carry on a conversation during a persistent downpour is beyond my powers. I might as well try to sing under water. Paragot, who ordinarily was indifferent to the seasons' difference, and would discourse gaily in a deluge, walked on in silence. We went along amid the umbrella-covered crowd, past the steaming terraces of cafés, whose lights set the kiosques in a steady glare and sent shafts of yellow from the tops of stationary cabs, and caught the wet passing traffic in livid flashes, and illuminated faces to an unreal significance; down the gloom-enveloped, silent quais frowned upon by the dim and monstrous masses of architecture, guarding the Seine like phantasmagorical bastions, none visible in outline, but only felt looming in the rain-filled night, until we reached the statue of Paragot's tutelary King. And the rain fell miserably.

We were wet through. I put my hand on his dripping sleeve.

"Master, let me see you home."

He shook me off roughly.

"You can go."

"But dear Master," I implored. He put both hands behind his head and threw out his arms in a great gesture.

"Boy! Can't you see," cried he, "that I am in agony of soul?"

I bent my head and went away. God knows what he said to Henri Quatre. I suppose each of us has a pet Gethsemane of his own.

One night, a few weeks later, Blanquette appeared in my little student's attic. Fired by the example of some of my comrades at Janot's who showed glistening five-franc pieces as the rewards of industry, I was working up a drawing which I fondly hoped I could sell to a comic paper. Youth is the period of insensate ambitions.

I put down my charcoal as Blanquette entered, bare-headed—wise girl, she scorned hats and bonnets—and as neatly dressed as her figure daily growing dumpier would allow. She was laughing.

"Guess what your concierge said."

"That it was improper for you to come to see me at this hour of the night."

"Improper? Bah!" cried Blanquette, for whom such conventions existed not. "But she told me that it was *un joli petit amant* that I had upstairs. What an idea!" She laughed again.

"You find that funny?" I asked, my dignity somewhat ruffled. "I suppose I am as pretty a little lover as anyone else."

"But you and me, Asticot, it is so droll."

"If you put it that way," I admitted, "it is. But the concierge doesn't think it possible that you are not my *maîtresse*. Why otherwise should you be running in and out of my room, as if it belonged to you?"

"You will be bringing a *maîtresse* of your own here soon, and then you won't want Blanquette any longer."

I dismissed the idea as one too remote for contemplation. At the same time I reflected that I kissed a pretty model at Janot's when we met alone on the stairs. I wondered whether the diabolical perspicacity of women had seen traces of the kiss on my lips.

"I disturb you?" she asked drawing up my other wooden chair to the deal table and sitting down.

"Why, no. I can work while you talk."

She put her elbow on a couple of pickled gherkins that remained casually on the table after a perambulatory meal.

"Oh, how dirty men are! You are worse than the Master. Oh la! la! and he puts his boots and his dirty plates together on his bed! It is time that you did have a *maîtresse* to keep the place in order."

"I believe you really do want to come here in that capacity," I said laughingly.

She flushed at the jest and drew herself up. "You have no right to say that, Asticot. I would sooner be the Master's servant than the mistress or even the wife of any man living. He is everything to me, my little Asticot, everything, do you hear? although he loves me just as he loves you and Narcisse. *Il ne faut pas te moquer de moi.* You must not laugh at me. It hurts me."

It was only then, for the first time, that I realised in Blanquette a grown woman. Hitherto I had regarded her merely as a female waif picked up like the dog and myself under Paragot's vagabond arm and attached to him by ties of gratitude. Now, lo and behold! she was a woman talking of deep things with a treacherous throb in her voice.

I reached across the table and took one of her coarse hands.

"*Mais tu l'aimes donc, ma pauvre Blanquette!*" I exclaimed in sympathy and consternation.

She looked down and nodded. I did not know what to say. A tear fell on my hand. I knew still less. Then crying out she was very unhappy, she began to sob.

"He does not want me—even to pass the time. It has never entered his head. I am too ugly. I do not demand that he should love me. It would be asking for the moon."

"But he does love you, like a father," I said, in vain consolation. "I love him like a son and you should love him like a daughter."

93

She did not even condescend to notice this counsel of perfection. She was too ugly. She was built like a hayrick. The Master had never cast his eyes on her, as doubtless he would have done, being a man, had she any of the qualities of allurement. She suffered, poor Blanquette, from the *spretæ injuria formæ* with reason even more solid than the forsaken Dido. She was humble, she sobbed; she did not demand a bit of love bigger than that—and she clicked her finger nail. With that she would be proud and happy.

"If the master were as gay as he used to be, I should not mind," she said, lifting a grotesquely stained face. "But when he goes drinking, drinking so as to drown his love for another woman, *c'est plus fort que moi*. It is more than I can bear."

"Which other woman?"

"You know very well. That beautiful lady. She has come more than once to fetch him away. She is a wicked woman, for she does not love him; she even detests him; one can see that. I should like to kill her," cried Blanquette.

The idea of anyone wanting to kill Joanna was so novel that I stared at her speechless. It took some time for my wits to accommodate themselves to the point of view.

"If I were a man I would not drink myself to death for the sake of a woman who treated me so," she remarked, recovering her composure.

"Is it as bad as that?" I asked.

She shrugged her shoulders. Men must drink. It is their nature. But there should be limits. One ought to be reasonable, even a man. Did I not think so? In her matter of fact way she gave me details of Paragot's habits. The one morning absinthe had grown to two or three. There was brandy too in his bedroom.

"And it eats such a deal of money, my little Asticot," she remarked.

After which, to relieve her feelings, she washed up my dirty plates, and discoursed on the economics of catering.

I walked with her through the two or three streets that separated me from the Rue des Saladiers, and went upstairs with her to see whether Paragot had returned. It was past midnight. There was no Paragot. I went to the Café Delphine profoundly depressed by Blanquette's story. Here was Blanquette eating her heart out for Paragot, who was killing his soul for Joanna, who was miserably unhappy on account of her husband, who was suffering some penalty for his scaly-headed vulturedom. It was a kind of House-that-Jack-built tale of misery, of which I seemed to be the foundation.

Save for Paragot the café was empty. He was asleep in his usual corner, breathing stertorously, his head against the wall. Madame Boin on her throne was busy over accounts. Hercule dozed at a table by the door, his napkin in the crook of his arm. He nodded towards Paragot as I entered and made a helpless gesture.

I looked at the huddled figure against the wall and wondered how the deuce I was to take him home. I had no money to pay for a cab. I tried in vain to rouse him.

"Monsieur had better let him stay here," said Hercule. "It won't be the first time." My heart grew even heavier than it was before. No wonder poor Blanquette was dismayed.

"He will catch his death of cold when the morning comes," said I, for the night was fresh and three years of warm lying had softened the Paragot of vagrant days.

"One must die sooner or later," moralised Hercule inhumanly.

I shook my master again. He grunted. I shook him more violently. To my relief he opened his eyes, smiled at me and waved a limp salutation.

"The Palace of Dipsomania," he murmured.

"No, Master," said I. "This is the Café Delphine and you live in the Rue des Saladiers."

"It is a nuisance to live anywhere. I was born to be a bird—to roost on trees." I had considerable difficulty in disentangling the words from his thick speech. He shut his eyes—then opened them again.

"How does a drunken owl stay on his twig?"

As I felt no interest in the domestic habits of dissolute owls, I set about getting him home. I took his green hat from the peg and put it on his head, and with Hercule's help drew away the table and set him on his feet.

"A man like that! It goes to my heart," said Madame Boin in a low voice.

I felt unreasonably angry that any one, save myself or perhaps Blanquette, should pity my beloved master. I did not answer, whereby I am afraid I was rude to the good Madame Boin. Paragot lurched forward and would have fallen had not Hercule caught and steadied him.

"Broken ankle," explained Paragot.

"You must try to walk, Master," I urged anxiously. How was I going to get him to the Rue des Saladiers? His arm round my neck weighed cruelly on my frail body.

"Put best foot forward," he murmured making a step and pausing. "That is very easy; but the devil of it is when time comes for worst foot."

"Try it, for goodness sake," said I.

He tried it with a silly laugh. Then the swing door of the café opened and Joanna with her sweet frightened face appeared on the threshold.

CHAPTER XIII

THE sight of Joanna froze Paragot into momentary sobriety. He stood rigid for a few seconds and then swayed into a chair by one of the tables and sat with his head in his hands. I went up to Joanna.

"He can't come to-night, Madame."

"Why not?"

"He is not fit."

As she realised my meaning a look of great pain and repulsion passed over her face.

"But he must come. Perhaps he will be better presently. You will accompany us and help me, Mr. Asticot, won't you?"

As usual the frost melted from her eyes and her voice—the silvery English voice—went to my heart. I bent over Paragot and whispered.

"Take her from this pigstye and the sight of the hog," muttered Paragot. His hands were clenched in a mighty effort to concentrate his wits. Joanna approached and touched him on the shoulder.

"Gaston."

Suddenly he relaxed his grip and broke into a stupid laugh.

"Very well. What does it matter? Sorry haven't got—velveteen suit."

"What does he say?" she asked turning to me.

"That he will come, Madame," said I.

Hercule aided me to frog-march him out of the café and across the pavement to the waiting carriage. Joanna took her seat by his side and I sat opposite. Hercule shut the carriage door and we drove off. Paragot relapsed into stupor.

"I don't know how to ask you to forgive me, Mr. Asticot, for keeping you out of your bed at this time of night," said Joanna. "But I am very friendless here in Paris."

We went along the Boul' Mich' by the quais to the Pont de la Concorde, crossed the vast and now silent expanse of the Place de la Concorde and, going by the Rue Royale and the long dull Boulevard Malesherbes and the Boulevard Haussmann, entered the Avenue de Messine. It is a long drive under the most cheerful circumstances; but at one o'clock in the morning in the company of the dearest thing in the world to me half drunk, and the dear lady whom he worshipped horrified and disgusted at the thought thereof, it seemed interminable. At last we arrived at No. 7. At my ring the door swung open drawn by the concierge within. I helped Paragot out of the carriage. He made a desperate effort to stand and walk steadily. Heaven knows how he managed to clamber with not too great indecency up the stairs to the Comte de Verneuil's flat on the first floor. Joanna opened the door with her latch key and we entered a softly-lit drawing room.

"Let me sit down," said Paragot. "I shall be better presently."

He sank an ashamed heap on a sofa by the wall, and with his fingers through his long black hair fought for mastery over his intoxication. The Comtesse de Verneuil left us and presently returned, having taken off her hat and evening wrap. She brought a little silver tray with Madeira wine and biscuits.

"We need something, Mr. Asticot," she said graciously.

We drank the wine and sat down to wait for Paragot's recovery. Although it was late May, a wood fire glowed beneath the great chimney-piece. This made of blue and white ware with corbels of cherubs caught my attention. I had seen things like it in the stately museums of Italy.

"But this is Della Robbia," I exclaimed.

She smiled, somewhat surprised. "You are a connoisseur as well as a philosopher, Mr. Asticot? Yes, it is Della Robbia. The Comte de Verneuil is a great collector."

Then for the first time I looked about the room, and I caught my breath as I realised its wealth and luxury. For a time I forgot Paragot, lost in a dream of Florentine tapestries, priceless cabinets, porcelain, silver, pictures, richly toned rugs, chairs with rhythmic lines, all softened into harmonious mystery by the shaded light of the lamps. At the end of a further room just visible through the looped curtains a great piece of statuary gleamed white. I had never entered such a room in my life before. My master had taken me through the show apartments of great houses and palaces, but they were uninhabited, wanted the human touch. It had not occurred to me that men and women could have such wonder as their daily environment, or could invest it with the indefinable charm of intimacy. I turned and looked at Joanna as she sat by the Della Robbia chimney-piece, gracious and distinguished, and Joanna became merged in the Countess de Verneuil, the great lady, as far removed from me as my little bare attic from this treasure house of luxury. She wore the room, so to speak, as I wore the attic. Overcome by sudden timidity I could barely reply to her remarks.

She was in no mood for conversation, poor lady; so there dropped upon us a dead silence, during which she stared frozenly into the fire while I, afraid to move, occupied the time by storing in my memory every bewitching detail of her dress and person. The oil sketch of her I made a day or two afterwards hangs before me as I write these lines. I prided myself on having caught the colour of her hair— black with the blue reflections like the blue of cigarette smoke.

Suddenly the quietness was startled by loud groans of agony and unintelligible speech coming from some room of the flat. Paragot staggered noisily to his feet, a shaking, hairy, dishevelled spectre, blinking glazed eyes.

Madame de Verneuil started and leaned forward, her hands on the arms of her chair.

"My husband," she whispered, and for a few seconds we all listened to the unearthly sounds. Then she rose and turned to me.

"You had better see it through."

She crossed to Paragot.

"Are you better now?"

"I can do what is required of me," said my master, humbly, though in his ordinary voice. He was practically sober.

"Then come," said Joanna.

We followed her out of the room, through softly carpeted corridors full of pictures and statues and beautiful vases, and entered a dimly lit bedroom. A nurse rose from a chair by the bed, where lay a bald-headed, beaky-nosed man groaning and raving in some terrible madness. Joanna gripped my arm as Paragot went to the bedside.

"I am Gaston de Nérac," said he.

The Comte de Verneuil raised himself on his elbow and looked at him in a wild way. I too should have liked to grip someone's arm, for the sight of the man sent a shudder through me, but I braced myself up under the consoling idea that I was protecting Joanna.

"You are not dead then? I did not kill you?" said the Comte de Verneuil.

"No, since I am here to tell you that I am alive."

The sweat poured off the man's face. He lay back exhausted.

"I do not know why," he gasped, "but I thought I had killed you." He closed his eyes.

"That is enough," said the nurse.

Without a word, we all returned to the drawing-room. It was an astounding comedy.

"I am grateful," said Joanna to my master. "I wish there were some means of repaying you."

"I thought," said he, with a touch of irony which she did not notice, "that it was I who was paying for a wrong I did you."

She drew herself up and surveyed him from head to foot, with a little air of disdain.

"I forget," she said icily, "that you ever did me any wrong."

"And I can't," said he; "I wish to heaven I could. You beheld me to-night in the process of trying—an unedifying sight for Madame la Comtesse de Verneuil."

"An unedifying sight for anybody," said Joanna.

He bowed his head. Something pathetic in his attitude touched her. She was a tender-hearted woman. Her hand caught his sleeve.

"Gaston, why have you come down to this? You of all men?"

"Because I am the one poor fool of all poor fools who takes life seriously."

Joanna sighed. "I can't understand you."

"Is there any necessity?"

"You belong to a time when one wanted to understand everything. Now nothing much matters. But curiously in your case the desire has returned."

"You understood me well enough to be sure that when you wanted me I would be at your service."

"I don't know," she said. "It was a desperate resort to save my husband's reason. Oh, come," she cried, moving to the chairs by the fire, "let us sit and talk for five minutes. The other times you came and went and we scarcely spoke a word. Besides," with a forced laugh, "it would not have been *convenable*. Now Mr. Asticot is here as chaperon. It doesn't seem like real life, does it, that you and I should be here? It is like some grotesque dream in which all sorts of incoherences are mixed up together. Don't you at least find it interesting?"

"As interesting as toothache," replied Paragot.

"If it is pain for you to talk to me, Gaston, I will not detain you," said Joanna, rising from her chair.

"Forgive me," said he; "I suppose my manners have gone with the rest. You may help me to recover them if you allow me to talk to you."

He passed his hand wearily over his face, which during the last minute or two had been overspread by a queer pallor. He looked ghastly.

"Tell me," said he, "why you come to that boozing-ken of a place? A note would reach me and I would obey."

She explained that there was no time for letter-writing. The Comte's attacks came on suddenly at night. To soothe him it was necessary to find the chief actor in the absurd comedy at once, at any cost to her reputation. Besides, what did it matter? The only person who knew of her escapade was the coachman, an old family servant of the Comte, as discreet as death.

"How long have these attacks been going on?" asked my master.

Joanna poured out her story with the pathetic eagerness of a woman who has kept hateful secrets in her heart too long and at last finds a human soul in whom she can confide. I think she almost forgot my presence, for I sat modestly apart, separated from them by the wide cone of light cast by the shaded lamp.

The first symptoms of mental derangement, she said, had manifested themselves two years ago. They had gradually increased in frequency and intensity. During the interval the Comte de Verneuil went about the world a sane man. The attacks, as she had explained, came on suddenly, always at night, and his fixed idea was that he had killed Gaston de Nérac. Before Paragot had appeared they lasted two or three days, till they spent themselves leaving the patient in great bodily prostration. When she had met me taking the Spring outside the Hôtel Bristol, a wild idea had entered her head that the confrontation of the Comte with the living Gaston de Nérac might end his madness. On the occasion of the next attack she had rushed in eager search for Paragot, had brought him to the raving bedside, and the result had been magical. She had thought the cure permanent; but a fortnight later the attack returned, as it had returned again and again, and as it had returned to-night.

"It is charitable of you to have come, Gaston," she said, in her sweet way, "and I must ask you to forgive me for anything unkind I may have said."

He made some reply in a low voice which I did not hear, and for a little time their talk was pitched in the same tone. I began to grow sleepy. I aroused myself with a jerk to hear Joanna say,

"Why did you play that detestable tune from 'Orphée aux Enfers'?"

"To see if you would recognise it. Some mocking devil prompted me. It was the last tune you and I heard together—the night of our engagement party. The band played it in the garden."

"Don't—don't!" exclaimed Joanna, putting up her hands to her face.

This then was why each had cried out at Aix-les-Bains against the merry little tune. It was interesting. I saw however that it must have jangled horribly on tense nerves.

She dashed away her hands suddenly and strained her face towards him.

"Why, Gaston—why did you?"

He rose with a deprecating gesture and there was a hunted look in his eyes. During all this strange scene he was no longer Paragot, my master, but Gaston de Nérac whom I did not know. His wild, picturesque speech, his dear vagabond manner had gone. The haggardness of some desperate illness changed his features and I grew frightened. I came to his side.

"Master—we must take a cab. Have you any money?"

"Yes," he said faintly, "let us go home."

"But you are ill! You look as white as a ghost!" cried Joanna, in alarm.

"I had a dinner of herbs—in the liquid form of absinthe," said my master with a clutch at Paragot. "How does it go? Better a dinner of herbs where love is——"

"Ah! Monsieur has not yet gone," said the nurse, hurrying into the room. "Monsieur le Comte begs me to give this to Monsieur."

She held out a letter.

"Monsieur le Comte made me open his despatch box, Madame," she added apologetically.

She left the room. Paragot stood twirling the letter between his fingers. Joanna bade him open it. It might be something important Paragot drew from the envelope half a sheet of note-paper. He looked at it, made a staggering step to the door and fell sprawling prone upon the carpet.

Joanna uttered a little cry of fright, and, as I did, cast herself on her knees beside him. He had fainted. Abstinence from food, drink, his tremendous effort of will towards sobriety, the strain of the interview, had brought him to the verge of the precipice, and it only required the shock of the letter to send him toppling over. We propped his head on cushions and loosened his collar.

"What can we do?" gasped my dear lady.

"I will call the nurse from Monsieur le Comte's room," said I.

"She will know," said Joanna hopefully.

I went to the Comte's room, opened the door and beckoned to the nurse. She gave a glance at her sleeping patient and joined me in the corridor. On my explanation she brought water and sal-volatile and returned with me to the drawing-room. It was a night of stupefying surprises. The *quartier* would have called it *abracadabrant* and they would not have been far wrong. There was necromancy in the air. I felt it, as I followed the nurse across the threshold. I anticipated something odd, some grotesque development. In the atmosphere of those I loved in those days I was as sensitive as a barometer.

Paragot lay still as death, his wild hairy head on the satin cushions, but Joanna was crouching on her knees in the midst of the cone of light cast by the shaded lamp, reading, with parted lips and blanched face, the half sheet of note-paper. As we entered she turned and looked at me and her eyes were frozen hard blue. The nurse bent over by my master's side.

Joanna stretched out her arms full length towards me.

"Read," she cried, and her voice was harsh with no silvery tone in it at all. I took the paper wonderingly from her fingers.

Why she should have shown it to me, the wretched little pasty-faced gutter-bred art student, I could not conceive for many of the after years during which I wrestled with the head- and heart-splitting perplexities of women. But experience has taught me that human beings, of whichever sex they may be, will do amazing things in times of spiritual upheaval. I have known the primmest of vicar's churchwardens curse like a coal-heaver when a new incumbent chose in his stead a less prim man than he.

I was just a human entity, I suppose, who had strayed into the sacred and intimate sphere of her life—the only one perhaps in the world who had done so. She was stricken to the soul. Instinct compelled my sharing of her pain.

She commanded me to read. I was only nineteen. Had she commanded me to drink up eisel or eat a crocodile, I would have done it. I read.

The address of the letter was Eaton Square: the date, the 20th of June thirteen years before. The wording as follows:—

"In consideration of the sum of Ten thousand pounds I the undersigned Gaston de Nérac promise and undertake from this moment not to hold any communication by word or writing with Miss Joanna Rushworth for the space of two years—that is to say until midnight of the 20th June 18—. Should however Miss Joanna Rushworth be married in the meantime, I solemnly undertake on my honour as a gentleman not of my own free will to hold any communication with her whatever as long as I live, or should circumstances force us to meet, not to acquaint her in any way with the terms of this agreement, whereof I hold myself bound by the spirit as well as by the letter. GASTON DE NÉRAC."

My young and unpractised mind required some minutes to realise the meaning of this precious agreement. When it had done so I stared blankly at Joanna.

The nurse in her businesslike fashion drew the curtains and flung the French windows wide open.

"He has only fainted. He will soon come round."

She returned to Paragot's side. Joanna and I remained staring at each other. She rose, took me by the sleeve and dragged me to the fireplace.

"The writing is my husband's," she said in a whisper. "The signature is his," pointing to Paragot. "He sold me to my husband for ten thousand pounds on the evening of our engagement party. What am I to do? I haven't a friend in this hateful country."

I longed to tell her she had at least one friend, but as I could neither help nor advise her I said nothing.

"No wonder he has a banking account," she said with a bitter laugh. I noticed then that a strained woman's humour is unpleasant. She sat down. The corners of her kind lips quivered.

"The world is turned upside down," she said piteously. "There is no love, honour or loyalty in it. I felt this evening as if I could forgive him; but now—" She rose and wrung her hands and exclaimed sharply, "Oh, it's hateful, it's hateful for men to be so base!"

That it was a base action to sell Joanna for any sum of money, however bewildering in largeness, I could not deny. But that Paragot should have been guilty of it I would not have believed had the accusation come from Joanna's own lips. The confounded scrap of paper, however, was proof. Therein he had pledged himself to give up Joanna for ten thousand pounds, and the scaly-headed vulture had paid the money. I turned away sadly and went to help the nurse minister to my master.

He opened his eyes and whispered that I must fetch a cab.

"Or a dung-cart," he added, characteristically.

Glad of action I went out into the long quiet avenue and after five minutes' walk hailed a passing fiacre. The nurse admitted me when I rang the bell. I found Paragot sitting on the sofa by the wall, and Joanna where I had left her, by the Della Robbia chimney-piece. Apparently they had not had a very companionable five minutes. He rose as I entered.

"I thought you were never coming," said he. "Let us go."

"I must say good-bye to Madame."

"Be quick about it," he whispered.

I crossed the room to Joanna's chair and made a French bow according to my instruction in manners.

"Good night, Madame."

She held out her hand to me—such a delicate soft little hand, but quite cold and nerveless.

"Good night, Mr. Asticot. I am sorry our friendship has been so short."

I joined Paragot. He said from where he stood by the door:—

"Good night, Madame la Comtesse."

She made no reply. Instinctively both of us lingered a second on the threshold, filling our eyes with the beauty and luxury that were all part and parcel of Joanna, and as the door closed behind us we felt like two bad angels turned out of Paradise.

CHAPTER XIV

I CAME across him the next afternoon sitting on a stone bench in the Luxembourg Gardens. His hat was slouched forward over his eyes. His hand supported his chin so that his long straggling beard protruded in a curious Egyptian horizontality. His ill-laced boots innocent as usual of blacking, for he would not allow Blanquette to touch them, were stuck out ostentatiously, and to the peril of the near passers-by. He had never during our acquaintance manifested any sense of the dandified; on our travels he had worn the casual, unnoticeable dress of the peasant, save when he had masqueraded in the pearl-buttoned velveteens; in London a swaggering air of braggadocio had set off his Bohemian garb: but never had the demoralised disreputability of Paragot struck me until I saw him in the Luxembourg Gardens.

Everything else wore a startlingly fresh appearance, after the heavy rains. The gravel walk had the prim neatness of a Peter de Hoogh garden path. The white balustrades and flights of steps around the great circle, the statuary and the fountains in the middle lake, flashed pure. The enormous white caps of nurses, their gay silk streamers fluttering behind them, the white-clad children, the light summer dresses of women; the patches of white newspaper held by other loungers on the seats; a dazzling bit of cirro-cumulus scudding across the clear Paris sky; the pale dome of the Panthéon rising to the East; the background of the Luxembourg itself in which one was only conscious of the high lights on the long bold cornices; all set the key of the picture and gave it symphonic value. The eye rejected everything but the whites and the pearl greys, subordinating all other tones to its impression of fantastic purity.

And there like an ink blot splashed on the picture, sat Paragot. The very foulest odd-volume of Montesquieu's "Esprit des Lois" which could be picked up on the quays lay unopened on his knee. Not until Narcisse, who was sleeping at his feet, jumped up and barked a welcome around me did Paragot notice my approach. He held out his hand, and the finger-nails seemed longer and dirtier than ever. He drew me down to the seat beside him.

"You were asleep when I ran in this morning, Master," said I apologetically, for it was the first time I had seen him that day.

"Since then I have been thinking, my little Asticot. It is a vain occupation for a May afternoon, and it makes your head ache. I should be much better employed carting manure for Madame Dubosc. We earned two francs. Do you remember?"

"I remember that my back ached terribly afterwards," said I laughing.

"Ah, but the ease and comfort in your soul! Perhaps there's nothing much the matter with yours yet, is there?"

"I think it's all right," I answered.

"Something must be wrong with mine," he remarked meditatively, "because at a crisis in my life I haven't had an inspiration. It is sluggish. I want a soul pill."

This time it was I who had an inspiration—one of terrifying audacity.

"Master, perhaps absinthe isn't good for it," said I all in a breath.

"Infant Solomon," replied Paragot ironically, "where have you gathered such a store of wisdom? Have you a scrap of paper in your pocket?"

"Yes, Master," said I, producing a sketch-book and preparing to tear out a leaf. He stopped my hand.

"Leave it in. All the better. As I am sure you don't remember the passage from Cicero's *De Natura Deorum* which I quoted to you some time ago, since you are unacquainted with the Latin tongue, I will dictate it to you, and you can learn it by heart and say it like a Pater or an Ave morning and evening."

I wrote down at his dictation the passage concerning the impossibility of judging between the false and true. And that is how I was able to set it down in its proper place in a previous chapter.

"Do you know why I have made you do this?"

"Yes, Master," said I, for I knew that he referred to the sale of Joanna for ten thousand pounds.

"Circumstance flattens a man out sometimes," said he, "like a ribbon—as if he had been carefully ironed by a hot steam roller. I suppose a flattened man can't have an inspiration. I am my own tomb-stone and you can chalk across me '*Hic jacet qui olim Paragotus fuit.*'"

His tone was so dejected that I felt a sinking at my heart, a scratchiness in my nose and a wateriness in my eyes. I suffered the pangs of suppressed sympathy. What could a boy of nineteen say or do in order to restore rotundity to a flattened hero?

"Years ago," he continued after a pause, "I found the world a Lie and I started off to chase the wild goose of Truth. I captured nothing but a taste for alcohol which brought me eventually beneath the steam roller. Were it not the silliest legend invented by man, I should say to you 'Beware of the steam roller.' But if a man's sober he can see the thing himself; if he isn't, he can't read the warning. I can only tell you to be unalcoholic and you'll be happy. You see, my little son Asticot, to what depths I have descended in that I can be the Apostle of the Platitudinous."

He leaned forward, chin on knuckles, and his beard again stuck out horizontally. Happy people passed us by. For many the work of the day was already over and they had the lingering magic of the sunshine for their own. A young blue-bloused workman and a girl hanging on his arm brushed close by our seat.

"*Si, nous aurons des enfants, et de beaux enfants,*" she cried.

"I hope they will," said Paragot, looking at them wistfully. Then after a pause: "Has the Comtesse de Verneuil any children?"

"No, Master," said I in a tone of conviction. It struck me later that I had spoken from blank ignorance. But at the moment the question seemed preposterous. In many ways I had still the unreasoning instincts of a child. Because I had never contemplated my dear lady Joanna in the light of a mother, I unhesitatingly proclaimed her childless. As a matter of fact I was right.

Paragot, satisfied with my reply, watched the endless stream of cheerful folk. Once he quoted to himself:—

"'The golden foot of May is on the flowers'—and on the heads of all but me."

Suddenly he sat back and seized me by the arm.

"Asticot, you are a man now, and you must see things with the eyes of a man. I have loved you like my son—if you should turn away, thinking evil things of me, like someone else, it would break my heart. Neither she nor you ought to have seen that accursed paper. You and Blanquette and the dog are all I have in the world to care for, and I want you all to think well of me."

Then the tears did spring into my eyes, for my beloved master's appeal went home to that which was truest and best in me. I stammered out something, I know not what; but it came from my heart. It pleased him. He jumped to his feet in his old impetuous way.

"Bravo, *petit Asticot de mon cœur!* The nightmare is over, and we can enjoy the sunshine again. We will drag Blanquette from the Rue des Saladiers which does not lay itself out for jollity, and we will dine at a reckless restaurant. Blanquette shall eat the snails which she adores and I shall eat pig's feet and you an underdone beefsteak to nourish your little body. And we shall all eat with our dinner '*le pain bénit de la gaîté.*'"

He strode off eager as usual to put his idea into immediate execution. He talked all the way to the Rue des Saladiers. Poor Blanquette! He had been neglecting her. A girl of her age needed some amusement; we would go to the Théâtre, the Porte Saint-Martin, like good bourgeois, and see a melodrama so that Blanquette could weep.

"They are playing 'Les Eventreurs de Paris.' I hear they rip each other up on the stage and everybody is reeking with blood—good honest red blood—carried in bladders under their costumes, my son. You turn up what you can of your snub little superior artistic nose—but Blanquette will be in Paradise."

Blanquette was in the slip of a kitchen and a flurried temper when we entered.

"But, Master, you said you would not be home for dinner. There is nothing in the house—only this which I was cooking for myself," and she dived her fork into the pot and brought up on the prongs a diminutive piece of beef. "And now you and Asticot demand dinner, as if dinners came out of the pot of their own accord. Ah men! They are always like that."

I put my arm round her waist. "We are all dining out together, Blanquette; but if you don't want to come, you shall stay at home."

"And without dinner," said Paragot, taking the fork from her hand and throwing the meat to Narcisse.

"*Ah, mais non!*" cried Blanquette, whose sense of economy was outraged. But when Narcisse sprang on the beef and finding it too hot, lay growling at it until it should cool, she broke out laughing.

"After all, it would have been very tough," she admitted.

"Then why in the sacred name of shoe leather were you going to eat it?" asked Paragot.

"Food is to be eaten, not thrown away, Master," she replied sententiously.

We took the omnibus and crossed the river and went up the Grands Boulevards, an unusual excursion for Paragot who kept obstinately to the Boulevard Saint-Michel and the poorer streets of the *quartier*, through fear, I believe, of meeting friends of former days. A restaurant outside the Porte Saint-Martin provided a succulent meal. The place was crowded. Two young soldiers sat at our table, and listened awe-stricken to Paragot's conversation and were prodigiously polite to Blanquette, who, they discovered, was from Normandy, like themselves. And when they asked, after the frank manner of their kind, which of us had the honour to be the lover of Mademoiselle, and she cried with scarlet face, "But neither, Monsieur!" we all shouted together and laughed and became the best friends in the world. Happy country of fraternity! The little soldiers—they were dragoons and wore helmets too big for them and long horsehair plumes—accompanied us with clanking sabres to the gallery of the theatre, and at Paragot's invitation sat one on each side of Blanquette, who, what with the unaccustomed bloodshed of the spectacle and the gallantry of her neighbours, passed an evening of delirious happiness. In those days I had an æsthetic soul above the 'Eventreurs de Paris,' and I made fun of it to Paragot, whose thoughts were far away. When I perceived this, I kept my withering sarcasm to myself, and realised that a flattened man cannot be blown like a bladder into permanent rotundity even by the faith and affection of a little art-student. But I marvelled all the more at his gaiety during the intervals, when we all went outside into the thronged boulevard and drank bocks on the terrace of the café, and I learned how great a factor in the continued existence of humanity is the Will-to-Laugh, which I think the German philosopher has omitted from his system.

I mention this incident to show how Paragot defied the effects of the steam roller and became outwardly himself again. He did not visit the Café Delphine that night, but went soberly home with Blanquette, and I believe read himself to sleep with his tattered odd volume of Montesquieu. The following evening however found him in his usual seat under the lee of Madame Boin's counter, arguing on art, literature and philosophy and consuming a vast quantity of ill-assorted alcohols. And then his life resumed its normal course.

It was about this time that Madame Boin seeing in Paragot an attractive adjunct to her establishment and, with a Frenchwoman's business instinct, desiring to make it permanent, paralysed him by an offer of marriage.

"Madame," said he, as soon as he had recovered, "if I accepted the great honour which you propose, you would doubtless require me to abandon certain personal habits which are dear to me, and also to trim my hair and beard and cut my finger-nails of whose fantastic length I am inordinately proud."

"I think I should ask you to cut your nails," said Madame Boin reflectively.

"Then, Madame," said Paragot, "it would be impossible. Shorn of these adornments I should lose the power of conversation and I should be a helpless and useless Samson on your hands."

"I don't see what long nails have to do with talking," argued Madame Boin.

"They give one the necessary thirst," replied Paragot.

"My son," said he when relating to me this adventure, "do not cultivate a habit of affability towards widows of the lower middle classes. There was once a murderer's widow of Prague—"

"I know," said I.

"How?"

"There was an old stocking."

"I forgot," said he, and his laughing face darkened and I saw that he fell to thinking of Joanna.

Although much of my leisure was absorbed by the companionship of my beloved Master and Blanquette, I yet had an individual life of my own. I made dozens of acquaintances and one or two friends. I had not a care in the world. Bisard, the great man attached to the life school in Janot's atelier, proclaimed me one of the best of my year, and sent my heart leaping sky-high. I worked early and late. I also played the fool as (worse luck) only boyhood can. With my fellows, arm in arm through the streets, I shouted imbecile songs. I went to all kinds of reprehensible places—to the *bals du quartier*, for instance, where we danced with simple-minded damsels who thought *choucroute garnie* a generous supper and a bottle of *vin cacheté* as setting the seal of all that was most distinguished upon the host. With the first five francs that I made by selling a drawing I treated Fanchette, the little model I kissed on the stairs, to a trip to Saint-Cloud. Five francs went prodigiously far in those days. They had to, as some of us were desperately poor and could afford but one meal a day. Fortunate youth that I was, whenever money ran short, instead of borrowing or starving, I had only to climb to Blanquette and open my mouth like a young bird and she filled it with nice fat things. Poor sandalled Cazalet of the yellow hair, on the other hand, lived sometimes for a week on dry bread and water. It was partly his own fault; for had he chosen to make saleable drawings he too might have had five francs wherewith to take Fanchette to Saint-Cloud. Pretty little Pierrettes in frills and pointed caps are more attractive to the cheap purchaser than ugly souls writhing in torment; and really they are quite as artistic. We quarrelled fiercely over this one day, and he challenged me to a duel. I replied that I had no money to buy pistols. Neither had he, he retorted, but I could borrow a sabre. He himself had one. His father had been an officer. Whereupon the studio bawled in gleeful unison "*Voici le sabre, le sabre de mon père*," and dragged us in tumult to the Café opposite where we swore eternal friendship over *grogs américains*.

From this I do not mean you to infer that I was a devil of a fellow, the mention of whose name spread a hush over godly families. God wot! I did little harm. I only ate what Murger calls "the Blessed bread of gaiety," the food of youth. Remember, too, it was the first time in my life that I had companions of my own age. Indeed, so nearly had I modelled myself on Paragot the ever young, that my comrades laughed at my old fashioned ideas, and I found myself hopelessly behind the times. Youth hops an inch sideways and thinks it has leaped a mile ahead. All is vanity, even youth.

'Tis a pleasant vanity though, on which the wise smile with regretful indulgence; and therein lay the wisdom of Paragot.

"Ah! confounded little cock-sparrow—I haven't seen you for a week," he said one morning, shaking me by the shoulders till my teeth chattered. "What about the other little sparrow you neglected me for on Sunday? Is she at least good-looking? A model? And she is a good girl and supports her widowed mother and ten brothers and sisters, I suppose? And she calls herself Fanchette? Narcisse, the lady of Monsieur Asticot's affections has the singular name of Fanchette."

Whereupon Narcisse uncurled himself from slumber and planted himself on his hindquarters in front of me and grinned at me with lolling tongue.

"But she is quite a different kind of girl from all the other models!" I cried eagerly.

"What does she pose for?"

"Well—of course—you know how it is—" I stammered, reddening.

Paragot laughed and quoted something in Latin about an ingenuous boy.

"Would she be a fit companion for Blanquette and Narcisse and myself?"

Having deep convictions as to the essential virtues of Fanchette, I swore that she could not disgrace so respectable a company.

"We will all picnic together in the woods of Fontainebleau on Sunday," said he.

We picnic-ed. Fanchette had no shynesses. She found Paragot peculiarly diverting, and though I enjoyed the day prodigiously, I realised afterwards that I had spent most of it in the company of Blanquette.

"My son," said he, "there never was a model so like all the other models that have posed for the well-of-course-you-know-how-it-is, since the world began."

A week later, when I found my particular friend Ewing, whom as a tongue-tied Englishman I had relieved of many embarrassments, and for whom I had secured an easel, branding it myself in twenty places with his name, and for whom I had engineered a good position next to mine in the Life School—when I saw Ewing hugging Fanchette on the stairs, on the very landing sacred to my embraces, I knew that Paragot was right, and that Fanchette was just a fickle, naughty little model like the others. But if Paragot had not taken her measure before my eyes at Fontainebleau and made a figured drawing so to speak of her heart and soul, shewing their exiguous dimensions, I might have cast myself beneath the wheels of an omnibus like the pig Népomucène, or blacked the eyes of Ewing who was smaller than myself. As it was, I put my hands in my trousers' pockets and surveyed the abashed couple in Paragot's best manner.

"Amuse yourselves well, my children," I laughed, in French, and turned away heart-whole.

This is an instance of the wisdom of Paragot. He smiled on the vanity of my youth, and personally conducted me to the barrenness whither it led. In this particular case the result was more positive still. Ewing in admiration of my magnanimity at the time, and a fortnight later of my profound knowledge of women—for he in his turn witnessed the alien osculations of Fanchette—cultivated my friendship to the extent of urging me to spend some of the summer recess at his father's country vicarage in Somerset.

"But you'll have to get some other togs," said he, eyeing my attire dubiously. "If you come like that to church on Sunday, my governor would forget and want to baptise you. He was once a missionary, you know."

When I mentioned the invitation, Paragot insisted on acceptance.

"The Latin Quarter confers an exuberance of tone which conflicts with the reposeful ideal of manners required in the *beau monde* which I destined you to grace when I took you from the maternal soapsuds. You will find an English Parsonage exerts a repressive influence. But for Heaven's sake don't fall in love with Ewing's eldest sister, who, I am sure, is addicted to piety and good works. She will try to make a good work of you and thus all my labour will have been in vain."

In his heart, however, I believe he was immensely proud at having trained me to meet gentlefolk on more or less equal terms. Ewing's invitation was a tribute to himself. To fit me for church on Sunday and other functions of civilisation he took Ewing (as counsellor) and myself to a tailor's and plunged enthusiastically into the details of my outfit. I can see him now, shaggy and shabby, fingering stuffs with the anxious solicitude of a woman at a draper's counter.

"That's a nice country suiting. It expresses its purpose, suggests the right gaiety of mood. What says *Arbiter elegantiarum?*"

"Don't you think it might make the cart-horses shy?" says Ewing, and Paragot drops reluctantly the thunder-and-lightning check that has seized his unaccustomed fancy.

My wardrobe included a dress suit.

At Paragot's bidding, I donned it when it arrived, and on my way to him transfixed the Rue des Saladiers with awe and wonder. Upstairs, Paragot twirled me slowly round as if I were a mannequin on a pivot, and called Blanquette to admire, and uttered strange oaths in the dozen languages of which he was master. Was I not beautiful?

Blanquette admitted that I was. All that was most beautiful; without a doubt. I resembled the stylish people who went to expensive funerals. In fact, she added with a sigh, I was too beautiful.

She saw her brother Asticot transfigured into the resplendent gentleman beyond her sphere, and sighed womanlike at my apotheosis. She could no longer walk by my side, bareheaded, in the streets. The dress suit was a symbol of change detested by woman. She gave the matter however her practical attention.

"He ought to have patent-leather shoes," she observed.

"That's true," said Paragot, pulling his beard reflectively. "Ewing should have mentioned it; but I have noticed a singular lack of universality in the sons of English clergymen."

"And now my son," said he on the eve of my departure, "I too have the nostalgia of green fields and the smell of hay and manure and the fresh earth after rain. I have at last an inspiration. As this confounded ankle will not let me walk, I shall hire a donkey and let him take me whither he will. Narcisse shall accompany me."

"And Blanquette, will she trudge beside the donkey?"

"I have arranged for Blanquette to go into villégiatura at the farm of La Haye."

"With Monsieur and Madame Dubosc?"

"Your logical faculty does you credit, my son. They are most excellent people, although they could not tell me how many towers the Cathedral of Chartres possessed. You will remember an excursion we made on Sunday, and I lectured learnedly on the archæology of the fabric. My learning impressed them less than my skill in curing a pig according to a Dalmatian recipe. They will board and lodge Blanquette for ten francs a week and she will be as happy as Marie Antoinette while haymaking at the Petit Trianon. She will occupy herself with geese and turkeys while I shall be riding my donkey."

"Master," said I, "I only have one fear. You will adopt that donkey and bring it to live in the Rue des Saladiers."

Paragot laughed, drained his glass of absinthe and ordered another.

CHAPTER XV

THUS the three of us were again separated. Blanquette was enjoying herself amongst the pigs and ducks of La Haye, whence she wrote letters in which her joy in country things mingled with anxiety as to the neglected condition of the Master; I led a pleasant but somewhat nervous life in Somersetshire, spending hours in vain attempts to reconcile the cosmic views of Paragot and an English vicar, and learning sometimes with hot humiliation the correctitudes of English country vicarage behaviour; and Paragot, his long legs dangling on each side of his donkey, rode, as I thought, picturesquely vagrant, through the leafy byways of France.

A fortnight after my arrival, however, he informed me by letter of his resolve to stay in Paris. He had failed to find an ass of the true vagabond character. The ideal ass he sought should be a companion as well as a means of locomotion. He would not take an urban donkey into the country against its will. To force any creature, man, woman, or ass, out of the groove of its temperament were a crime of which he could not be guilty. Then, again, Narcisse did not enter into the spirit of the pilgrimage. He laid his head along his forepaws and glowered sullenly instead of barking with enthusiasm. Again, when he announced his intention of leaving Paris, Hercule groaned aloud and Madame Boin wept so profusely that sitting beneath her counter he had to put up a borrowed umbrella. Cazalet too, and a few others too poor for railway fares, were staying in town. Also the Café Delphine had spoiled him for the horrible alcohols of wayside cafés. And, lastly, what did it matter where the body found itself so long as the soul had its serene habitations?

The letter depressed me. I was beginning to see Paragot with the eyes of a man. I felt that this inability to carry out an inspiration was a sign of decay. The springs of action had weakened. Though the spirit thirsted for sweet things, habit chained him to the squalor of the Café Delphine. When the quiet Somersetshire household knelt around the drawing-room for evening prayers, I speculated on the stage of intoxication at which my lonely master had arrived.

I was a million miles from speculating on what was really happening, and when I received a curt uncharacteristic note from Paragot a fortnight later begging me to return to Paris at once, a day or two before the formal expiry of my visit, it only occurred to me that he might be ill.

The crowded train steamed into the Gare Saint-Lazare at half past seven in the morning. I was desperately anxious to get to Paragot, and bag in hand I stood with a sickening feeling of suspense by the open door, waiting for the train to slow down. I sprang out. In an instant the line of porters were odd dots of blue in the throng that swarmed out of the carriages. I became a mere ant in the heap, and struggled with the others towards the barrier. After giving up my ticket, I set down my bag to rest my strained arm for a minute, and looked around me. Then I noticed a stranger approaching whose smiling face had an air of uncanny familiarity. Where had I seen the long gaunt man before? He wore a silk hat and a frock coat. My acquaintance with silk-hatted gentlemen in Paris was limited. I picked up my bag.

"Ah! My little Asticot," cried the stranger. "How good it is to see you."

I dropped my bag. I dropped my jaw. I would have dropped my brains had they been loose. This cadaverous image of respectability was Paragot—but a Paragot transmogrified beyond recognition even by me. His hair was cropped short. His face was clean shaven. On his transfigured head shone a flat brimmed silk hat. He wore a villainously fitting frock coat buttoned across his chest, with long wrinkly creases stretching horizontally from each button. His hands were encased in lemon coloured gloves a size too large for him. When he extended his hand even my bewilderment did not blind me to the half-inch of flat dead tips to the fingers. Beneath his arm was an umbrella—on a broiling August morning! He wore spats—in mid-summer! His trousers were fawn coloured. I could only gape at him as he wrung me by the hand.

"You are surprised, my son."

"I did not expect you to meet my train, Master," said I.

"If one could anticipate all the happenings of life it would lose its fascination. My son, go your way and do your duty, but believe in the unexpected."

"But what has happened?" I asked, again surveying his ill-fitting glory.

"The Comte de Verneuil is dead," he answered.

"Are you going to his funeral?"

"In these?" he cried holding up the lemon kids, "and this cravat?"

I noticed that he wore a floppy purple tie adorned with yellow spots, outside the lapels of his coat. It required more than two glances to take in all his detail.

"Besides," he added, "my distinguished patient was buried a fortnight ago."

He looked at me with an amused smile, enjoying my mystification like a child.

"You didn't know me."

"No, Master." I rubbed my eyes. "In fact I scarcely recognise you now."

"That is because I am again Gaston de Nérac," said he magnificently.

I had an idea that he must have come into the family fortune. But what had the death of the Comte de Verneuil to do with it? I picked up my bag again and walked with him to the exit. The hurrying crowd of passengers by my train and of clerks and work-people pouring from suburban platforms rendered conversation impossible.

At the station gates Paragot stood and watched the brisk life that swarmed up and down the Rue Saint-Lazare and the Rue du Havre. Paris awakens a couple of hours earlier than London. Clerks hurried by with flat leather portfolios under their arms. Servants trotted to market, or homewards, with the end of a long golden loaf protruding from their baskets. Work-girls sped by in all directions. Omnibuses lumbered along as at midday. Before the great cafés opposite, the tables were already set out on the terrace and the awnings lowered, and white-aproned waiters stood expectant. The whole scene was bathed in the gay morning sunshine.

"It is good to be alive, Asticot," said my master. "It is good to be in Paris. It is good to get up early. It is good to see the world's work beginning. It is also good to feel infernally hungry and to have the means of satisfying one's desires. But as, in the absence of Blanquette, my establishment is disorganised, I think we had better have our breakfast at a *crêmerie* than in the Rue des Saladiers. We can talk over our coffee."

I accompanied him across the street in a muddled condition of intellect, casting sidelong glances at him from time to time, as if to assure myself that he was real. Having just come from an English environment where the niceties of costume were as rigidly observed as the niceties of religion, I could not help marvelling at Paragot's attire. He looked like a tenth-rate French provincial actor made up to represent a duke, and in a country where none but actors and footmen are clean-shaven this likeness was the more accentuated. Also the difference between Paragot hairy and bearded and Paragot in his present callow state was that between an old unbroken hazel nut and its bald, shrivelled kernel.

We entered the *crêmerie*, sat down and ordered our coffee and crisp horse-shoe loaves. I think the *petit déjeuner* at a *crêmerie* is one of the most daintily served meals in France. The morning dew glistens so freshly on the butter, the fringed napkin is so spotless, the wide-mouthed cups offer themselves so delicately generous. If everyone breakfasted there crime would cease. No man could hatch a day's iniquity amid such influences.

When we were half-way through, Paragot unbuttoned his frock coat and took from his pocket a black-edged letter which he flourished before my eyes. It was then that I noticed, to my great surprise, that he had cut his finger-nails. I thought of Madame Boin.

"It is from the Comtesse de Verneuil, and it gives you the word of the enigma."

"Yes, Master," said I, eyeing the letter.

"Confess, my little Asticot," he laughed, "that you are dying of curiosity."

"You would tell me," said I, "that it was no death for a gentleman."

"You have a way of repeating my unsaid epigrams which delights me," said he, throwing the letter on the table. "Read it."

I read as follows:

"CHÂTEAU   MARLIER
près   de   Nevers.
13th Aug. 18—

"MY DEAR GASTON:

"The newspapers may have told you the news of my husband's death on the 1st August. Since then I have been longing to write to you but I have not found the strength. Yet I must.

"Forgive me for the cruel things I said on the last unhappy night we met. I did not know what I do now. Before my husband died he told me the true circumstances of the money transaction. My husband bought me, it is true, Gaston, but you did not sell me. You sacrificed all to save my father from prison and me from disgrace. You have lived through everything a brave, loyal gentleman, and even on that hateful night you kept silent. But oh, my friend, what misery it has been to all of us!

"I shall be in Paris on the 28th—Hôtel Meurice. If you care to see me will you make an appointment? I would meet you at any place you might suggest. The flat in the Avenue de Messine is dismantled and, besides, I shrink from going back there.   Yours sincerely,

"JOANNA DE VERNEUIL."

"You see, my son, what she calls me—a brave, loyal gentleman," he cried, with his pathetic boastfulness. "Thank Heaven she knows it. I have kept the secret deep in my heart all these years. One must be a man to do that, eh?" He thumped his heart and drank a draught of coffee. Then he wiped his mouth with the back of his hand.

He eyed the brown stain disgustedly.

"That," said he, "is Paragot peeping out through Gaston de Nérac. You will have observed that in the polite world they use table-napkins."

"The Comtesse de Verneuil," said I, bringing back the conversation to more interesting matters, "writes that she will be in Paris on the 28th. It was the 28th yesterday."

"I am aware of it. I have been aware of it for a fortnight. Yesterday I had a long interview with Madame la Comtesse. It was very satisfactory. To-day I pay her a ceremonious visit at eleven o'clock. At twelve I hope you will also pay your respects and offer your condolences to Madame. You ought to have a silk hat."

"But, Master," I laughed, "If I went down the Boul' Mich' in a silk hat, I should be taken up for improper behaviour."

"You at least have gloves?"

"Yes, Master."

"Remember that in this country you wear both gloves while paying a call. You also balance your hat on your knees."

"But Madame de Verneuil is English," I remarked.

"She has learned correct behaviour in France," he replied with the solemnity of a professor of deportment. "You will have noticed in her letter," he continued, "how delicately she implies that the Hôtel Meurice would not be a suitable rendezvous. In my late incarnation I doubtless should have surprised the Hôtel Meurice. I should have pained the Head Porter. In my live character of Gaston de Nérac I command the respect of flunkeydom. I give my card——"

He produced from his pocket and flourished in the air an ornate, heavily printed visiting-card of somewhat the size and appearance of the Three of Spades. I felt greatly awed by the sight of this final emblem of respectability.

"I give my card," he repeated, "and the Hôtel Meurice prostrates itself before me."

While Paragot was playing on the lighter side of the conjuncture, my mind danced in wonder and delight. I read the letter, which he left in my hands, several times over. He was cleared in Joanna's eyes; nay more, he stood revealed a hero. The generous ardour of youth bedewed my eyelids.

"Master," I cried, "this must be wonderful news for you."

He nodded over his coffee cup.

"You are right, my little Asticot; it is," he answered gravely.

When I called at the Hôtel Meurice at noon, I was conducted with embarrassing ceremony to Madame de Verneuil's private sitting-room, and on my way I rehearsed, in some trepidation, the polite formula of condolence which Paragot had taught me. When I entered, the sight of Joanna's face drove polite formulæ out of my head. She was dressed in black, it is true, but the black only set off the shell pink of her cheeks and the blue of her eyes which were no longer frozen, but laughed at me, as if a visit of condolence were the gayest event possible.

"It is so good of you, Mr. Asticot, to come and see me. Mr. de Nérac tells me you have travelled straight from Somerset in order to do it. How is the West Country looking? I am of the West Country myself—one of these days you will let me shew it you. I like him much better, Gaston, dressed like an Englishman, instead of in that dreadful student get-up, which makes him look like a brigand. Yes, England has agreed with him. Oh! do take off your gloves and put your hat down. I am not a French mamma with a daughter whose hand you are asking. Gaston, I am sure you told him to keep on his gloves!"

"I am responsible for his decorum, Joanna," said my Master, solemnly.

I noticed that he too had discarded hat, gloves and umbrella which lay forlorn on a distant table. Still his coat was buttoned, and he sat bolt upright on his chair. Madame de Verneuil's silvery voice rippled on. She was girlishly excited.

"I have persuaded Mr. de Nérac to lunch with me," she said happily. "And you must do the same. Will you ring the bell? We'll have it up here. And now tell me about Somerset."

Never was there a sweeter lady than mine. Yes, I call her mine; and with reason. Was she not the first vision of gracious womanhood that came into my childhood's world? Up to then woman to me was my mother and Mrs. Housekeeper. Joanna sprang magically, as in an Arabian Night, out of an old stocking. Never was there a sweeter lady than mine. She welcomed me as if such things as wash-tubs, tambourines, Café Delphines and absinthiated Paragots had never existed, and I were one of her own people.

"How I long to get back," she cried when I had told her of my modest exploits at the Ewings. "I have not been to Melford for five years. When will you come, Gaston?"

They had evidently made good use of their previous interviews.

"I am going to live in England," she explained. "At first I shall stay with my mother at Melford. She is an old friend of Mr. de Nérac's. Oh, Gaston, she does so want to see you—I have told her the whole story—of course she knew all my poor father's affairs. And I have a cousin whose people live at Melford too, Major Walters—I don't think you know him—a dear fellow. He has just been at Nevers helping me to settle up things. He is my trustee. You must be great friends."

"I remember the name," said Paragot.

"Why of course you ought to," she cried prettily with a laugh and a blush. "I had forgotten. You were pleased to be jealous of him. Mr. Asticot, you will have to forgive us for dragging memories out of the dust heap. It is all so very long ago. Dear me!" Her face grew pathetic. "It is very long ago, Gaston."

"Thirteen years," said he.

I calculated. Joanna was a grown-up woman about to be married when my age was six. I suddenly felt very young indeed.

The waiters set the lunch. Joanna, most perfect of hostesses, presided gaily, cracked little jokes for my entertainment and inspired me with the power of quite elegant conversation. Paragot preserved his correct demeanour and, to my puzzledom, spoke very little. I wondered whether the repressive influence lay in the spats or the purple cravat with the yellow spots. As a painter I didn't like the cravat. He drank a great deal of water with his wine. I noticed him once pause in the act of conveying to his mouth a bit of bread held in his fingers with which he had mopped up the sauce in his plate, and furtively conceal it between his cutlet bones—a manœuvre which, at the time, I could not understand. In the *Quartier*

Latin we cleaned our plates to a bright polish with bits of bread. How else could you consume the sauce?

At the end of the meal Joanna gave us permission to smoke.

"I won't smoke, thank you," said Paragot politely.

"Rubbish!" laughed Joanna, whereupon Paragot produced a cigarette case from the breast pocket of his frock coat. Paragot and a cigarette-case! Once more it was *abracadabrant!* He also refused cognac with his coffee.

After a time, still feeling that I was very young, and that my seniors might have further confidential things to say to each other, I rose to take my leave. Paragot rose too.

"I would ask you to stay, Gaston, if I hadn't my wretched lawyer to see this afternoon. But you'll come in for an hour after dinner, won't you? No one knows I'm in Paris. Besides, at this time of year there is no one in Paris to know."

"Willingly," said Paragot, "but *les convenances*——"

Joanna's pretty lips parted in astonishment.

"You—preaching the proprieties?—My dear Gaston!"

I turned to the window and looked at the Tuileries Gardens which baked in the afternoon sun. The two spoke a little in low voices, but I could not help overhearing.

"Is it true, Gaston, that you have wanted me all these years?"

"I want you as much now as I did then."

"I, too," whispered Joanna.

CHAPTER XVI

As we emerged from the Hôtel Meurice I turned instinctively to the left. Paragot drew me to the right.

"Henceforward," said he, "I resume the Paris which is my birthright. We will forget for a moment that there are such places as the Boulevard Saint-Michel and the Rue des Saladiers."

We walked along the Rue de Rivoli and taking the Rue Royale passed the Madeleine and arrived at the Café de la Paix. It was a broiling afternoon. The cool terrace of the café invited the hot wayfarer to repose.

"Master," said I, "isn't it almost time for your absinthe?"

He raised his lemon kids as if he would ban the place.

"My little Asticot, I have abjured absinthe and forsworn cafés. I have broken my new porcelain pipe and have cut my finger-nails. As I enter on the path of happiness, I scatter the dregs and shreds and clippings of the past behind me. I divest myself of all the crapulous years."

If he had divested himself of the superfluous trappings of respectability beneath which he was perspiring freely, I thought he would have been happier. The sight of the umbrella alone made one feel moist, to say nothing of the spats.

"We might have some grenadine syrup," I suggested ironically.

"Willingly," said he.

So we sat and drank grenadine syrup and water. He gave me the impression of a cropped lion sucking lollipops.

"It is peculiarly nasty and unsatisfying," he remarked after a sip, "but doubtless I shall get used to it. I shall have to get used to a devil of a lot of things, my son. As soon as the period of her widowhood has elapsed I hope to marry Madame de Verneuil."

"Marry Madame de Verneuil?" I cried, the possibility of such an occurrence never having crossed my mind.

"Why not? When two people of equal rank love and are free to marry, why should they not do so? Have you any objection?"

"No, Master," said I.

"I shall resume my profession," he announced, lighting a cigarette, "and in the course of a year or two regain the position to which an ancient *Prix de Rome* is entitled."

I was destined that day to go from astonishment to astonishment.

"You a *Prix de Rome*, Master?"

"Yes, my son, in Architecture."

He was clothed in a new and sudden radiance. To a Paris art student a *Prix de Rome* is what a Field Marshal is to a private soldier, a Lord Chancellor to the eater of dinners in the Temple. I must confess that though my passionate affection for him never wavered, yet my childish reverence had of late waned in intensity. I saw his faults, which is incompatible with true hero-worship. But now he sprang to cloud summits of veneration. I looked awe-stricken at him and beheld nothing but an ancient *Prix de Rome*. Then I remembered our enthusiasm over the Palace of Dipsomania.

"They said you were an architect that night at the Café Delphine," I exclaimed.

"I was a genius," said Paragot modestly. "I used to think in palaces. Most men's palaces are little buildings written big. My small buildings were palaces reduced. I could have roofed in the whole of Paris with a dome. My first commission was to put a new roof on a Baptist Chapel in Ireland. It was then that I met Madame de Verneuil after an interval of five years. We are second cousins. Her father and my mother were first cousins. I have known her since she was born. When I was at Rugby, I spent most of my holidays at her house. You must take all this into account, my little Asticot, before you begin to criticise my plans for the future."

By this time the nerve or brain cell whereby one experiences the sensation of amazement was numb. If Paragot had informed me that he had been a boon companion of King Qa and had built the pyramids of Egypt I should not have been surprised. I could only record the various facts.

Paragot was at Rugby.

Paragot was Joanna's second cousin.

Paragot was a *Prix de Rome*.

Paragot was a genius who had put a new roof to a Baptist Chapel in Ireland.

Paragot was going to marry Joanna.

How he proposed to start in practice at his age, with no connection, I did not at the moment enquire. Neither did Paragot. It was Paragot's easy way to leap to ends and let the means take care of themselves. He drained his glass meditatively and then with a wry face spat on the ground.

"If I don't have a cognac, my little Asticot," said he, "I shall be sick. To-morrow I may be able to swallow syrup without either salivation or the adventitious aid of alcohol."

He summoned the languid waiter and ordered *fine champagne*. Everything seemed languid this torrid afternoon, except the British or American tourists who passed by with Baedekers under their arms. The cab-horses in the file opposite us dropped their heads and the glazed-hatted cabmen regarded the baking Place de l'Opéra with more than their usual apathy. It looked more like the market place of a sleepy provincial town than the heart of Paris. When the waiter had brought the little glass in a saucer and the *verseur* had poured out the brandy, Paragot gulped it down and cleared his throat noisily. I drowsed in my chair, feeling comfortably tired after my all night journey. Suddenly I awakened to the fact that Paragot was telling me the story of Joanna and the Comte de Verneuil.

She was exquisite. She was fragrant. She was an English rosebud wet with morning-dew. She had all manner of attributes with which I was perfectly well acquainted. They loved with the ardour of two young and noble souls. (Your ordinary Englishman would not thus proclaim the nobility of his soul; but Paragot, remember, was half French—and Gascon to boot—and the other half Irish.) It was more than love—it was a consuming passion; which was odd in the case of an English rosebud wet with morning-dew. However, I suppose Paragot meant that he swept the beloved maiden off her feet with his own vehemence; and indeed she must have loved him truly. He was fresh from the Villa Medici, the Paradise where all the winners of the *Prix de Rome* in the various arts complete their training; he had won an important competition; fortune smiled on him; he had only to rule lines on drawing paper to become one of the great ones of the earth. He became engaged to Joanna.

Now, Joanna's father, Simon Rushworth, was a London solicitor in very fashionable practice; a man of false geniality, said Paragot, who smiled at you with lips but seemed always to be looking at some hell over your shoulder. He also promoted companies, and the Comte de Verneuil, an Anglo-French financier, stood ever by his elbow, using him as his tool and dupe and drawer in general of chestnuts from the fire. The Comte wanted to marry Joanna, "which was absurd, seeing that I was his rival," said Paragot simply.

One of Mr. Rushworth's companies failed. Mr. Rushworth's fashionable clients grew alarmed. He gave a party in honour of Joanna's engagement and invited all his clients. Ugly rumours spread among the guests. The presage of disaster was in the air. Paragot began to suspect the truth. It was a hateful party. The band in the garden played selections from "Orphée aux Enfers," and the mocking refrain accompanied the last words he was to have with Joanna. The Comte de Verneuil called him aside, explained Rushworth's position. Ten thousand pounds of his clients' money which he held in trust had gone in the failure of the company. If that amount was not at his disposal the next morning, he was finished, snuffed out. It appeared that no one in Paris or London would lend him the money, his credit being gone. Unless M. de Nérac could find the ten thousand pounds there was the gaol yawning with horrible certainty for M. de Nérac's prospective father-in-law. As Paragot's patrimony, invested in French government securities, was not a third of this sum, he could do nothing but wring his hands in despair and call on Providence and the Comte de Verneuil. The former turned a deaf ear. The latter declared himself a man of business and not a philanthropist; he was ready however to purchase an option on the young lady's

121

affections. Did not M. de Nérac know what an option was? He would explain. He drafted the famous contract. In return for Paragot's signature he would hand him a cheque drawn in favour of Simon Rushworth.

"*Nom de Dieu!*" cried Paragot, banging the marble table, with his fist, "Do you see in what a vice he held me? He was a devil, that man! The only human trait about him was a passion for rare apes of which he had a collection at Nevers. Thank Heaven they are dead! Thank Heaven he is dead! Thank Heaven he lost most of the money for which he preyed on his kind. He was a vulture, a scaly-headed vulture. He was the carrion kite above every rotten financial concern in London and Paris. That which went near to ruin my poor vain fool of a father-in-law filled his bulging pockets. I hated him living and I hate him dead!"

He tore open his frock coat and pushed the flat brimmed silk hat to the back of his head and waved his lemon kids in his old extravagant gestures.

"What did the stolen ten thousand pounds matter to him? It mattered prison to Rushworth, Joanna's father—think of the horror of it! She would have died from the disgrace—her mother too. And the devil jested, Asticot. He talked of Rushworth being smitten with the slings and black arrows of outrageous fortune. *Nom de Dieu*, I could have strangled him! But what could I do? Two years! To go out of her life for two years as if I had been struck dead! Yet after two years I could come back and say what I chose. I signed the contract. I went out of the house. I kept my word. *Noblesse oblige.* I was Gaston de Nérac. I came back to Paris. I worked night and day for eighteen months. I had genius. I had hope. I had youth. I had faith. She would never marry the Comte de Verneuil. She would not marry anybody. I counted the days. Meanwhile he posed as the saviour of Simon Rushworth. He poisoned Joanna's mind against me. He lied, invented infamies. This I have heard lately. He confessed it all to her before the devil took him as a play-fellow. Of one who had so cruelly treated her all things were possible. She half believed them. At last he told her I was dead. An acquaintance had found me in a Paris hospital and had paid for my funeral. She had no reason for disbelief. He pressed his suit. Her father and mother urged her—the fool Rushworth soon afterwards came to another crisis, and de Verneuil again stepped in and demanded Joanna as the price. She is gentle. She has a heart tenderer than that of any woman who ever lived. One day I heard she had married him. My God! It is thirteen years ago."

He poured some water into the syrup glass and gulped it down. I remained silent. I had never seen him give way to violent emotion—save once—when he broke the fiddle over Mr. Pogson's head.

Presently he said with a whimsical twist of his lips:

"You may have heard me speak of a crusader's mace."

"Yes, Master."

"That's when I used it. I had an inspiration," he remarked quietly.

"Master," said I after a while, "if Madame de Verneuil believed you to be dead, it must have been a shock to her when she saw you alive at Aix-les-Bains."

"She learned soon after her marriage that her husband had been mistaken. Her mother had caught sight of me in Venice. Madame de Verneuil never forgave him the lie. She is gentle, my son, but she has character."

It was after that, I think, that the frozen look came into her eyes. Thenceforward she was ice to the Comte de Verneuil, who for pleasant, domestic companionship had to resort to his rare apes. No wonder his madness took the form of the fixed idea that he had murdered Paragot.

"After all," he mused, "there must have been some good in the man. He desired to make amends. He sent me the old contract, so that his wife should not find it after his death. He confessed everything to her before he died. There is a weak spot somewhere in the heart of the Devil himself. I shouldn't wonder if he were devoted to a canary."

"Master," said I, suddenly bethinking me of the canary in the Rue des Saladiers, "if you marry Madame de Verneuil, what will become of Blanquette?"

"She will come and live with us, of course."

"H'm!" said I.

Respect forbade downright contradiction. I could only marvel mutely at his pathetic ignorance of woman. Indeed, his reply gave me the shock of an unexpected stone wall. He, who had but recently taught me the chart of Fanchette's soul, to be unaware of elementary axioms! Did I not remember Joanna's iciness at Aix-les-Bains when I told her of his adoption of my zither-playing colleague? Was I not aware of poor Blanquette's miserable jealousy of the beautiful lady who enquired for her master? To bring these two together seemed, even to my boy's mind, a ludicrous impossibility. Yet Paragot spoke with the unhumorous gravity of a Methodist parson and the sincerity of a maiden lady with a mission to obtain good situations for deserving girls; a man, so please you, who had gone into the holes and corners of the Continent of Europe in search of Truth, who had come face to face with human nature naked and unashamed, who had run the gamut of femininity from our rare princess Joanna to the murderer's widow of Prague; a man who ought to have had so sensitive a perception that the most subtle and elusive harmonies of woman were as familiar to him as their providential love of babies or their ineradicable passion for new hats.

He lit another cigarette, having dallied in a somewhat youthful fashion with the newly acquired case, and blew two or three contented puffs.

"I believe in the Roman conception of the *familia*, my son. You and Blanquette are included in mine. You being a man must go outside the world and make your way; but Blanquette, being a woman, must remain under the roof of the *paterfamilias* which is myself."

I foresaw trouble.

When he left me after dinner to pay his promised visit to Joanna, I went in quest of Cazalet of the sandals, with whom I spent a profitable evening discussing the question of Subject in Art. Bringard and Bonnet and himself had rented a dilapidated stable in Menilmontant which they had fitted up as a studio, and, as his two colleagues were away, Cazalet had displayed his own horrific canvases all over the place. The argument, if I remember right, was chiefly concerned with Cazalet's subject in art over which we fought vehemently; but though the sabre of his father hung proudly on the wall, he did not challenge me to a duel. Instead, he invited me to join the trio in the rent of the studio, and I, suddenly struck with the advantage and importance of having a studio of my own, gladly accepted the proposal. When one can say "my studio," one feels that one is definitely beginning one's professional career. I left him to sleep on some contrivance of sacking which he called a bed, and trudged homewards to the Boulevard Saint-Michel. Curiosity tempted me to look into the Café Delphine. It was deserted. Madame Boin opened her fat arms wide and had it not been for the intervening counter would have clasped me to her bosom. What had become of Monsieur Paragot? It was more than a fortnight since he had been in the café. I lied, drank a glass of beer and went home. I could not take away Paragot's character by declaring his reversion to respectability.

CHAPTER XVI

MY taking the share of the stable-studio in Menilmontant had one unlooked-for result.

"You must paint my portrait," said Joanna.

"Madame," I cried, "if I only could!"

"What is your charge for portraits, Mr. Asticot?"

Paragot set down his tea-cup and looked at me with a shade of anxiety. We were having tea at the Hôtel Meurice.

"The pleasure of looking a long time at the sitter, Madame," said I.

"That is very well said, my son," Paragot remarked.

"You will not make a fortune that way. However, if you *will* play for love this time—"

She smiled and handed me the cakes.

"Where did you say your studio was?"

"But, Madame, you can't go there!" I expostulated. "It is in the slums of Menilmontant beyond the Cemetery of Père Lachaise. The place is all tumbling down—and Cazalet sleeps there."

"Who is Cazalet?"

"A yellow-haired Caliban in sandals," said Paragot.

Joanna clapped her hands like a child.

"I should love to go. Perhaps Mr. de Nérac would come with me, and protect me from Caliban. If you won't," she added seeing that Paragot was about to raise an objection, "I will go by myself."

"There are no chairs to sit upon," I said warningly.

"I will sit upon Caliban," she declared.

Thus it came to pass that I painted the portrait of Madame de Verneuil in periods of ecstatic happiness and trepidation. She came every day and sat with unwearying patience on what we called the model throne, the one comfortless wooden arm-chair the studio possessed, while Paragot mounted guard near by on an empty box. Everything delighted her—the approach through the unsavoury court-yard, the dirty children, the crazy interior, Cazalet's ghastly and unappreciated masterpieces, even Cazalet himself, who now and then would slouch awkwardly about the place trying to hide his toes. She expressed simple-hearted wonder at the mysteries of my art, and vowed she saw a speaking likeness in the first stages of chaotic pinks and blues. I have never seen a human being so inordinately contented with the world.

"I am like a prisoner who has been kept in the dark and is let out free into the sunshine," she said one day to Paragot, who had remarked on her gaiety. "I want to run about and dance and smell flowers and clap my hands."

In these moments of exuberance she seemed to cast off the shadow of the years and become a girl again. I regarded her as my contemporary; but Paragot with his lined time-beaten face looked prematurely old. Only now and then, when he got into fierce argument with Cazalet and swung his arms about and mingled his asseverations with the quaint oaths of the Latin Quarter, did he relax his portentous gravity.

"That is just how he used to go on," she laughed confidentially to me, her pink-shell face close to mine. "He was a whirlwind. He carried everybody off their feet."

She caught my eye, smiled and flushed. I quite understood that it was she who had been carried off her feet by my tempestuous master.

"*Mais sacré mille cochons, tu n'y comprends rien du tout!*" cried Paragot, at that moment. I, knowing that this was not a proper expression to use before ladies, kept up the confidential glance for a second.

"I hope he didn't use such dreadful language."

"You couldn't in English, could you? He always spoke English to me. In French it is different. I like it. What did he say? *'Sacré mille cochons'!*"

She imitated him delightfully. You have no idea what a dainty musical phrase this peculiarly offensive expletive became when uttered by her lips.

"After all," she said, "it only means 'sacred thousand pigs'—but why aren't you painting, Mr. Asticot?"

"Because you have got entirely out of pose, Madame."

Whereupon it was necessary to fix her head again, and my silly fingers tingled as they touched her hair. It is a good thing for a boy of nineteen to be romantically in love with Joanna. He can thus live spiritually beyond his means, without much danger of bankruptcy, and his extravagance shall be counted to him for virtue. Also if he is painting the princess of his dreams, he has such an inspiration as is given but to the elect, and what skill he is possessed of must succeed in its purpose.

One morning she found on her arrival a bowl of roses, which I had bought in the markets, placed against her chair on the dais. She uttered a little cry of pleasure and came to me both hands outstretched. Taking mine, she turned her head, in an adorable attitude, half upwards to Paragot.

"I believe it is Mr. Asticot who is in love with me, Gaston. Aren't you jealous?"

I blushed furiously. Paragot smiled down on her.

"Hasn't every man you met fallen in love with you since you were two years old?"

"I forgive you," she cried, "because you still can make pretty speeches. Thank you for the roses, Mr. Asticot. If I wore one would you paint it in? Or would it spoil your colour scheme?"

I selected the rose which would best throw up the pink sea-shell of her face, and she put it gaily in her corsage. She pirouetted up to the dais and with a whisk of skirts seated herself on the throne.

"If any of my French friends and relations knew I were doing this they would die of shock. It's lovely to defy conventions for a while. One will soon have to yield to them."

"Conventions are essential for the smooth conduct of social affairs," remarked Paragot.

She looked at him quizzically. "My dear Gaston, if you go on cultivating such unexceptional sentiments, they'll turn *you* into a churchwarden as soon as you set foot in Melford."

I had seen, for the first time in my life, a churchwarden in Somerset, a local cheesemonger of appalling correctitude. If Paragot ever came to resemble him, he was lost. There would be an entity who had passed through Paragot's experiences; but there would be no more Paragot.

"You must save him, Madame," I cried, "from being made a churchwarden."

Paragot lit a cigarette. I watched the first few puffs, awaiting a repartee. None came. I felt a qualm of apprehension. Was he already becoming de-Paragot-ised? I did not realise then what it means to a man to cast aside the slough of many years' decay, and take his stand clean before the world. He shivers, is liable to catch cold, like the tramp whose protective hide of filth is summarily removed in the workhouse bath. Nor did my dear lady realise this. How could she, bright freed creature, hungering after the long withheld joyousness of existence, and overwilling to delude herself into the belief that every shadow was a ray of sunlight? She had no notion of the man's grotesque struggles to conceal the shivering sensitiveness of his roughly cleaned soul.

She twitted him merrily.

"You can argue like a tornado with Monsieur Cazalet, but you think I must be talked to like this country's *jeune fille à marier*. Isn't he perverse, Mr. Asticot? I think I am quite as entertaining as Caliban."

Well you see, when he talked to Cazalet, he slipped on the slough again and was comfortable.

He waited for a moment or two as if he were composing a speech, and then rose and drawing near her, said in a low voice, thinking that as I was absorbed in my painting I could not hear:—

"This new happiness is too overwhelming for fantastic talk."

"Oh no it isn't," she declared in a whisper. "We have put back time thirteen years—we wipe out of our minds all that has happened in them, and start just where we left off. You were fantastic enough then, in all conscience."

"I had the world at my feet and I kicked it about like a football." He hunched up his shoulders in a helpless gesture. "Somehow the football burst and became a helpless piece of leather."

"I haven't the remotest idea what you mean," laughed Joanna.

"Madame," said I, "if you turn your head about like that I shall get you all out of drawing."

"Oh dear," said Joanna, resuming her pose.

These were enchanted days, I think, for all of us. Even Cazalet felt the influence and put on a pair of gaudily striped socks over which his sandals would not fit. Joanna was very tender to him, as to everybody, but she appeared to draw her skirts around her on passing him by, as if he were a slug, which she did not love but could not harm for the world. Paragot, having for some absurd reason forsworn his porcelain pipe, smoked the cigarette of semi-contentment and fulfilled his happiness by the contemplation of Joanna and myself. I verily believe he was more at his ease when I was with them. As for the portrait, he viewed its progress with enthusiastic interest. Now and then he would forget himself and discourse expansively on its merits, to the delight of Joanna. He regarded it as his own production. Had he not bought this poor little devil and all his works for half-a-crown? Ergo, the work taking shape on the canvas was his, Paragot's. What could be more logical? And it was he who had given me my first lessons. No mother showing off a precocious brat to her gossips could have displayed more overweening pride. It was pathetic, and I loved him for it, and so did Joanna.

The time came however—all too soon—-when Madame de Verneuil could live in her Land of Cockaigne no longer. Convention claimed her. Her cousin, Major Walters, was coming from England to aid her in final arrangements with the lawyers, and he was to carry her off in a day or two to Melford. At the end of the last sitting she looked round the dismal place—it had discoloured, uneven, bulging whitewashed walls, an unutterably dirty loose plank floor, and a skylight patched with maps of hideous worlds on Mercator's projection, and was furnished with packing cases and grime and the sacking which was Cazalet's bed—and sighed wistfully, as if she had been an unoffending Eve thrust out of Eden.

"I have been so happy here," she said to me. "I wonder whether I shall ever be so happy again! Do you think I shall?"

I noticed her give a swift, sidelong glance—almost imperceptible—at Paragot, who had sauntered down the studio to look at one of Cazalet's pictures.

"The first time you saw me," she added, as I found nothing to say, "you announced that you were learning philosophy. Haven't you learned enough yet to answer me?"

"Madame," I replied, driven into a corner, "happiness is such an awfully funny thing. You find it when you least expect it, and when you expect it you often don't find it."

"Is that supposed to be comforting or depressing, Mr. Asticot?"

"I think we had better ask my master, Madame," I said. "He can tell you better than I."

But she shook her head and did not ask Paragot.

"My son," said Paragot that evening by his window in the Rue des Saladiers, trying to disintegrate some fresh air from the fetid odours that rose from the narrow street below, "you have won Madame de Verneuil's heart. You are a lucky little Asticot. And I am proud of you because I made you. You are a proof to her that I haven't spent all my life in absorbing absinthe and omitting to decorate Europe with palaces. Instead of bricks and mortar I have worked in soul-stuff and my masterpiece is an artist,—and a great artist, by the Lord God!" he cried with sudden access of passion, "if you will keep 'the sorrowful great gift' pure and undefiled as a good woman does her chastity. You must help me in my work, my son. Let me be able to point to you as the one man in the world who does not prostitute his art for money or reputation, who sees God beneath a leper's skin and proclaims Him bravely, who reveals the magical beauty of humanity and compels the fool and the knave and the man with the muck-rake and the harlot to see it, and sends them away with hope in their hearts, and faith in the destiny of the race and charity to one another—let me see this, my son, and by heavens! I shall have done more with my life than erect a temple made by hands—and I shall have justified my existence. You will do this for me, Asticot?"

I was young. I was impressionable. I loved the man with a passionate gratitude. I gave my promise. Heaven knows I have tried to keep it—with what success is neither here nor there.

The fantastic element in the psychological state of Paragot I did not consider then, but now it moves me almost to tears. Just think of it. I was his one *apologia pro vita sua;* his one good work which he presented with outstretched hands and pleading eyes, to Joanna. I love the man too well to say more.

Madame de Verneuil went away leaving both of us desolate. Even the prospect of visiting Melford a month hence—at Mrs. Rushworth's cordial invitation—only intermittently raised Paragot's spirits. It did not affect mine at all. I felt that a glory had faded from Menilmontant. Still, I had the portrait to finish, and the preliminary sketches to make of a deuce of a mythological picture for which Cazalet and Fanchette (who for want of better company had become addicted during August to my colleague) were to serve as models. I had my head and hands full of occupation, whereas the reorganized Paragot had none. He talked in a great way of resuming his profession, and even went the length of buying drawing-paper and pins, and drawing-board and T-squares and dividers and other working tools of the architect. But as a man cannot design a palace or a pigstye and put it on the market as one can a book or a picture, he made little headway with his project. He obtained the conditions of an open competition for an Infectious Diseases Hospital somewhere in Auvergne, and talked grandiosely about this for a day or two; but when he came to set out the plan he found that he knew nothing whatever about the modern requirements of such a building and cared less.

"I will wait, my son, until there is something worthy of an artist's endeavour. A Palace of Justice in an important town, or an Opera House. Hospitals for infectious diseases do not inspire one, and I need inspiration. Besides, the visit to Melford would break the continuity of my work. I begin, my son Asticot, when I come back, and then you will see. An ancient Prix de Rome, *nom de nom!* has artistic responsibilities. He must come back in splendour like Holger Danske when he wakes from his enchanted slumber to conquer the earth."

Poor Holger Danske! When he does wake up he will find his conquering methods a trifle out of date. Paragot did not take this view of his simile. I believed him, however, and looked forward to the day when his winning design for a cathedral would strike awe into a flabbergasted world.

"My son," said he a day or two after he had resolved upon this Resurrection in State, "I want Blanquette. An orderly household cannot be properly conducted by the intermittent ministrations of a concierge."

Our good Blanquette, believing as I had done, that the Master was riding about France on a donkey, was still in villégiatura with our farmer friends near Chartres, and in order that she should have as long a holiday as possible he had hitherto forbidden me to enlighten her as to his change of project.

"Besides," he added, "Blanquette has a place in my heart which the concierge hasn't. I also want those I love to share the happiness that has fallen to my lot. You will write to her my son and ask whether she wants to come home."

"She will take the first train," said I.

"Blanquette is a curious type of the absolute feminine," he remarked. "She is never happier than when she can regard us as a couple of babies. Her greatest delight would be to wash us and feed us with a spoon."

"Master," said I, somewhat timidly, "I think Blanquette is sometimes just a little bit miserable because you don't seem to care for her."

He regarded me in astonishment.

"I not care for Blanquette? But you ridiculous little lump of idiocy! will you never understand? She, like you, is part of myself." He thumped his chest as usual.

130

"In the name of petticoats, what does she want? In Russia I met an honest German artisan who had married a peasant girl. After a month's unclouded existence she broke down beneath the load of misery. Her husband didn't love her. Why? Because they had been married a whole month and he hadn't beaten her yet! Does the child want me to beat her? I believe lots of women do. And you, mindless little donkey, what do you want me to make of her? Your head is full of the imbecilities of the studio. Because I keep her here like my daughter, and have not made her my mistress, you take it upon yourself to conclude that I have no affection for her. Bah! You know nothing. You have lived with me all these years, and you know nothing whatever about me. You don't even know Blanquette. Beneath an unprepossessing exterior she has a heart of gold. She has every large-souled quality that a woman can stuff into her nature. She would live on cheese-rind and egg shells, if she thought it would benefit either of us. I not care for Blanquette? You shall see."

So the following afternoon when we met Blanquette's train at the Gare Saint-Lazare, Paragot had taken her into his arms and planted a kiss on each of her broad cheeks before she realised who the magnificent, clean-shaven welcomer in the silk hat really was.

When he released her, she stared at him even as I had done.

"*Mais—qu'est-ce que c'est que ça?*" she cried, and I am sure that the comfort of his kisses was lost in her entire bewilderment.

"It is the Master, Blanquette," said I.

"I know, but you are no longer the same. I shouldn't have recognised you."

"Do you prefer me as I used to be?"

"*Oui, Monsieur*," said Blanquette.

I burst out laughing.

"She is saying '*Monsieur*' to the silk hat."

"*Méchant!*" she scolded. "But it is true." She turned to the master and asked him how he had enjoyed his holiday.

"I never went, my little Blanquette."

"You have been in Paris all the time?"

"Yes."

"And you only send for me now? But *mon Dieu!*—how have you been living?"

Visions of hideous upheaval in the Rue des Saladiers floated before her mind, and she hurried forward as if there was no time to be lost in getting there. When we arrived she held up horror-stricken hands. The dust! The dirt! The state of the kitchen! The Master's bedroom! Oh no, decidedly she would not leave him again! She would only go to the country after she had seen him well started in the train with a ticket for a long way beyond Paris. There was a week's work in front of her.

"Anyway, my little Blanquette," said Paragot, "you are glad to be with me?"

"It is never of my own free will that I would leave you," she replied.

CHAPTER XVIII

"You perceive," said Paragot, waving a complacent hand, as soon as Blanquette had retired to make the necessary purchases for the evening meal, "you perceive that she is perfectly happy. You were entirely wrong. All is for the best in this best of all possible worlds."

When my master adopted the Panglossian view of the universe I used no arguments that might cloud his serenity. I acquiesced with mental reservations. We talked for a time, Paragot sitting primly on a straight-backed chair. He had abandoned his sprawling attitudes, for fear, I suspect, of spoiling his new clothes. The position, however, not making for ease of conversation, he presently took up a book and began to read, while I amused myself idly by making a furtive sketch of him. Since his metamorphosis he was by no means the entertaining companion of his unregenerate days. He himself was oppressed, I fancy, by his own correctitude. The eternal reading which filled so much of his life did not afford him the same wholehearted enjoyment now, as it did when he lolled dishevelled, pipe in mouth and glass within reach, on bed or sofa. This afternoon, I noticed, he yawned and fidgeted in his chair, and paid to his book the distracted attention of a person reading a back number of a magazine in a dentist's waiting room. My sketch, which I happen to have preserved, shows a singularly bored Paragot. At last he laid the book aside, and gathering together hat, gloves, and umbrella, the precious appanages of his new estate, he announced his intention of taking the air before dinner. I remained indoors to gossip with Blanquette during its preparation. I had considerable doubts as to her optimistic view of things, and these were confirmed as soon as the outer door closed behind my master, and the salon door opened to admit Blanquette.

She came to me with an agitated expression on her face which did not accord with perfect happiness of spirit.

"*Dis donc, Asticot*," she cried. "What does it mean? Why did the master not go on his holiday? Why did he not send for me? Why has he cut off his hair and beard and dressed himself like a *Monsieur?* I know very well the master is a gentleman, but why has he changed from what he used to be?"

I temporised. "My dear," said I, "when you first knew me I wore a blue blouse and boots with wooden soles. Almost the last time you had the happiness of beholding me, I was clad in the purple and fine linen of a dress-suit. You weren't alarmed at my putting on civilised garments, why should you be excited at the master doing the same?"

"If you talk like the master, I shall detest you," exclaimed Blanquette. "You do it because you are hiding something. *Ah, mon petit frère,*" she said with a change of tone and putting her arm round my neck, "tell me what is happening. He is going to be married to the beautiful lady, eh?"

She looked into my eyes. Hers were deep and brown and a world of pain lay behind them. I am a bad liar. She freed me roughly.

"I see. It is true. He is going to be married. He does not want me any longer. It is all finished. O *mon Dieu, mon Dieu!* What is to become of me?"

She wept, rubbing away the tears with her knuckles. I tried to comfort her and lent her my pocket-handkerchief. She need have no fear, I said. As long as the master lived her comfort was assured. She turned on me.

"Do you think I would let him keep me in idleness while he was married to another woman? But no. It would be *malhonnête.* I would never do such a thing."

She looked at me almost fiercely. There was something noble in her pride. It would be dishonourable to accept without giving. She would never do that, never.

"But what will become of you, my dear Blanquette?" I asked.

"Look, Asticot. I would give him all that he would ask. I am his, all, all, to do what he likes with. I have told you. I would sleep on the ground outside his door every night, if that were his good pleasure. It is not much that I demand. But he must be alone in the room, *entends-tu?* Another woman comes to cherish him, and I no longer have any place near him. I must be far away. And what would be the good of being far away from him? What shall I do? *Tiens,* as soon as he marries, *je vais me fich' à l'eau.*"

"You are going to do *what?*" I cried incredulously.

She repeated that she would "chuck" herself into the river—"*Se fich à l'eau*" is not the French of Racine. I remonstrated. She retorted that if she could not keep the master's house in order there was nothing left to live for. Much better be dead than eat your heart out in misery.

"You are talking like a wicked girl," said I severely, "and it will be my duty to tell the master."

She gave her eyes a final dab with my handkerchief which she restored to me with an air of scornful resentment.

"If you do, you will be infamous, and I will never speak to you again as long as I live."

I descended from my Rhadamanthine seat and reflected that the betrayal of Blanquette's confidence would not be a gallant action. I maintained my dignity, however.

"Then I must hear nothing more about you drowning yourself."

"We will not talk of it any longer," said Blanquette, frigidly. "I am going to cook the dinner."

As the prim salon provided little interest for an idle youth, I followed her into the slip of a kitchen, where I lounged in great contentment and discomfort. Blanquette relapsed into her fatalistic attitude towards life and seemed to dismiss

133

the disastrous subject from her mind. While she prepared the simple meal she entertained me with an account of the farm near Chartres. There were so many cows, so many ducks and hens and so many pigs. She rose at five every morning and milked the cows. Oh, she had milked cows as a child and had not forgotten the art. It was difficult for those who did not know. *Tiens!* She demonstrated with finger and thumb and a lettuce how it was done.

"I shall not forget it," said I.

"It is good to know things," she remarked seriously.

"One never can tell," said I, "when a cow will come to you weeping to be milked: especially in the Rue des Saladiers."

"That is true," replied Blanquette. "The oddest things happen sometimes."

Light satire was lost on Blanquette.

After dinner she continued the recital of her adventures for the Master's delectation. The old couple no longer able to look after the farm were desirous of selling it, so that they could retire to Evreux where their only son who had married a rich wife kept a prosperous hotel.

"Do you know what they said, Master. 'Why does not Monsieur Paragot, who must be very rich, buy it from us and come to live in the country instead of that dirty Paris?' *C'est drôle, hein?*"

"Why do they think I am very rich?"

"That is what I asked them. They said if a man did not work he must be either rich or a rogue; and they know you are not a rogue, *mon Maître.*"

"They flatter me," said Paragot. "Would you like to live in the country, Blanquette?"

"Oh yes!" she cried with conviction. "*Il y a des bêtes. J'adore ça.* And then it smells so good."

"It does," he sighed. "I haven't smelt it for over three years. Ah! to have the scent of the good wet earth in one's nostrils and the sound of bees in one's ears. For two pins I would go gipsying again. If I were a rich man, my little Blanquette, I would buy the farm, and give it you as your dowry, and sometimes you would let me come and stay with you."

"But as I shall never marry, *mon Maître*, there will be no need of a dowry."

She said it smilingly, as if she welcomed her lot as a predestined old maid. There was not a sign on her plain pleasant face of the torment raging in her bosom. In my youthful ignorance I did not know whether to deplore woman's deceit or to admire her stout-heartedness.

"My child," said Paragot, "no human being can, without arrogance, say what he will or what he will not do. Least of all a woman."

Having uttered this profound piece of wisdom my master went to bed.

During the next few weeks Paragot suffered the boredom of a provisional condition of existence. He went to bed early, for lack of evening entertainment, and rose late in the morning for lack of daily occupation. With what he termed "the crapulous years," he had divested himself of his former associates and habits. Friends that would harmonise with his gloves and umbrella he had none as yet. If he ordered an *apéritif* before the midday meal, it was on the terrace of a café on the Boulevard Saint-Germain, where he sat devouring newspapers in awful solitude. Sometimes he took Blanquette for a sedate walk; but no longer Blanquette *en cheveux*. He bought her a mystical headgear composed as far as I could see of three plums and a couple of feathers, which the girl wore with an air of happy martyrdom. He discoursed to her on the weather and the political situation. At this period he began to develop republican sympathies. Formerly he had swung, according to the caprice of the moment, from an irreconcilable nationalism to a fantastic anarchism. Now he was proud to identify himself with the once despised *bourgeoisie*. He would have taken to his bosom the draper papa of Hedwige of Cassel.

Most of his time he spent in the studio at Menilmontant; there at any rate he was at ease. We were not too disreputable for the umbrella, and though he deprecated the loose speech of Bringard and Bonnet who had returned to Paris, and the queer personal habits of Cazalet, he appeared to find solace in oursociety. At any rate the visits gave him occupation. He also posed for the body of M. Thiers in an historical picture which Bringard proposed to exhibit at the Salon the following spring.

"*L'homme propose et Dieu expose*," said Paragot.

"If he is anything of a judge this ought to be hung on the line," said Bonnet.

I regret to say the picture was rejected.

At last the time came for the Melford visit. Paragot consulted Ewing and myself earnestly as to his outfit, and though he clung to his frock-coat suit as a garb of ceremony, we succeeded in sending him away with a semblance of English country-house attire. He took with him my portrait of Joanna, packed in a wooden case and bearing, to my great pride, the legend, "Precious. Work of Art. With great care," in French and English.

When he had gone I moved my belongings from my attic to the Rue des Saladiers, and gave myself up to the ministrations of Blanquette.

A little while later I received from my dear lady an invitation to visit Melford and paint the portrait of her mother, who regarded my portrait of Joanna as a work of genius. If you are a young artist it makes your head spin very pleasantly to hear yourself alluded to as a genius. Later in life you do not quite like it, for you have bitter knowledge of your limitations and are mortally afraid your kind flatterers will find you out. But at twenty you really do not know whether you are a genius or not. Mrs. Rushworth, however, backed her opinion with a hundred guineas. A hundred guineas! When I read the words I uttered a wild shriek which brought Blanquette in a fright from the bedroom. It was a commission, Joanna explained, and I was to accept it just like any other artist, and I was to stay with them, again like any other artist, during the sittings.

"I am to go to England to paint another portrait, Blanquette. How much do you think I shall be paid for it?"

"Much?" queried Blanquette, in her deliberate way.

I indicated with swinging arms a balloon of gold. Blanquette reflected.

"Fifty francs?"

"Two thousand six hundred and twenty five francs," I cried.

Blanquette sat down in order to realise the sum. It was difficult for her to conceive thousands of francs.

"That will make you rich for the rest of your life."

"It is only the beginning," I exclaimed hopefully.

Blanquette shook a reproachful head.

"There are some folks who are never satisfied," she said.

CHAPTER XIX

WHEN I arrived at Melford my head was full of painting and self-importance; and for the first week or so, Mrs. Rushworth, my subject, occupied the centre of my stage. She was a placid lady of sixty, whose hair, once golden, had turned a flossy white, and whose apple cheeks, though still retaining their plumpness, had grown waxen and were criss-crossed by innumerable tiny lines. The light blue of her eyes had faded, and the rich redness of her lips had turned to faint coral. One could trace how Time had day by day touched her with light but unfaltering fingers, now abstracting a fleck of brightness, now lowering by an imperceptible shade a tone of colour, until she had become what I saw her, still the pink and white beauty, but with rose all deadened into white, like a sick pink pearl. Her pink and white character had also suffered the effacement of the years. She was as dainty and as negative as a piece of Dresden China. She loved to dress in lilac and old lace: and that is how I painted her, regarding her as a bit of exquisite decoration to be treated flat like a panel of Puvis de Chavannes.

My young head, I say, was full of the masterpiece I was about to execute, and though I found much joy in renewed intercourse with my beloved lady and my master, I took no particular note of their relations. We met at meals, sometimes in the afternoons, and always of evenings, when I played dutiful piquet with Mrs. Rushworth, while Joanna made music on the piano, and Paragot read Jane Austen in an arm-chair by the fire. To me the quietude of the secluded English home had an undefinable charm like the smell of lavender, for which I have always had a cat-like affection. Not having the Bohemian temperament—I am now the most smugly comfortable painter in Europe—I was perfectly happy. I took no thought of Paragot, whose temperament was essentially Bohemian; and how he enjoyed the gentle monotony of the days it did not occur to me to consider. Outwardly he shewed no sign of impatience. A dean might have taken him as a model of decorum, and when he drove of afternoons with Joanna in the dog-cart, no dyspeptic bishop could have assumed his air of grim urbanity. But after a while I realised that the old Paragot still smouldered within him; and now and then it burst into unregenerate flame.

Mrs. Rushworth had inherited from her father an old Georgian Bath-stone house at the end of the High Street of Melford. He had been the Duke of Wiltshire's agent and a person of note in the town. Mrs. Rushworth also was a person of note, and her beautiful daughter, the Countess, a lady of fortune, became a person of greater note still. Now on Tuesday afternoons Mrs. Rushworth was "at home." We saw a vast deal of Society, ladies of county families, parsons' wives, doctors' wives and the female belongings of the gentlemen farmers round about. There were also a stray hunting man, a curate or two and Major Walters. The callers sat about the drawing room in little groups drinking tea and discoursing on unimportant and unintelligible matters, and seemed oddly shy of

Paragot and myself, whom Joanna always introduced most graciously. They preferred to talk among themselves. I considered them impolite, which no doubt they were; but I have since reflected that Paragot was an unusual guest at an English country tea-party, and if there is one thing more than another that an English country tea-party resents, it is the unusual. I am sure that a square muffin would be considered an indelicacy. On the second of these Tuesday gatherings which I was privileged to attend, Joanna presented me to two well-favoured young women, the daughters, I gathered, of people who had country places near by.

"Mr. Pradel is the artist from Paris who is painting mamma's portrait," she explained.

I bowed and remarked that I was enchanted to make their acquaintance. They stared. I know now that this Gallic mode of address is not usual in Melford. One young woman, recovering from the shock, said she would like to be an artist. The other asked me whether I had been to the Academy. I said, no. I lived in Paris. Then had I been to the Salon?

"At Janot's," said I, with the idiot egregiousness of youth, "we don't go to the Salon."

"Why?" asked the first, looking across the room, apparently at a curate.

"On principle," I answered. "In the first place it costs a franc which might be spent in food and raiment, and in the second we desire to preserve our ideals from the contaminating spectacle of commercial art."

"Do you play much tennis?" asked Number Two, with no desire to snub me (as I deserved) for fatuity, but through sheer lack of interest in my observation.

"No," said I.

"Shoot?"

"No; there is not much shooting to be got in the Boulevard Saint-Michel."

"Oh," she remarked. "Where's that?"

"Paris," said I.

"Oh yes. You live in Paris." And she regarded me with the expression of bored curiosity exhibited by a superior child before the Yak's enclosure at the Zoological Gardens. An English country-bred maiden's cosmic horizon was sadly limited in those days. Now I believe she has extended it to include the more depressing forms of drama when she pays her annual visit to London. There was a silence after which she enquired whether I fished. As my ideas of fishing were restricted to the patient hosts—pale shades of Acheron—who have angled off the quays of the Seine for centuries and have till now caught nothing, I smiled and shook my head.

"The Browns have taken a fishing in Scotland," observed Number One taking her eyes from the curate, "and I'm to join them next month."

"Myra Brown is going to be married, I hear."

"At Christmas."

"What is he like?"

The hitherto unspeculative eyes of the young woman lit up; an answering gleam awoke in the other's. Myra Brown and her engagement absorbed their attention, and I slunk back in my chair, forgotten. I suffered agonies of shyness. I disliked these foolish virgins and longed to flee from them; but how to rise and make my escape, without rudeness, passed my powers of invention. I looked around me. At the tea-table on the farther side of the room stood Joanna and Major Walters. He was a tall soldierly man with a blond moustache and fair hair thinning on the crown. There are about two thousand like him at the present moment on the active and retired list of the British Army. He seemed to be talking earnestly to her, for her eyes were fixed on the point of her shoe, which she moved slightly, from side to side. Presently she flashed a glance at him somewhat angrily and her lips moved as though she said:—

"What right have you to speak like that?"

He made the Englishman's awkward paraphrase of the shrug, looked swiftly over at Paragot, and turned to her with a remark. Then for the first time since the Comte de Verneuil's death, the glacier blue came into her eyes. She said something. He executed a little stiff bow and walked away. Joanna, bearing herself very haughtily, crossed the room with a cup of tea for a new arrival.

Paragot, gaunt and tight-buttoned in his famous frock coat—he had donned it for the ceremonious afternoon, but Joanna (I think) had suppressed the purple cravat with the yellow spots—was talking to an elderly and bony female owning a great beak of a nose. I wondered how so unprepossessing a person could be admitted into a refined assembly, but I learned later that she was Lady Molyneux, one of the Great Personages of the county. The lady seemed to be emphatic; so did Paragot. She regarded him stonily out of flint-blue eyes. He waved his hands; she raised her eyebrows. She was one of those women whose eyebrows in the normal state are about three inches from the eyelids. I understood then what superciliousness meant. Paragot raised his voice. At that moment one of those strange coincidences occurred in which the ends of all casual conversations fell together, and a shaft of silence sped through the room, killing all sound save that of Paragot's utterance.

"But Great Heavens, Madam, babies don't grow in the cabbage patch, and you are all well aware they don't, and it's criminal of your English writers to mislead the young as to the facts of existence. Charlotte Yonge is infinitely more immoral than Guy de Maupassant."

Then Paragot realized the dead stillness. He rose from his chair, looked around at the shocked faces of the women and curates, and laughing turned to Mrs. Rushworth.

"I was stating Zola to be a great ethical teacher, and Lady Molyneux seemed disinclined to believe me."

"He is an author very little read in Melford," said the placid lady from her sofa cushions, while the two or three women with whom she was in converse gazed disapprovingly at my master.

"It would do the town good if it were steeped in his writings," said he.

As this was at a period when like hell you could not mention the name of Zola to ears polite, no one ventured to argue the matter. Mrs. Rushworth's plump faded lips quivered helplessly, and it was with a gush of gratitude that she seized the hand of one of the ladies who rose to take her leave, and save the situation. The little spell of shock was broken. Groups resumed their mysterious conversations, and Paragot swung to the hearth-rug and stood there in solitary defiance. I seized the opportunity to escape from my two damsels. As I passed Lady Molyneux, she turned to her neighbour.

"What a dreadful man!" she said. "I entirely disapprove of Mrs. Rushworth having such persons in her house."

I could have wept with rage. Here was this turtle-brained, ugly woman (so, in my presumption, I called her) daring to speak slightingly of my beloved master who had condescended to speak out of his Olympian wisdom, and no fire from Zeus shrivelled her up! She signified her disapproval with the air of a law-giver, and the other woman acquiesced. I longed to flame into defence of Paragot; but remembering how ill I fared on a similar occasion when a member of the Lotus Club accused him of having led a bear in Warsaw, I wisely held my peace. But I was very angry.

I joined Paragot on the hearth-rug. Presently Joanna came with her silvery laugh.

"You mustn't be so dreadfully emphatic, Gaston," she said.

"Unintelligent women must not lay down the law on matters they don't understand," said Paragot.

"But it was Lady Molyneux."

"Which signifies?"

"The sovereign lady of Melford."

"God help Melford!" ejaculated my master.

When the ladies had left us that evening after dinner, Paragot poured out a glass of port and pushed the decanter across to me.

"My son," said he, "as a philosopher and a citizen of the world you will find Melford repay patient study as much as Chambéry or Buda-Pesth or the Latin Quarter. It is a garden of Lilliput. Here you will see Life in its most cultivated littleness. A great passion bursting out across the way would convulse the town like an earthquake. Observe at the same time how constant a factor is human nature. However variable the manifestation may be, the degree is invariable. In spacious conditions it manifests itself in passions, in narrow ones in prejudices. The females in and out of petticoats who were here this afternoon experience the same thrill in expressing their dislike of me as a person foreign to their convention, as the Sicilian who plunges his dagger into a rival's bosom. When I am married, my son, I shall not live at Melford."

"Where do you propose to live, Master?" I enquired.

He made a great gesture and drew a deep breath.

"On the Continent of Europe," said he, as if even a particular country were too cabined to satisfy his nostalgia for wide spaces. "I must have room, my son, for the development of my genius. I must dream great things, and immortal visions are blasted under the basilisk eye of Lady Molyneux."

"She is a *vieille pimbêche!*" I cried.

"She is the curse of England," said Paragot.

After this it occurred to me that I might take more note of Melford and its ways than I had done hitherto, and the more I observed it the less did it appear to resemble either Eden or the Boulevard Saint-Michel. At times I felt dull. I would lean over the parapet of the bridge at the other end of the High Street, and watch the tower and decorated spire of the old parish church rise from the gold and russet bosom of the church-yard elms, and wish I were back on the Pont Neuf with the tumultuous life of Paris around me. There was a lack of breeziness in the social air of Melford.

Meanwhile Paragot and Joanna continued the romance of long ago. They walked together in the garden like lovers, his arm around her waist, her delicate head lightly leaning on his shoulder. Once when I made my presence known, he withdrew his arm, but Joanna laughingly replaced it.

"What does it matter? Asticot is in our confidence," she remarked. "Isn't he going to be your best man? You will bring him over for the wedding, Gaston."

"You cling to the idea of being married in Melford?" he asked.

"Of course."

"By that dry, grey-whiskered gentleman who treats me as if I were a youth he would like to prepare for confirmation? And all these dreadful people to look on? My dear, doesn't the thought of it chill you into the corpse of a Melfordian?"

"I should have imagined that so long as we were married the 'how' would not matter to you."

"Quite so," said he. "Why does the 'how' matter so much to you?"

"It is different," said Joanna. "It is right for me to be married here."

"We must do what is right at all costs," assented my master in an ironical note, which she was quick to detect. She swerved from his encircling arm.

"You would not be married under a bush like a beggar?" she quoted.

"I wish to heaven I could!" he exclaimed with sudden spirit. "It is the only way of mating. I would take you to a little village I know of in the Vosges, overhanging a precipice, with God's mountains and sky above us, and not a schedule of regulations for human conduct within thirty miles, and Monsieur le Maire would tie his tricolor scarf around him and marry us, and we would go away arm in arm and the cow-bells overhead would ring the wedding peal, and there would be just you and I and the universe."

"We'll compromise," said Joanna, smiling. "We'll spend our honeymoon in your village in the Vosges after we are well and duly and respectably married in Melford. Don't you think I am reasonable, Asticot?"

"My dear Joanna," said Paragot, "you have infatuated this boy to such an extent that he would agree with you in anything. Of course he will say that the Reverend and respectable Mr. Hawkfield is better than the picturesque Monsieur le Maire, and that a wedding cake from Gunter's is preferable to the curdled cheese of Valdeauvau. He would perjure his little soul to atoms for your sake."

"I thought somebody else would too," whispered Joanna softly.

Paragot yielded as he looked down at her sea-shell face.

"So he would. For your sake he would go through Hell and the Church of England service for the Solemnization of Matrimony."

We were walking round and round the broad gravel path that enclosed the tennis lawn. Land was cheap in the days when the Georgian houses of the High Street were built, and people took as much for garden purposes as they desired. The gardens were the only truly spacious things in Melford. There was a long silence. The lovers seemed to have forgotten my existence. Presently Joanna spoke.

"You must remember that I am still a member of the Church of England, and look at the religious side of marriage. It would be very pretty to be married by Monsieur le Maire, but I could not reconcile it to my conscience. So when you speak scoffingly of a marriage in church you rather hurt me, Gaston."

"You must forgive me, ma chérie," said he, humbly. "I am a happy Pagan and it is so long since I have met anyone who belonged to the Church of England that I thought the institution had perished of inanition."

"Why, you went with me to church last Sunday."

"So I did," said he, "but I thought it was only to worship the Great British God Respectability."

Joanna sighed and turned the conversation to the autumn tints and other impersonal things, and I noticed that she drew Paragot's arm again around her waist, as if to reassure herself of something. As we passed by the porch, I entered the house; but loving to look on my dear lady, I lingered, and saw her hold up her lips. He bent down and kissed them.

"Don't think me foolish, Gaston," she said, "but I have starved for love for thirteen years."

By the gesture of his arm and the working of his features, I saw that he rhapsodised in reply.

To the sentimental youngster who looked on, this love-making seemed an idyll without a disturbing breath. Joanna, though she had lost the gay spontaneity of her Paris holiday, smiled none the less adorably on Paragot and myself. She wore a little air of defiant pride when she introduced him to her acquaintance as "my cousin, Monsieur de Nérac," which was very pretty to behold. Convention forbade the announcement of their engagement at so early a stage of her widowhood, but anyone of rudimentary intelligence could see that she was presenting her future husband. Few women can hide that triumphant sense of proprietorship in a man, especially if they have at the same time to hold themselves on the defensive against the possible fulminations of Lady Molyneux. Joanna proclaimed herself a champion. Even when Paragot forgot his social reformation and banged his fist down on the dinner table till the glasses rang again, with a great *nom de Dieu!* her glance swept the company as if to defy them to find anything uncommon in the demeanour of her guest. It was only towards the end of my stay that she began to wince. And Paragot, save on occasion of outburst, went through the love-making and the social routine with the grave but contented face of a man who had found his real avocation.

Looking back on these idyllic days I realise the greatness of Paragot's self-control. In his domestic habits he was less a human being than a mechanical toy. At half past eight every morning he entered the breakfast-room. At half past nine he went into the town to get shaved. Had he an appointment with Joanna, he was there to the minute. He clothed himself in what he considered were orthodox garments. He even folded up his trousers of nights. He limited his smoking to a definite number of cigarettes consumed at fixed hours. Apparently he had never heard of the reprehensible habit of drinking between meals. If he only went to church to worship the British God Respectability, he did so with impeccable unction. No undertaker listened to the funeral service with more portentous solemnity than Paragot exhibited during the Vicar's sermon. Indeed, sitting bolt upright in the pew, his lined, brown face set in a blank expression, his ill-fitting frock coat buttoned tight across his chest, his hair—despite the barber's pains—struggling in vain to obey the rules of the unaccustomed parting, he bore considerable resemblance to an undertaker in moderate circumstances. Of the delectable vagabond in pearl-buttoned velveteens fiddling wildly to capering peasants; of the long-haired, unkempt Dictator of the Café Delphine roaring his absinthe-inspired judgments on art and philosophy for the delectation of his disciples, not a trace remained. He sang the hymns. It was a pity they did not invite him to go round with the plate. Yet the signs of a rebellious spirit continued now and then to manifest themselves. He asked me, one day, with a groan whether he was condemned to a daily clean collar for the rest of his life. Another day he seized me by the arm, as we were lounging on the porch, and dragged me out of earshot of the house.

"My good Asticot," said he in a dramatic whisper, "if I don't talk to a man, I shall go mad. I shall dance around the flower beds and scream. I have a yearning to converse with the host of the Black Boar, a fat Rabelaisian scoundrel who has piqued my imagination. And besides, if Shadrach, Meshach and Abednego were cast into my throat this minute they would find it quite a different thing from Nebuchadnezzar's ineffectual bonfire."

"There is no reason why we should not go to the Black Boar," said I.

He clapped me on the shoulder, calling me a Delphic oracle, and haled me from the premises through the garden gate, with the lightning rapidity of the familiar Paragot.

"Master," said I, as we hastened down the High Street—the Black Boar stood at the other end, by the bridge—"if you want a man to talk to, there is always Major Walters."

Paragot threw out his hand.

"He is a man, in that he is brave and masculine; in that he is intelligent, he is naught. He is a machine-gun. He fires off rounds of stereotyped conversation at the rate of one a minute, which is funereal. I also have the misfortune, my little Asticot, to be under the ban of Major Walters' displeasure. Your British military man is prejudiced against anyone who is not cut out according to pattern."

"Madame de Verneuil is not cut out according to pattern," said I maliciously.

"Your infant eyes have noticed it too? But I, my son, am Gaston de Nérac, a vidame of Gascony, *nom de Dieu! et il aura affaire à moi, ce pantin-là! Sacredieu!* Do you know what he had the impertinence to ask me yesterday? What settlements I proposed to make on Madame de Verneuil. Settlements, *mon petit* Asticot! He spoke as trustee, whatever that may be, under her husband's will. 'Sir,' said I, 'I will settle my love and my genius upon her, and thereby insure her happiness and her prosperity. Besides, Madame de Verneuil has a fortune which will suffice her needs and of which I will not touch a penny.'"

I smiled, for I could see Paragot in his grand French manner, one hand thrust between the buttons of his coat and the other waving magnificently, as he proclaimed himself to Major Walters.

"I explained," he continued, "in terms which I thought might reach his intelligence, that I only had to resume my profession and my financial position would equal that of Madame de Verneuil. 'And, Sir,' said I, 'I will not suffer you to say another word.' We bowed, and parted enemies. Wherefore the conversation of the excellent Major Walters does not appeal to me as attractive."

At the time I thought this very noble of Paragot. In a way it was so, for my master, who had never committed a dishonourable action in his life, was genuine in his scorn of the insinuation that he proposed to live on Joanna's money. He verily believed himself capable of reattaining fame and fortune. It was only the nuisance of having to do so that, at introspective times, disconcerted him. He knew that to break away from a thirteen-year-old habit of idleness would need considerable effort. But he was a man, *nom d'un chien!*

To prove it he called for a quart of ale in the bar-parlour of the Black Boar, an old coaching inn, set back from the road. The little eyes of the fleshy rubicond host, loafing comfortably in shirt-sleeves, glistened as he received the Pantagruelian order and brought the great tankard with a modest half pint for me, and a jorum of rum for himself. Paragot was worthy of a host's attention.

Paragot pledged him and literally poured the contents of the tankard down his throat.

The landlord stared in an ecstasy of admiration.

"Well, I'm damned," said he.

"I'll take another," said Paragot.

The landlord brought another tankard.

"How do you manage it?" he asked.

Paragot explained that he had learned the art in Germany. You open your throat to the good beer without moving the muscles whereby you swallow, and down it goes.

"Well, I'm jiggered," said mine host.

"Have you no pretty drinkers hereabouts?" asked my master, sipping the second quart.

"They lots of 'em comes here and gets fuddled, if that's what you mean."

Paragot waved an impatient hand. "To get fuddled on beer is not pretty drinking. Haven't you any hard-headed topers who are famous in the neighborhood? Men who can carry their liquor like gentlemen and whose souls expand as they get more and more filled with the alcohol of human kindness? If so, I should like to meet them."

"There isn't any as could toss off a quart like that."

"Have you always lived in Melford?"

"Oh no," replied the landlord, as if resenting the suggestion, "I was born and bred in Devizes."

"It must be a devil of a place, Devizes," said Paragot.

145

"It be none so bad," assented the landlord. A woman's voice from the bar summoned him away. Paragot pushed his unfinished quart from him and rose. He shook his head sadly.

"I am disappointed in that man. He is a mere bucolic idiot. I shall waste my talents intellectual and bibulous on him no longer. Our excursion into the Bohemia of Melford is a failure, my little Asticot, and the beer is confoundedly sour. I am glad I did not vagabondise in rural England."

"Why?" I asked.

"To avoid an asylum for idiots I should have rushed into the dissenting ministry. I might have expected mine host to be a dullard. In this country the expected always happens, which paralyses the brain. Now let us go home to lunch."

He paid the bill, and as we issued from the door of the inn we fell into the arms of Joanna and Major Walters.

The latter regarded us superciliously, and Joanna catching his glance flushed to the wavy hair over her forehead. The ordinary greetings having been exchanged, she proudly and markedly drew Paragot ahead, leaving me to follow with Major Walters. As he made no remark of any kind during our little walk, I did not find him an exhilarating companion.

CHAPTER XX

I HAD worked till the last glimmer of daylight at the portrait, which was now approaching completion.

"That's the end of it for to-day," said I, laying my palette and brushes aside, and regarding the picture.

Joanna rose from her chair by the fire where she had been sewing for the last hour and stood by my side. The morning-room, which had a clear north-east light through the French window leading into the garden, had been assigned to me as a studio, and here, sometimes on a murky afternoon, Joanna, who preferred the bright, chintz-covered place to the gloomy drawing-room, honoured me with her company. Mrs. Rushworth was asleep upstairs, and Paragot had gone for a solitary walk. We were cosily alone.

It pleased my lady to be flattering.

"It is wonderful how a boy like you can do such work—for you *are* a boy, Asticot," she said with one of her bright comrade-like smiles. "In a few years you will have the world at your feet imploring you to paint its portrait. You will fulfil the promise, won't you?"

"What promise, Madame?" I asked.

"The promise of your life now. It is not everyone who does. You won't allow outside things to send you away from it all."

She had slung the stole which she was embroidering for the vicar across her shoulders, and holding the two ends looked at me wistfully.

"I owe it to my master, Madame," said I, "to work with all my might."

"If only he had had a master in the old days!" she sighed, "He would have been by now a famous man full of honours, with all the world can give in his possession."

"Hasn't he the best the world can give now that he has found you again?" said I, somewhat shyly.

Joanna gave a short laugh. "You talk sometimes like one's grandfather. I suppose that is because you became a student of philosophy at a tender age. Yes, your master has found me again; but after all, what is a woman? Just a speck of dust on top of the world."

She half seated herself on my painting stool, her back to the picture.

"Tell me, Asticot, is he at least happy?"

"Can you doubt it, Madame?" I cried warmly.

"I do so want him to be happy, Asticot. You see it was all through me that he gave up his career and took to the strange life he has been leading, and I feel doubly responsible for his future. Can you understand that?"

Her blue eyes were very childish and earnest. For all my love of Paragot, I suddenly felt something like pity for her, as for one who had undertaken a responsibility that weighed too heavily on slender shoulders. For the first time it struck me that Paragot and Joanna might not be a perfectly matched couple. Intuition prompted me to say:—

"My master is utterly happy, but you must give him a little time to accustom himself to the new order of things."

"That's it," she said. Then there was a pause. "You are such a wise boy," she continued, "that perhaps you may be able to do something for me. I can't do it myself—and it's horrid of me to talk about it—but do you think you might suggest to him that people of our class don't visit the Black Boar? I don't mind it a bit; but other people—my cousin Major Walters said something a day or two ago—and it hurt. They don't understand Gaston's Continental ways. It is natural for a man to go to a café in France; but in England, things are so different."

I promised to convey to Paragot the tabu of the Black Boar, and then I asked her which she preferred, England or France. She shivered, and a gleam of frost returned to her eyes.

"I never want to see France again. I was so unhappy there. I am trying to persuade Mr. de Nérac to live in London. He can find as much scope for his art there as in Paris, can't he?"

"Surely," said I.

"And you'll come too," she said with the flash of gaiety that was one of her charms. "You'll have a beautiful studio near by and we'll all be happy together."

She jumped off the painting stool and having bidden me light the gas, resumed her task of embroidering the stole, by the fireside.

"It's pretty, isn't it?" she asked, holding it up for my inspection.

I agreed. She had considerable talent for art needlework.

"Gaston doesn't appreciate it," she remarked, laughing. "He disapproves of clergymen."

"They have scarcely been in his line," I answered apologetically.

"They will have to be. Oh, you'll see. I'll make him a model Englishman before very long."

"I'm afraid you will find it rather difficult, Madame," said I.

"Do you think I'm afraid of difficulties? Isn't everything difficult? Is it easy for you to get everything to come out on that canvas just as you want it? If you could dash it off in a minute it wouldn't be worth doing. As you yourself said, I'll have to give Gaston time."

I seated myself on the fender-seat close by her chair, and for some minutes watched the clever needle work its golden way through the white silk. No one has ever had such dainty fingers and delicate wrists.

"You mustn't think, because I have spoken about Mr. de Nérac, that I am discontented. I wouldn't have him a bit altered integrally, for there is no one like him living. And I'm utterly happy in the fulfilment of the great romance of my life. Isn't it wonderful, Asticot? Have you ever heard the like outside a story book? To meet again after thirteen years and to find the old—the old——"

"Love," I whispered, as I saw that she suddenly blushed at the word.

"As strong and true as ever. It is the inner things that matter, Asticot. The outside ones are nothing. Dreadful things have happened to each of us during those years, but they haven't clouded the serenity of our souls."

"Ah, Madame," said I, with a smile—it strikes me now that I was slightly impertinent—"I am sure my master said that."

"Yes," she admitted, raising wide innocent eyes. "How did you guess?"

"You yourself once detected echoes in me!"

We both laughed.

"That is what brought us together, Asticot. You seemed to regard him as a god rather than as a man—and I loved you for it."

She put out her left hand. I touched it with my lips.

"That's a charming French way we haven't got in England. And—you did it very nicely, Asticot."

I almost scowled at the servant who entered with the announcement that tea was waiting in the drawing-room.

I think of all human utterances I have heard fall from the lips of those I love and honour, that formula of Paragot's echoed by Joanna was the most pathetically vain. And they believed it. Indeed it was the vital article of their faith. On its truth the whole fabric of their love depended.

It counted for nothing in Joanna's romantic eyes that the brilliant eager youth, "rich in the glory of his rising-sun," who had won her heart long ago—(she shewed me his photograph: alas poor Paragot!)—was now the tongue-tied spectre, the tale of whose ungentle past was scarred upon his face: who stalked grotesquely comfortless in his ill-fitting clothes: who with the art of dress had lost in the boozing-kens of Europe the graces of social intercourse. It counted for nothing that he was middle-aged, deserted forever by the elusive wanton, inspiration, condemned (she knew it in her heart) to artistic barrenness in perpetuity. It

149

counted for nothing that her gods awakened his contempt, and his gods her fear. It counted for nothing that they had scarcely a single taste or thought in common—half-educated, half-bred boy that I was, I vow I entered a sweeter chamber of intimacy in my dear lady's heart than was open to Paragot.

You see, in spite of all the deadening influences, all the horror of her married life, she had remained a child. When the Comte de Verneuil had found her unforgiving in the matter of the false announcement of Paragot's death, he had left her pretty much to herself, and had gone after the strange goddesses, the ignoble Astaroths, beloved by a man of his type. Month had followed month and year had followed year, and she had not developed. His family, nationalist and devout, of the old school, regarded him, rightly, as a renegade from their traditions, and regarded Joanna, wrongly, as the English heretic who had seduced him from the paths of orthodoxy. Their relations with Joanna were of the most frigid. On the other hand, the society of Hebraic finance in which the Comte de Verneuil found profit and entertainment was repugnant to the delicately nurtured Englishwoman. She led a lonely existence. "I have so few friends in Paris," were almost her first words to me on the day of our meeting outside the Hôtel Bristol. She went through the world, her lips set in a smile, and her dear eyes frozen, and her heart yearning for the sheltered English life with its rules for guidance and its barriers of convention, its pleasant little routine of duties, and its gentle communion of unemotional temperaments. Her eleven years married life had been merely a suspension of existence. Her few excursions into the unusual had been the scared adventures of a child. Her romance was the romance of a child. Her gracious simplicity, and her caressing adorableness which made my boy's love for her a passionate worship which has lasted to this day, when we both are old and only meet to shake heads together in palsied sympathy, were the essential charms of a child. How should she understand the Paragot that I knew? His soul still shone the stainless radiance that had dazzled her young eyes. That was all that mattered. It was easy to convert the outer man to convention. It was the simplest thing in the world to make the chartered libertine of talk accept the Index Expurgatorius of subjects mete for discussion: to regulate the innate vagabond by the clock: to bring the pantheistic pagan of wide spiritual sympathies (for Paragot was by no means an irreligious man) into the narrowest sphere of Anglicanism. The colossal nature of her task did not occur to her; and there again she exhibited a child's unreasoning confidence. Nor did it occur to her to bid him throw off his undertaker's garb and gloom and to adopt his free theories of life and conduct. At her mother's knee she had learned the First Commandment, "Thou shalt have none other gods but me"; and Joanna's god, though serving her sweet innocent soul all the reasonable purposes of a deity, was Matthew Arnold's gigantic clergyman in a white tie. In obedience to his maxims alone lay salvation: Joanna's conviction was unshakable. As a matter of course Paragot must walk the same path. There was not another one to walk.

Paragot accepted meekly my report of Joanna's tabu of the Black Boar.

"Whatever Madame de Verneuil says is right. I was forgetting that the refrain of the ballade of the immortal Villon '*Tout aux tavernes et aux filles*' which was that of my life for so many years is so no longer, I wonder what the devil the refrain is now? Ha!" he exclaimed clapping his hand on my shoulder in his old violent way, "I have it! also Villon. Guess. Didn't I teach you all the ballades by rote as we wandered through Savoy?"

"Yes, Master," said I; but I could only think of the one that came into my Byronic little head on the occasion of my first meeting with Joanna, "*Bien heureux qui rien n'y a*," which in the present circumstances was clearly not applicable. The romantic lover does not base his conduct on the formula that blessed is he who has nothing to do with women.

"What is it, Master?" I asked.

"'*En ceste foy je veuil vivre et mourir.*'"

I did not understand. "In which faith do you wish to live and die?" I asked.

He made a gesture of disappointment. He too was a child in many respects.

"You must go back to Paris to sharpen your wits, my son. I thought I had trained you to catch allusion, one of the most delicate and satisfying arts of life. Did I not preface my remarks by saying that Madame de Verneuil was infallible? By which I mean that she is the mouthpiece of all the sweeter kinds of angels. That is the faith, my little Asticot," and he repeated to himself the rascal poet's refrain to his most perfect poem: "*En ceste foy je veuil vivre et mourir.*"

"But that," said I, wishing to prove that I had not forgotten my scholarship, "is a prayer to Our Lady made by Villon at the request of his mother."

"You are as hopeless as mine host of the Black Boar," said my master, and being wound up to talk—it was during the after-dinner interval before joining the ladies—he launched into a half hour's disquisition on the philosophic value of allusiveness, addressing me as if I had been his audience at the Lotus Club or a choice band of disciples at the Café Delphine.

In the drawing-room I played my piquet with Mrs. Rushworth, while Paragot sat with Joanna in a far corner. I could not help noticing how little they spoke. Paragot's torrent of words had dried up, and the talk seemed to flow in unsatisfying driblets. Why did he not entertain her with his newly adopted romantical motto from Villon? Why did he not express, in terms of which he was such a master, his fantastic adoration? Why even did he not continue his disquisition on the philosophic value of allusiveness? Anything, thought I, as I declared a *quinzième* and fourteen kings, rather than this staccato exchange of commonplaces which I was sure neither Joanna nor himself in the least enjoyed. In fact, my dear Joanna yawned.

Presently Major Walters was announced. He had come, he explained apologetically, on trustee business and required Joanna's signature to an

151

important document. She flew to him with a pretty air of delight, drew him by the arm to an escritoire in a corner of the room, and laughed girlishly as she inked her fingers and confessed her powerlessness to comprehend the deed she was signing. Paragot, after a very cold exchange of greetings with Major Walters, sat down by our card-table, and watched the game with the funereal expression he always wore when he desired to exhibit his entire correctness of demeanour. To Mrs. Rushworth's placid remarks during the deals he made the politest of monosyllabic replies. Meanwhile his dingy white tie, which he never could arrange properly (he dressed for dinner each night without a murmur) had worked up beyond his collar, and encircling his lean neck like a pussy-cat's ribbon, gave him a peculiarly unheroic appearance.

The signing over, Joanna kept Major Walters by the escritoire and chatted in a lively manner. As far as I could hear—and I am afraid my attention was sadly abstracted from my game—they talked of the same unintelligible things as the Tuesday afternoon guests, personalities, local doings and what not. She ran to fetch the stole, over which Paragot had not glowed with rapturous enthusiasm; apparently Major Walters said just the thing concerning it her heart craved to hear; her silvery voice rippled with pleasure. A while later he must have returned to some business matter which he declared settled, for she put her hand on his sleeve in her impulsive caressing way and her eyes beamed gratitude.

"I don't know what I should do without you, Dennis. You bear all my responsibilities on your strong shoulders. How can I thank you?"

He bent down and said something in a low voice, at which she blushed and laughed reprovingly. His remark did not offend her in the least. She was enjoying herself. He drew himself up with a smile. It was then that I noted particularly how well bred and clean-limbed he was; how easily his clothes fitted. It seemed as impossible for Major Walters' tie to work up round his neck as for his toes to protrude through his boots. He gave one the impression of having followed cleanliness of thought and person all his life. I began to have a sneaking admiration for the man. I beheld in its openness that which I had often seen pierce through Paragot's travesty of mountebankery or rags, but which singularly enough seemed hidden beneath his conventional garb—the inborn and incommunicable quality of the high-bred gentleman. I set to dreaming of it and scheming out a portrait in which that essential quality could be expressed; whereby I played the fool with my hand and incurred the mild rebuke of my adversary, as she repiqued and capoted me and triumphantly declared the game.

There was a short, general conversation. Then Major Walters, declining the offer of whisky and soda in the dining-room, took his leave. Paragot accompanied him to the front door. When he returned, Mrs. Rushworth retired, as she always did after her game, and Joanna instead of remaining with us for an hour, as usual, pleaded fatigue and went to bed.

"Master," said I, boyishly full of my new idea, "do you think Major Walters would sit to me? I don't mean as a commission—of course I couldn't ask him—but for practice. I should like to paint him as a knight in armour."

"Why this lunatic notion?" asked my master.

I explained. He looked at me for some time very seriously. There was a touch of pain in his tired blue eyes.

"You are right, my little Asticot," he said, "and I was wrong. My perception is growing blunt. I regarded our friend as having fallen out of the War Office box of tin soldiers. Your vision has been keener. Breed counts for much; but for it to have full value there must be the *life* as well. All the same, the notion of asking Major Walters to pose to you in a suit of armour is lunatic, and the sooner you finish Mrs. Rushworth and get back to Janot's the better. There is also Blanquette who must be bored to death in the Rue des Saladiers, with no one but Narcisse to bear her company."

He put a cigarette into his mouth, but for some time did not light it although he held a match ready to strike in his fingers. His thoughts held him.

"My son," he said at last, "I would give the eyes out of my head to have my violin."

"Why, Master?" I asked.

"Because," said he, "when one is afflicted with a divine despair, there is nothing for it like fiddling it out of the system."

CHAPTER XXI

PARIS again; Janot's; the organized confusion of the studio; the boisterous comradeship of my coevals; the Monday morning throng of models in all stages of non-attire crowding the staircases; the noisy café over the way; the Restaurant Didier where those of us, young men and maidens, who had princely incomes dined marvellously for one franc fifty, *vin compris*—such wine!—I writhe sympathetically at its memory; the squabbles, the new romances, the new slang on the tip of everyone's tongue; the studio in Menilmontant where the four of us slaved at never-to-be-purchased masterpieces; the dear, full-blooded, inspiring life again. Paris, too, which meant the Rue des Saladiers and Blanquette and Narcisse, and the grace of dear familiar things.

It must not be counted to me for ingratitude that I was glad to be back. I was still a boy, under twenty. My pockets bulged with the bank notes into which I had converted Mrs. Rushworth's cheque, and I found myself master of infinite delight. I presented Blanquette with a tortoise-shell comb and Narcisse with a collar, and I electrified my intimate and less fortunate friends by giving them a dinner in the dismal entresol at Didier's which was superbly styled the "*Salle des Banquets.*" Fanchette and one or two of her colleagues being of the party, I fear we behaved in a disreputable manner. If Melford had looked on it would have blushed to the top of its decorated spire. We put the table aside and danced eccentric quadrilles. We shouted roystering songs. When Cazalet tried to sing a solo we held him down and gagged him with his own sandals. We flirted in corners. A goodly portion of Rosaria, a Spanish model born and bred in the Quartier Saint-Antoine, we washed in red wine. It was a memorable evening. The next day Blanquette listened with great interest to my expurgated account of the proceedings, and in her good unhumorous way prescribed for my headache. When one is young, such a night is worth a headache. I am unrepentant, even though I am old and the almond tree flourishes and the grasshopper is trying to be a nuisance. I don't like your oldsters who pretend to be ashamed of the follies of their youth. They are humbugs all. There is no respectable elderly gentleman in the land who does not inwardly chuckle over the chimes he has heard at midnight.

Though I always had Joanna's gracious personality at the back of my mind, and the love of my good master as part of my spiritual equipment, yet I must confess to concerning my thoughts very little with the progress of their romance. I took it for granted as I took many things in those unspeculative days. The actual whirl of Paris caught me and left me little time for conjecture. I wrote once or twice to Joanna; but my letters were egotistical outpourings; the mythological picture at Menilmontant inspired sheets of excited verbiage. She replied in her pretty sympathetic way, but gave me little news of Paragot. It was hardly to be expected that she should write romantically, like a young girl foolishly in love, gushing to a bosom friend. Paragot himself, who disliked pen, ink, and paper, merely sent me the casual messages of affection through Joanna. He took the view of the Duenna in "Ruy Blas" as to the adequacy of the King's epistle to the Queen: "Madame. It is very windy and I have killed six wolves. Carlos." What more was necessary? asked the Duenna. So did Paragot.

When I was with Blanquette I avoided the subject of the impending marriage as much as possible. She looked forward with dull fatalism to the day when another woman would take the master into her keeping and her own occupation would be gone.

"But, Blanquette, we shall go on living together just as we are doing now," I cried in the generosity of youth.

"And when a woman comes and takes you too?"

I swore insane vows of celibacy; but she laughed at me in her common-sense way, and uttered blunt truths concerning the weaknesses of my sex.

"Besides, my little Asticot," she added, "I love you very much; you know that well; but you are not the Master."

Once I suggested the possibility of her marrying some one else. There was a cheerful *quincaillier* at the corner of the street who, to my knowledge, paid her assiduous attentions. He was evidently a man of substance and refinement, for a zinc bath was prominently displayed among his hardware. But Blanquette's love laughed at tinsmiths. She who had lived on equal terms with the Master and myself (I bowed my acknowledgment of the tribute) to marry a person without education? *Ah! mais non! Au grand nom! Merci!* She was as scornful as you please, and without rhyme or reason plucked a bunch of Christmas roses from a jug on the table and threw them into the stove. Poor *quincaillier!* There was nothing for it but to *se fich' à l'eau*—to chuck herself into the river. That was the end of most of our conversations on the disastrous subject.

It was the end of a talk on one November evening, about three weeks after I had returned to Paris. I had dined at home with Blanquette, and was in the midst of a drawing which I blush to say I was doing for *Le Fou Rire,* an unprincipled comic paper fortunately long since defunct—(fortunately? Tartuffe that I am. Many a welcome louis did I get from it in those necessitous days)—when she looked up from her sewing and asked when the Master was coming back. The question led to an answer, the answer to an observation, and the observation to the discussion of the Subject.

"There is no way out of it, *mon pauvre Asticot, je vais me fich' à l'eau, comme je l'ai dit.*"

"In the meanwhile, my dear," said I, throwing down the crow-quill pen and pushing my drawing away, "if you remain in this pestilential condition of morbidness, you will die without the necessity of drowning yourself. Instead of making ourselves miserable, let us go and dance at the Bal Jasmin. *Veux-tu?*"

"This evening?" she asked, startled. She had never grown accustomed to the suddenness of the artistic temperament.

"Of course this evening. You don't suppose I would ask you to dance next month so as to cure you of indigestion to-night."

"But nothing is wrong with my stomach, *mon cher*," said the literal Blanquette.

"It is indigestion of the heart," said I, after the manner of Paragot, "and dancing with me at the Bal Jasmin will be the best thing in the world for you."

"It would give you pleasure?"

This was charmingly said. It implied that she would sacrifice her feelings for my sake. But her eyes brightened and her cheeks flushed a little. Women are rank hypocrites on occasion.

Ten minutes later Blanquette, wearing her black Sunday gown set off by a blue silk scarf embroidered at the edges with a curious kind of pink forget-me-not, her hair tidily coiled on top and fixed with my tortoise-shell comb, announced that she was ready. We started. In those days I did not drive to balls in luxurious hired vehicles. I walked, pipe in mouth, correctly giving my arm to Blanquette. No doubt everybody thought us lovers. It is odd how wrong everybody can be sometimes.

The Bal Jasmin was situated in the Rue Mouffetard. It has long since disappeared with many a haunt of my youth's revelry. The tide of frolic has set northward, and Montmartre, which to us was but a geographical term, now dazzles the world with its venal splendour. But the Moulin de la Galette and the Bal Tabarin of the present day lack the gaiety of the Bal Jasmin. It was not well frequented; it gathered round its band-stand people with shocking reputations; the sight of a man in a dress coat would have transfixed the assembly like some blood-curdling ghost. The ladies would have huddled together in a circle round the wearer and gazed at him open-mouthed. He would subsequently have had to pay for the ball's liquid refreshment. The Bal Jasmin did not employ meretricious ornament to attract custom. A low gallery containing tables ran around the bare hall, the balustrade being of convenient elbow height from the floor, so that the dancers during intervals of rest could lounge and talk with the drinkers. In the middle was a circular bandstand where greasy musicians fiddled with perspiring zeal. At the doors a sergent de ville stood good-humouredly and nodded to the ladies and gentlemen with whom he had a professional acquaintance.

Everybody came to dance. If good fortune, such as a watch or a freshly subventioned student, fell into their mouths, they swallowed it like honest, sensible souls; but they did not make reprehensible adventure the main object of their evening. They danced the quadrilles, not for payment and the delectation of

156

foreigners as at the Jardin de Paris, but for their own pleasure. A girl kicked off your hat out of sheer kindness of heart and animal spirits; and if you waltzed with her, she danced with her strange little soul throbbing in her feet. There were, I say, the most dreadfully shocking people at the Bal Jasmin; but they could teach the irreproachable a lesson in the art of enjoyment.

As I came with Blanquette, and danced only with Blanquette, and sat with Blanquette over bock or syrup in the gallery, the unwritten etiquette of the place caused us to be undisturbed. Like the rest of the assembly we enjoyed ourselves. Dancing was Blanquette's one supreme accomplishment. Old Père Paragot had taught her to play the zither indifferently well, but he had made her dance divinely: and Blanquette, I may here mention incidentally, had been my instructress in the art. Seeing her thick-set, coarse figure, and holding your arm around her solid waist as you waited for the bar, you would not have dreamed of the fairy lightness it assumed the moment feet moved in time with the music. If life had been a continuous waltz no partner of hers less awkward than a rhinoceros could have avoided falling in love with her. But waltzes ended all too soon and the thistle-down sylph of a woman became my plain homely Blanquette, uninspiring of romance save in the hardware bosom of the *quincaillier* at the corner of the Rue des Saladiers.

The *bal* was crowded. Gaunt ill-shaven men, each a parody of one of the Seven Deadly Sins, capered grotesquely with daughters of Rahab in cheap hats and feathers. Shop assistants and neat, bare-headed work-girls, students picturesquely long-haired and floppily trousered and cravated, and poorly clad models, a whole army of nondescripts, heaven knows with what means of livelihood, all dancing, drinking, eating, laughing, jesting, smoking, primitively love-making, moving, shouting, a phantasmagoria of souls making merry beyond the pale of reputable life; such were the frequenters of the Bal Jasmin. Gas flared in two concentric circles of flame around the hall and around the central bandstand. There was no ventilation. The *bal* sweltered in perspiration. Hollow-voiced abjects hawked penny paper fans between the dances, and the whole room was a-flutter.

Blanquette, who had forgotten tragedy for the time, sat with me at a table by the balustrade and alternately sipped her syrup and water and looked, full of interest, at the scene below, now and then clutching my arm to direct my attention to startling personalities. The light in her eyes and the colour in her coarse cheeks made her almost pretty. You have never seen ugliness in a happy face. And Blanquette was happy.

"Don't you want to go and dance with any other *petite femme?*" she asked generously. "I will wait for you here."

I declined with equal magnanimity to leave her alone.

"Suppose some rapscallion came up and asked you to dance?"

157

"I can take care of myself, *mon petit* Asticot," she laughed, bracing her strong arms. "And suppose I wanted to go off with him? They are amusing sometimes, people like that. There is one. *Regarde-moi ce type-là.*"

The "*type*" in question was a fox-faced young man, unwashed and collarless, wearing the peaked cap of Paris villainy. He crossed the hall accompanied by two of the brazenest hussies that ever emerged from the shadow of the fortifications. As they passed the sergent de ville they all cocked themselves up with an air of braggadocio.

"He makes me shiver," said I. Blanquette shrugged her shoulders.

"One must have all sorts of people in the world, as there are so many things to make people different. It is only a chance that I have not become like those girls. It's no one's fault."

"'There, but by the grace of God, goes John Bunyan,'" I quoted reflectively. "You are developing philosophy, Blanquette *chérie*, and your gentle toleration of the infamous does you credit. But only the master would get what wasn't infamous out of them."

The band struck up a waltz. Blanquette drank her syrup quickly and rose.

"Come and dance."

We descended and soon were swept along in the whirl of ragamuffin, ill-conditioned couples dancing every step in the tradition of Paris. Steering was no easy matter. After a while, we were hemmed in near the side of the hall, and were just on the point of emerging from the crush when the sound of a voice brought us to a dead stop which caused us to be knocked about like a pair of footballs.

"My good Monsieur Bubu le Vainqueur, you do me infinite honour, but until I have devoured the proceeds of my last crime I lead a life of elegant leisure."

We escaped from danger and reaching the side stood and looked at each other in stupefaction. Blanquette was the first to see him. She seized my arm and pointed.

"It is he! *Sainte Vierge*, it is he!"

It was he. He was sitting at a table a few yards off, and his companions were the fox-faced youth and the two girls over whom Blanquette had philosophised. He wore his silk hat. Brandy was in front of him. He seemed to be on familiar terms with his friends. For a long time we watched him, fascinated, not daring to accost him and yet unwilling to edge away out of his sight and make our escape from the ball. I saw that he was incredibly dirty. His beard of some days growth gave him a peculiarly grim appearance. His hat had rolled in the mud and was everything a silk hat ought not to be. His linen was black. Never had the garb of respectability been so battered into the vesture of disrepute.

Suddenly he caught sight of us. He hesitated for a moment; then waved us a bland, unashamed salutation. We went up the nearest steps to the gallery and

158

waited. After a polite leave-taking he bowed to his companions, and reeled towards us. I knew by the familiar gait that he had had many cognacs and absinthes during the day.

But what in the name of sanity was he doing here?

"*Mon dieu, mon dieu, qu'est-ce qu'il fait ici?*" asked Blanquette.

I shook my head. It was stupefying.

"*Eh bien, mes enfants*, you have come to amuse yourselves, eh? I too, in the company of my excellent friend Bubu le Vainqueur, whose acquaintance together with that of his fair companions I would not advise you to cultivate."

"But Master," I gasped, "what has happened?"

"I'll veil it, my son," said he, laying his hand on my shoulder, "in the decent obscurity of a learned language, '*Canis reversus ad suum vomitum et sus lota in volutabro luti.*'"

"*Oh, mon Dieu,*" sighed Blanquette again, as if it were something too appalling.

"But why, Master?" I entreated.

"Why wallow? Why not? And now, my little Blanquette, we will all go home and you shall make me some good coffee. Or do you want to stay longer and dance with Asticot?"

"Oh, let us go away, Master," said Blanquette, casting a scared glance at Bubu le Vainqueur, who was watching us with an interested air.

"*Allons,*" said Paragot, blandly.

The dance stopped, and the thirsty crowd surged to the gallery. We threaded our way towards the door, and I thought with burning cheeks that the eyes of the whole assembly were turned to my master's mud-caked silk hat. It was a relief to escape from the noise and gas-light of the *bal*, which had suddenly lost its glamour, into the cool and quiet street. After we had walked a few yards in silence, he hooked his arms in Blanquette's and mine, and broke into a loud laugh.

"But it is astonishing, the age of you children! You might be fifty, each of you, and I your little boy whom you had discovered in an act of naughtiness and were bringing home! Really are you as displeased with me *à ce point-là? C'est épatant!* But laugh, my little Blanquette, are you not glad to see me?"

"But yes, Master," said Blanquette. "It is like a dream."

"And you, Asticot of my heart?"

"I find it a dream too. I can't understand. When did you leave Melford?"

"About five days ago. I would tell you the day of the week, if I had the habit of exactness."

"And Madame de Verneuil?"

"Is very well, thank you."

After this rebuff I asked no more questions. I remarked that the weather was still cold. Paragot laughed again.

"He has turned into a nice little bourgeois, hasn't he, Blanquette? He knows how to make polite conversation. He is tidy in his habits in the Rue des Saladiers, eh? He does not spit on the floor or spill absinthe over the counterpane. *Ah! je suis un vieux salaud, hein?* Don't say no. And Narcisse?"

"It is he who will be contented to see you," cried Blanquette. "And so are we all. *Ah oui, en effet, je suis contente!*" She heaved a great sigh as though she had awakened from the night-mare of seeing herself a dripping corpse in the Morgue. "It is no longer the same thing when you are not in the house. Truly I am happy, Master. You can't understand."

There was a little throb in her voice which Paragot seemed to notice, for as he bent down to her, his grip of my arm relaxed, and, I suppose, his grip of hers tightened.

"It gives you such pleasure that I come back, my little Blanquette?" he said tenderly.

I craned my head forward and saw her raise her faithful eyes to his and smile, as she pronounced her eternal "*Oui, Maître.*"

"It is only Asticot who does not welcome the prodigal father."

I protested. He laughed away my protestations. Then suddenly he stopped and drew a long breath, and gazed at the tall houses whose lines cut the frosty sky into a straight strip.

"Ah! how good it smells. How good it is to be in Paris again!"

The door of a *marchand de vin* swung open just by our noses to give exit to a reveller, and the hot poisoned air streamed forth.

"And how good it is, the smell of alcohols. I could kiss the honest sot who has just reeled out and is skating across the road. *A bas les bourgeois!*"

He did not carry out his unpleasing desire, but when we reached the salon in the Rue des Saladiers, and we had lit the lamp, he kissed Blanquette on both cheeks, still crying out how good it was to be back. Narcisse, mad with delight, capered about him and barked his rapture. He did not in the least mind a master lapsed from grace.

Paragot threw himself on a chair, his hat still on his head. Oh, how dirty, dilapidated and unshaven he was! I felt too miserable with apprehension to emulate Narcisse's enthusiasm. It was cold. I opened the door of the stove to let the glowing heat come out into the room. Blanquette went to the kitchen to prepare the coffee.

Suddenly Paragot leaped to his feet, cast his silk hat on the floor and stamped it into a pancake. Then he thrust it into the stove and shut the door.

"*Voilà!*" he cried.

Before I could interfere he had taken off his frock-coat and holding one skirt in his hands and securing the other with his foot had ripped it from waist to neck. He was going to burn this also, when I stopped him.

"*Laisse-moi!*" said he impatiently.

"It will make such a horrid smell, Master," said I.

He threw the garment across the room with a laugh.

"It is true." He stretched himself and waved his arms. "Ah, now I am better. Now I am Paragot. Berzélius Nibbidard Paragot, again. Now I am free from the forms and symbols. Yes, my son. That hat has been to me Luke's iron crown. That coat has been the *peine forte et dure* crushing my infinite soul into my liver." He tore off his black tie and hurled it away from him. "This has been strangling every noble inspiration. I have been swathed in mummy bands of convention. I have been dead. I have come to life. My lungs are full. My soul regains its limitless horizons. My swollen tongue is cool, and *nom de Dieu de nom de Dieu*, I can talk again!"

He walked up and down the little salon vociferating his freedom, and kicking the remains of the frock-coat before him. With one of his sudden impulses he picked it up and threw it out of a quickly opened window.

"The sight of it offended me," he explained.

"Master," said I, "where are your other things?"

"What other things?"

"Your luggage—your great coat—your umbrella."

"Why, at Melford," said he with an air of surprise. "Where else should they be?"

I had thought that no action of Paragot could astonish me. I was wrong. I stared at him as stupefied as ever.

"Usually people travel with their luggage," said I, foolishly.

"They are usual people, my son. I am not one of them. It came to a point when I must either expire or go. I decided not to expire. These things are done all in a flash. I was walking in the garden. It was last Sunday afternoon—I remember now: a sodden November day. Imagine a sodden November Sunday afternoon English country-town garden. Joanna was at a children's service. Ah, *mon Dieu!* The desolation of that Sunday afternoon! The *death*, my son, that was in the air! Ah! I choked, I struggled. The garden-wall, the leaden sky closed in upon me. I walked out. I came back to Paris."

"Just like that?" I murmured.

"Just like that," said he. "You may have noticed, my son, that I am a man of swift decisions and prompt action. I walked to the Railway Station. A providential London train was expected in five minutes. I took it. *Voilà.*"

"Did you stay long in London?" I asked by way of saying something; for he began to pace up and down the room.

"Did I see anything worth seeing at the theatres? And did I have a good crossing? My little Asticot, I perceive you have become an adept at conventional conversation. If you can't say something original I shall go back to Bubu le Vainqueur, whose society for the last three days has afforded me infinite delectation. Although his views of life may be what Melford would call depraved, at any rate they are first-hand. He does not waste his time in futile politeness." Suddenly he paused, and seized me by the shoulder and shook me, as he had often done before. "Creep out of that shell of gentility, you little hermit-crab," he cried, "and tell me how you would like to live in Melford for the rest of your natural life."

"I shouldn't like it at all," said I.

"Then, how do you expect me to have liked it?"

Blanquette entered with the great white coffee jug and some thick cups and set the tray on the oilskin-covered table. Seeing Paragot in his grubby shirt-sleeves, she looked around, with her housewifely instinct of tidiness, for the discarded garments.

"Where are—"

"Gone," he shouted, waving his arms. "Cast into the flames, and rent in twain, and scattered to the winds of Heaven."

He laughed, seeing that she did not understand, and poured out a jorum of coffee.

"The farcical comedy is over, Blanquette," said he gently, "I'm a *Monsieur* no longer, do you see? We are going to live just as we did before you went away in the summer, and I am not going to be married. I am going to live with my little Blanquette for ever and ever *in sæculo sæculorum, amen.*"

She turned as white as the coffee jug. I thought she was about to faint and caught her in my arms. She did not faint, but burying her head against my shoulder burst into a passion of tears.

"What the devil's the matter?" asked Paragot. "Are you sorry I'm not going to be married?"

"*Mais non, mais non!*" Blanquette sobbed out vehemently.

"I think she's rather glad, Master," said I.

He put down his coffee-cup, and laid his hands on her as if to draw her comfortingly away from me.

"My dear child—" he began.

162

But she shrank back. "*Ah non, laissez-moi,*" she cried, and bolted from the room.

Paragot looked at me inquiringly, and shrugged his shoulders.

"The eternal feminine, I suppose. Blanquette like the rest of them."

"It's odd you haven't noticed it before, Master."

"Noticed what?"

I lit a cigarette.

"The eternal feminine in Blanquette," I answered.

"What the deuce do you mean?"

"She was jealous even of my friendship with Madame de Verneuil," said I diplomatically, realising that I was on the point of betraying Blanquette's confidences.

"It never struck me that she was jealous," he remarked simply.

He took his coffee-cup to the rickety sofa and sat down with the sigh of a tired man. I took mine to the chair by the stove, and we drank silently. I have never felt so hopelessly miserable in my life as I did that night. I was old enough, or perhaps rather I had gathered experience enough, to feel a shock of disgust at Paragot's return *in volutabro luti*. In what sordid den had he found shelter these last days of reaction? I shuddered, and loving him I hated myself for shuddering. Yet I understood. He was a man of extremes. Having fled from the intolerable virtues of Melford, with the nostalgia of the vagabond life devouring him like a flame, he could not have been expected to return tamely to the Rue des Saladiers. He had plunged head foremost into the depths. But Bubu le Vainqueur! The Latin Quarter was not exactly a Sunday School; very probably it flirted with Bubu's lady companions; but between Bubu and itself it raised an impassable barrier.

The idyll too was over. He had left my dear lady Joanna without drum or trumpet. As my destiny hung with his, I should never behold her adored face again. All the graciousness seemed suddenly to be swept out of my life. I pictured her forsaken, heartbroken, for the second time, weeping bitterly over this repetition of history, and including me in her indictment of my master. At nineteen we are all presumptuous egotists: if I mixed pity for myself with sorrow for Joanna and dismay for my master, I am not too greatly to be blamed. The best emotions of older, wiser and better men than I are often blends of queer elements.

The romance was dead. There was no more Joanna. I broke down and shed tears into my coffee-cup.

Paragot snored.

CHAPTER XXII

I SPENT the night on the sofa, as the only bed in the establishment belonged to Paragot. The next morning I took my scanty belongings to my old attic, which fortunately happened to be unlet, and left my master in undisturbed possession of his apartment. In the evening, calling to make polite inquiries as to his health, I found him still in bed looking grimier and bristlier than the night before.

"My son," said he, "the bread of liberty is sweet, but when you are starving you should not over-eat yourself. An old French writer says:

'*Après le plaisir vient la peine, Après la peine la vertu.*'

I've had the pain that follows pleasure, but whether I shall attain the consequential virtue I don't know. For the present, however, I am condemned to it against my will."

"How so?" I asked.

"I have a great desire to rise and seek the Nepenthe of the Café Delphine, but a whimsical fate keeps me coatless and hatless in a virtuous house. I am also comparatively shirtless, which does not so much matter."

"I'm afraid my things wouldn't fit you, Master," said I sitting on the edge of the bed.

"The only coat which the good Blanquette has preserved is the pearl-buttoned velveteen jacket in which I fiddled away so many happy hours."

"Why not wear it, until your bag arrives from Melford?"

"In Arcadian villages," he replied, "it commanded respect. In the Café Delphine I'm afraid it would only excite derision."

Presently a strong odour of onions gave promise of an approaching meal, and a little while afterwards Blanquette entered with the announcement that soup was on the table. Paragot rose, donned trousers and slippers and went forth into the salon to dine.

"Simplicity is one of the canons of high art. Life is an art, as I have endeavoured to teach you. Therefore in life we should aim at simplicity. To complicate existence into the intricacy of a steam-engine with white ties and red socks is an offence against art of which I will never again be guilty. It is also more comfortable to eat soup with your elbows on the table. *N'est-ce pas*, Blanquette?"

"*Bien sûr*," she replied, bending over her bowl, "where else could one put them?"

This pleased Paragot, who continued to talk in high good humour during the rest of the meal. Afterwards, he filled a new porcelain pipe, which Blanquette had purchased, and smoked contentedly the rest of the evening. Blanquette sat dutifully on a straight-backed chair, her hands in her lap, listening as she had so often done before to our inspiring conversation, and adding her word whenever it entered the area of her comprehension. If we had lectured each other alternately on the Integral Calculus, Blanquette would have given us her rapt and happy attention. This evening she would not have minded our talking English; the mere sound of the Master's voice was sweet: sweeter than ever, now that the other woman had been "planted there" (she thought of it with a fierce joy), and the master had come back to her for ever and ever, *in sæculo sæculorum, amen*. Like many peasant women of strong nature, she had the terrible passion of possession. In her soul she would rather have had the most degraded of Paragots in her arms, as her own unalienable property, than have seen him honourable and prosperous in the arms of another. Had she been of a nervous and emotional temperament there might have been tragedy in the Rue des Saladiers, and the newspapers of Paris might have chronicled yet another *crime passionnel* and the appearance of Blanquette before a weeping jury. But the days of tragedy were over. Paragot thundered invectives against insincerity in Art (we were discussing my famous mythological picture still on the easel at Menilmontant) and Blanquette beamed approval. She remarked, referring to my picture, that she didn't like so many unclad ladies. It was not decent. Besides, if they lay in the grass like that, they would catch cold.

"And they have no pocket-handkerchiefs to blow their noses," cried Paragot.

Whereat Blanquette's sense of humour being tickled she screamed with laughter. Narcisse sprang from sleep and barked, and there reigned great happiness, in which even I, still reproachful of my master, had my share.

"What a thing it is to be at home!" observed Paragot.

I had never heard him utter so domestic a sentiment.

"'After pleasure follows pain and after pain comes virtue.' This is virtue with a vengeance," I reflected cynically.

"*Bien sûr*," was Blanquette's inevitable response.

When she bade us good night, Paragot drew her down and kissed her cheek, which was an unprecedented mark of domesticity. Blanquette turned brick-red, and I suppose her foolish heart beat wildly. I have known my own heart to beat wildly for far less, and I am not a woman; but I have been in love.

"It is because you belong to me, my little Blanquette, and I am among mine own people. We understand one another, don't we? *Et tout comprendre c'est tout pardonner*."

When she had gone he smoked reflectively for a few moments.

"I never realised till now," said he, "the sense of stability and comfort that Blanquette affords me. She is unchangeable. God has given her a sense whereby she has pierced to the innermost thing that is I, and externals don't matter. She has got nearer the true Paragot than you, my son, although I know you love me."

"What is the true Paragot, Master?" I asked.

"There are only two that know it—Blanquette and the *bon Dieu*. I don't."

"I only know," said I, "that I owe my life to you and that I love you more than any one else in the world."

"Even more than Mme. de Verneuil?" he asked with a smile.

I blushed. "She is different," said I.

"Quite different," he assented, after a long pause. "My son," he added, "it is right that you should know why the end came. One generally keeps these things to oneself—but I see you are blaming me, and a barrier may grow up between us which we should both regret. You think I have treated your dear lady most cruelly?"

"I can't judge you, Master," said I, terribly embarrassed.

"But you do," said he.

Paragot was in one of his rare gentle moods. He spoke softly, without a trace of reproach or irony. He spoke, too, lying pipe in mouth on the old rep sofa, instead of walking about the room. He told me his story. Need I repeat it?

They had escaped a life-long misery, but on the other hand they had lost a life-long dream. She was still in his eyes all that is beautiful and exquisite in woman; but she was not the woman that Berzélius Nibbidard Paragot could love. The twain had been romantic, walking in the Valley of Illusion, wilfully blinding their eyes to the irony of Things Real. Love had flown far from them during the silent years and they had mistaken the afterglow of his wings for the living radiance. They had begun to realise the desolate truth. They read it in each other's eyes. She had been too loyal to speak. She would have married him, hoping as a woman hopes, against hope. Paragot, whose soul revolted from pretence, preferring real mire to sham down, fled from the piteous tragedy.

He might have retired more conventionally. He might have had a dismal explanatory interview with Joanna, and ordered a fly to convey himself and his luggage to the Railway Station the next morning. Perhaps if Joanna had found him in the November Sunday afternoon garden this might have occurred. But Joanna did not find him. His temperament found him instead; and when you have a temperament like Paragot's, it plays the very deuce with convention. It drew him out of the garden, across the Channel and into the society of Bubu le Vainqueur. But, all the same, in the essential act of leavingMelford, Paragot behaved like the man of fine honour I shall always maintain him to be.

How many men of speckless reputation, though feeling the pinch of poverty, would not have married Joanna for the great wealth her husband left behind? Answer me that.

I know that Joanna wept bitterly over her lost romance. But she has owned to me that the words written on a scrap of paper by Paragot and posted from London were tragically true:

"My dear. It is only the shadows of our past selves that love. You and I are strangers to each other. To continue this sweet pretence of love is a mockery of the Holiest. God bless you. Gaston."

"If you love a Dream Woman," said Paragot, "let her stay the divine Woman of the Dream. To awaken and clasp flesh and blood, no matter how delicately tender, and find that love has sped at the dawn is a misery too deep for tears."

And Paragot, lying unshaven, unwashed, in grimy shirt and trousers, smoked silently and stared into a future in which the dear sweet Dream Woman with "the little feet so adored" would never, never again have a place.

"If I had a coat to my back," said he, after nearly half an hour's silence, "I verily believe I would go to the Pont Neuf and talk to Henri Quatre."

Le Fou Rire had given me a commission for a front page in colours; and I was deep in the disreputable task on the following evening when Paragot appeared in my attic. He wore a jacket, his bag having arrived from Melford.

"My soul hungers," said he, "for the Café Delphine, and my throat thirsts for sociable alcohol. If you can cease the prostitution of your art to a salacious public for an hour or two, I shall be very glad of your company."

"I think it's rather good," said I complacently, regarding the drawing with head bent sideways. "It's an old theme, but it's up to date. At Janot's they would say it was palpitating with modernity."

"That's what makes it vile," said Paragot.

We were thrown into immediate argument. One of the flying art notions of the hour was to revive the old subjects which contained the eternal essentials of life and present them in "palpitatingly modern" form. I eloquently developed my thesis. We were sick to death, for instance, of the quasi-scriptural Prodigal Son, sitting half-naked in a desert beside a swine trough. Was it not more "palpitating" to set the prodigal in modern Paris?

"Your moderns can't palpitate with dignity, my son," replied Paragot. "Take Susannah and the Elders. Classically treated the subject might yet produce one of the greatest pictures of all time. Translate it into the grocer's wife and the two churchwardens and you cannot escape from bestial vulgarity."

Conscious of the wide horizon of extreme youth, I sighed at my master's narrowness. He was hopelessly behind the times. I dropped the argument and hunted for my cap.

We found the Café Delphine fairly full. Madame Boin, whom the past few months had provided with a few more rolls of fat round her neck, gave a little gasp as she caught sight of Paragot, and held out her hand over the counter.

"Is it really you, Monsieur Paragot? One sees you no more. How is that? But it is charming. Ah? You have been *en voyage?* In England? *On dit que c'est beau là-bas.* And where will you sit? Your place is taken. It is Monsieur Papillard, the poet, who has sat there for a month. We will find another table. There is one that is free."

She pointed to a draughty, unconsidered table by the door. Paragot looked at it, then at Madame Boin and then at his own private and particular table usurped by Monsieur Papillard and his associates, and swore a stupefied oath of considerable complication. A weird, pug-nosed, pig-eyed, creature with a goatee beard scarce masking a receding chin, sat in the sacred seat against the wall. His hat and cloak were hung on Paragot's peg. He was reading a poem to half a dozen youths who seemed all to be drinking *mazagrans*, or coffee in long glasses. They combined an air of intellectual intensity with one of lyrical enthusiasm, like little owls pretending to be larks. Not one of the old set was there to smile a welcome.

We stood by the counter listening to the poem. When Monsieur Papillard had ended, the youths broke into applause.

"*C'est superbe!*"

"*Un chef d'œuvre, cher maître.*"

They called the pug-nosed creature, *cher maître!*

"It is demented idiocy," murmured my astounded master.

At that moment entered Félicien Garbure, a down-at-heel elderly man, who had been wont to sit at Paragot's table. He was one of those parasitic personages not unknown in the *Quartier*, who contrived to attach themselves to the special circle of a café, and to drink as much as possible at other people's expense. His education and intelligence would have disgraced a Paris cabman, but an ironical Providence had invested him with an air of wisdom which gave to his flattery the value of profound criticism.

This sycophant greeted us with effusion. Where had we been? Why had the delightful band been dispersed? Did we know Monsieur Papillard, the great poet? Before we could reply he approached the chair.

"*Cher maître*, permit me to present to you my friends Monsieur Berzélius Paragot and Monsieur Asticot."

"*Enchanté, Messieurs*," said the great poet urbanely.

We likewise avowed our enchantment, and Paragot swore beneath his breath. The waiter—no longer Hercule, who had been dismissed for petty thievery some time before—but a new waiter who did not know Paragot—set us chairs at the end of the table far away from the great man. We ordered drinks. Paragot emptied his glass in an absent-minded manner, still under the shock of his downfall. But a few short months ago he had ruled in this place as king. Now he was patronizingly presented to the snub-nosed, idiot usurper by Félicien Garbure. *His* friend, Berzélius Paragot! *Nom de Dieu!* And he was assigned a humble place below the salt. Verily the world was upside down.

"Give me another *grog*," said Paragot, "a double one."

The poet read another poem. It was something about topazes and serpents and the twilight and the pink palms of a negress. More I could not gather. The company hailed it as another masterpiece. Félicien Garbure called it a supreme effort of genius. A young man beside Paragot vaunted its witchery of suggestion.

"It is absolute nonsense," cried my master.

"But it is symbolism, Monsieur," replied the young man in a tone of indulgent pity.

"What does it mean?"

The young man—he was very kind—smiled and shrugged his shoulders politely.

"What in common speech is the meaning of one of Bach's fugues or Claude Monet's effects of sunlight? One cannot say. They appeal direct to the soul. So does a subtle harmony of words, using words as notes of music, or pigments, what you will, arranged by the magic of a master. These things are transcendental, Monsieur."

"*Saperlipopette!*" breathed Paragot. "My little Asticot," he whispered to me, "have I really come to this, to sit at the feet of an acting pro-sub-vice-deputy infant Gamaliel and be taught the elements of symbolic poetry?"

"But Master," said I, somewhat captivated by the balderdash, "there is, after all, colour in words. Don't you remember how delighted you were with the name of a little town we passed through on our way to Orléans—Romorantin? You were haunted by it and said it was like the purple note of an organ."

"Which shews you my son that I was aware of the jargon of symbolism before these goslings were hatched," he replied.

He drained his tumbler, called the waiter and paid the reckoning.

"Let us go to Père Louviot's in the Halles where we can meet some real men and women."

We went, and the Café Delphine knew Paragot no more.

After this he took to frequenting indiscriminately the various cafés of the neighbourhood, wandering from one to the other like a lost soul seeking a habitation. Now and again he hit upon fragments of the old band, who had migrated from the Café Delphine when it became the home of the symbolic poets.

169

He tried in vain to collect the fragments together in a new hostelry. But the cohesive force had gone. These queer circles of the Latin Quarter are organisms of spontaneous growth. You cannot create them artificially or re-create them when once they are disintegrated. The twos and threes of students received him kindly and listened to his talk; but his authority was gone. Once or twice when I accompanied him I fancied that he had lost also the peculiar magic of his vehement utterances. Cazalet also noticed a change.

"What is the matter with Paragot? He no longer talks. He preaches. *Ça ennuie à la fin.*"

Paragot a bore! It was unimaginable.

Was he paying the penalty of his past respectability? Had Melford repressed his noble rage and frozen the genial current of his soul? It is not unlikely. He often found himself condemned to solitary toping over a stained newspaper, one of the most ungleeful joys known to man. Sometimes he played dominoes with Félicien Garbure, now icily received by the symbolists on account of an unpaid score. Whether desperation drove him occasionally to Bubu le Vainqueur and his friends I do not know. He was not really proud of his acquaintance with Bubu. Once he whimsically remarked that as he was half way between Gaston de Nérac and Berzélius Paragot, and therefore neither fish nor fowl, he could not find an appropriate hole in Paris. But when his hair and his beard and his finger nails had attained their old luxuriance of growth, and he was in every way Paragot again, the desired haven remained still unfindable. There were taverns without number and drink in oceans, and the life of Paris surged up and down the Boulevards as stimulating as ever: but the heart of Paragot cried out for something different. He took the old violin from its dirty case and spent hours in the Rue des Saladiers trying to fiddle the divine despair out of his system. Sometimes he would call upon Blanquette to accompany him on her almost forgotten zither.

One day he was with me at the Café opposite Janot's, when two or three of the studio came in and sat at our table. There was the usual eager talk. The subject, the new impressionism.

"But to understand it, you must be in the movement," cried Fougère, not dreaming of discourtesy.

But Paragot took the saying to heart.

"I see it now," said he afterwards. "I am no longer in the movement. You young men have passed me by. I am left stranded. You may ask why I don't seek the company of my own contemporaries? Who are they that know me, save worthless rags like Félicien Garbure? Stranded, my son. I have had my day."

After that he refused to talk at such social gatherings as chance afforded, and moodily listened, while he consumed profitless alcohol. Then he began to frequent the low-life cafés of the Halles. When he had nearly poisoned himself with vile absinthe and sickened himself with the conversation of fishwives, he sent for me in despair.

I found him half-dressed walking up and down the salon. He looked very ill.

"I am going to leave Paris to-day," he began, as soon as I entered. "It is a city of Dead Sea apples. It has no place for me, save the sewer. I don't like the sewer. I am going away. I shall never come back to Paris again."

"But where are you going, Master?" I asked in some surprise.

He did not know. He would pack his bundle and flee like Christian from the accursed city. Like Christian he would go on a Pilgrim's Progress. He would seek sweet pure things. He would go forth and work in the fields. The old life had come to an end. The sow had been mistaken. It could not return to its wallowing in the mire. Wallowing was disgustful. Was ever man in such a position? The vagabond life had made the conventions of civilisation impossible. The contact with convention and clean English ways had killed his zest for the old order of which only the mud remained. There was nothing for it but to leave Paris.

He poured out his heart to me in a torrent of excited words, here and there none too coherent. He must work. He had lost the great art by which he was to cover Europe with palaces. That was no longer.

"My God!" said he stopping short. "The true knowledge of it has only come to me lately. I was living in a Fool's Paradise. I could never have designed a building. I should have lived on her bounty. Thank God I was saved the shame of it."

He went on. Again he repeated his intention of leaving Paris. I must look after Blanquette for the present. He must go and dree his weird alone.

"And yet, my little Asticot, it is the dreadful loneliness that frightens me. Once I had a dream. It sufficed me. But now my soul is empty. A man needs a woman in his life, even a Dream Woman. But for me, *ni-ni, c'est fini.* There is not a woman in the wide world who would look at me now."

"Master," said I, "if you are going to settle down in the country, why don't you marry Blanquette?"

"Marry Blanquette! Marry——"

He regarded me in simple, undisguised amazement which took his breath away. He passed his hand through his hair and sat on the nearest seat.

"*Nom de Dieu!*" said he, "I never thought of it!"

Then he leaped up and caught me in the old way by the shoulders, and cried in French, as he did in moments of great excitement:

"But it's colossal, that idea! It is the solution of everything. And I never thought of it though it has been staring me in the face. Why I love her, our little Blanquette. I have loved her all the time without knowing it as the good Monsieur

Jourdain spoke prose. *Sacré nom d'un petit bonhomme!* Why didn't you tell me before, confounded little animal that you are?"

He swung me with a laugh, to the other side of the room, and waved his arms grotesquely, as he continued his dithyrambic eulogy of the colossal idea. I have never seen two minutes produce a greater change in a human countenance. Ten years fell from it. He looked even younger than when he had broken his fiddle over Mr. Pogson's head and received the inspiration of our vagabondage. His blue eyes cleared, and in them shone the miraculous light of laughter.

"But it was written, my son Asticot. It was preordained. She is the one woman in the world to whom I need not pretend to be other than I am. She is real, *nom de Dieu!* What she says is Blanquette, what she does is Blanquette, and her sayings and doings would grace the greatest Queen in Christendom. But, have you thought of it? I have come indeed to the end of my journey. I started out to find Truth, the Reality of Things. I have found it. I have found it, my son. It is a woman, strong and steadfast, who looks into your eyes; who can help a man to accomplish his destiny. And the destiny of man is to work, and to beget strong children. And his reward is to have the light in the wife's eyes and the welcome of a child's voice as he crosses the threshold of his house. And it cleanses a man. But Blanquette——" he smote his forehead, and burst into excited laughter. "Why did it not enter into this idiot head before?"

The laughter ceased all of a sudden, and at least three years returned to his face.

"It takes two parties to make a marriage," said he in a chastened tone. "Blanquette is young. I am not. She may be thinking of a future quite different. It is all very well to say I will marry Blanquette, but will Blanquette marry me?"

"Master," said I, feeling a person of elderly experience, "it was entirely on your account that Blanquette refused the *quincaillier* at the corner of the street."

I had learned from her the day before that the superior hardware merchant had recently made her a ceremonious offer of marriage.

"A sense of duty, perhaps," said Paragot.

I laughed at his seriousness.

"But, Master, she has been eating her heart out for you since the wedding at Chambéry."

"Asticot," said he, planting himself in front of me, "are you jesting or speaking what you know to be the truth?"

"The absolute truth."

"And you never told me? You knew that a real woman loved me, and you let me chase a will-o'-the-wisp with gloves and an umbrella? Truly a man's foes are of his own household."

"But, Master——" I began.

He laughed at the sight of my dejected face.

"No, you were loyal, my son. The man who gives away a woman's confidence, even when she avows the poisoning of her husband and the strangulation of her babes, is a transpontine villain."

He took up his porcelain pipe and filled it from the blue packet of caporal that lay on the table with the oilskin cover. He struck a match and was about to apply it to the bowl, when one of his sudden ideas caused him to blow out the match and lay down the pipe. Then with his old lightning swiftness he strode to the door and flung it open.

"Blanquette! Blanquette!" he cried.

"*Oui, maître,*" came from the kitchen, and in a moment Blanquette entered the room.

He took her by the hand and led her to the centre, while she regarded him somewhat mystified. With his heels together, he made her a correct bow.

"Blanquette," said he, "in the presence of Asticot as witness I ask you to do me the honour to become my wife."

It was magnificent; it was what Paragot would have called *vieille école;* but it was not tactful. It was half an hour before Blanquette fully grasped the situation.

CHAPTER XXIII

JOANNA married Major Walters, as soon as the conventionalities would permit.

She wrote then, for the first time, to Paragot.

"I bear you no malice, my dear Gaston, and I am sure you bear me none. Your breaking off of our engagement was the only way out of a fantastic situation. You might have broken it less abruptly; but you were always sudden. If I may believe Asticot, your own marriage was a lightning incident. I can laugh now, and so I suppose can your wife; but believe me this sort of thing does leave a woman rather breathless.

"Wish me happiness, as I wish you. If ever we meet it will be as loyal friends."

Could woman have spoken more sweetly?

"My dear Joanna," replied Paragot, "I do wish you all the happiness in the world. You can't fail to have it. You have a real husband as I have a real wife. Let us thank heaven we have escaped from the moon vapour of the Ideal, in which we poor humans are apt to lose our way and stray God knows whither. I am sending you a real marriage gift."

"My dear Asticot," wrote Joanna from an hotel in Florence, "what do you think your delightful but absurd master has sent me as a wedding present? It arrived here this morning, to the consternation of the whole hotel. A crate containing six live ducks. The label stated that they were real ducks fed by his own hand.

"But what am I to do with six live ducks on a wedding journey, my dear Asticot? I can't sell them. I hate the idea of eating them—and even if I didn't, Major Walters and I can't eat six. And I can't put blue ribbons round their necks, and carry them about with me on my travels as pets. Can't you see me walking over the Ponte Vecchio followed by them as by a string of poodles? And they are so voracious. The hotel people are already charging them full pension terms. Oh, dear! Do tell me what I am to do with these dreadful fowl!"

"My dearest Lady," I answered. "Offer the ducks like the Dunmow flitch of bacon to the most happily married couple in Florence."

Whether Joanna acted on my brilliant suggestion I cannot say. A little while ago I enquired after their ultimate destiny; but Joanna had forgotten. I believe Major Walters and herself fled from them secretly.

Paragot on his label stated that he had fed the ducks with his own hand. This was practically true; indeed, in the case of those who declined to nourish themselves to the requisite degree of fatness, it was literally true. I have beheld him since perform the astounding operation, a sight *Dis hominibusque;* but not in the Rue des Saladiers. It was on his own farm, the farm near Chartres, which he bought, in his bewildering fashion, as soon as lawyers could prepare the necessary documents. He took train the day after his proposal of marriage to Blanquette, and returned, I remember, somewhat crestfallen, because he could not conclude the purchase then and there.

"My dear sir," said the lawyer whom he consulted, "you can't buy landed property as you can a pound of sugar over a counter."

"Why not?" asked Paragot.

"Because," said the lawyer, "the law of France mercifully concedes to men of my profession the right of gaining a livelihood."

"I see that you are a real lawyer," said Paragot, pleased by the irony, "and it is an amiable Providence that has guided my steps to your *cabinet*."

But Paragot was married, and the little *appartement* in the Rue des Saladiers passed into alien hands, and the newly wedded pair settled down on the farm, long before all the legal formalities of purchase were accomplished. It takes my breath away, even now, to think of the hurry of those days. He decided human destinies in the fraction of a second.

"My son," said he, "when I have paid for this farm, I shall have very little indeed of the capital, on the interest of which we have been living. I am now a married man, with the responsibilities of a wife and a future family. I have put £200 to your credit at the Crédit Lyonnais and that is all your fortune. If art can't support you, when you have spent it, you will have to come to La Haye (the farm) and feed pigs. You'll be richer if you paint them; the piggier they are, and the heavier the gold watch chains across their bellies, the richer you will be; but you'll be happier if you feed them. *Crede experturo*."

I went to bed that night swearing a great oath that I would neither paint pigs nor feed pigs, but that I would prove myself worthy of the generosity of my master and benefactor. I felt then that his goodness was great; but how great it was I only realised in after years when I came to learn his financial position. Bearing in mind the relativity of things, I know that few fathers have sent their sons out into the world with so princely a capital.

Fortune smiled on me; why, I don't know; perhaps because I was small and sandy haired and harmless, and did not worry her. I sold two or three pictures, I obtained regular employment on an illustrated journal, and raised my price for contributions to *Le Fou Rire*. Bread and butter were assured. There was never prouder youth than I, when one August morning I started from Paris for Chartres, with fifty superfluous pounds in my pocket which I determined to restore to Paragot.

The old Paragot of the high roads, hairy and bronzed, and wearing a great straw hat with wide brim turned down, met me at the little local station. He forgot that he was half British and almost hugged me. At last I had come—it was my third

175

visit—at last I had torn myself away from that *sacré* Paris and its flesh-pots and its paint-pots and its artificialities.

"Nothing is real in Paris, whether it be the smile on the painted lady's lips or the dream of the young poet. Here, in the midst of God's fields, there is no pretending, no shamming, no lying, none of your confounded idealism. All is solid, *mon gars*. Solid like that," and he thumped his chest to illustrate the argument.

"Bucéphale, too?" I queried with a laugh, as we fetched up beside the most ancient horse in the Department, drooping between the shafts of a springless cart. Needless to say, Bucéphale had been rechristened in his extreme old age.

"He is a living proof," cried Paragot, "of the solidity *rerum agrestium*. Look at him! Shew me a horse of his age in Paris. The Paris horses, like Youth in the poem, grow pale and spectre thin and die of premature decay. Here, *mon petit*," said he giving a sou to a blue bloused urchin who was restraining the impetuous Bucéphale from a wild gallop over the Eure et Loire, "when you have spent that come to La Haye and I will give you another."

He threw my bag into the cart, and we took our places on the plank that served as a seat.

"*En route*, Bucéphale!" cried Paragot, gathering up the reins. "Observe the kindly manners of the country. If I had addressed him like your Paris cabman with a '*Hue Cocotte!*' it would have wounded his susceptibilities."

Bucéphale started off jog-trot down the straight white road edged with poplars, while Paragot talked, and the sun blazed down upon us from a cobalt sky. All around the fertile plain laughed in the sunshine—a giant, contented laugh, like that of its broad-faced, broad-hipped daughters who greeted Paragot as we raced by at the rate of five miles an hour. Did I ever meet a Paris horse that went this speed? asked Paragot, and I answered him truthfully, "Never."

We stopped in a white-walled, red-roofed village, beside a tiny shop gloriously adorned with a gilt bull's head. The butcher's wife came out. "*Bonjour*, Monsieur Paragot."

"*Bonjour*, Madame Jolivet, have you a nice fatted calf for this young Prodigal from Paris? If you haven't, we can do with four kilos of good beef."

And the result of ten minutes talk was a great lump of raw meat, badly wrapped in newspaper, which Paragot, careless of my Paris clothes, thrust on my knees, while he continued to drive Bucéphale. I dropped the beef into the back of the cart. Paragot shook his head.

"To-morrow, my son, you shall be clothed in humility and shall clean out the cow pen."

"I should prefer to accept your original invitation, Master," said I, "and help with the corn."

For Paragot, besides Bucéphale and cows and ducks and pigs and fowls and a meadow or two, possessed a patch of cornfield of which he was passionately proud. He had sown it himself that spring and now was harvest. He pointed to it with his whip as soon as we came in sight of the farm.

"*My* corn, my little Asticot. It is marvellous, eh? Who says that Berzélius Nibbidard Paragot can't make things grow? I was born to it. *Nom de Dieu* I could make anything grow. I could plant your palette and it would come up a landscape. And *sacré mille cochons*, I have done the most miraculous thing of all. I am the father of a human being, a real live human being, my son. He is small as yet," he added apologetically, "but still he is alive. He has teeth, Asticot. It is the most remarkable thing in this astonishing universe."

The dim form of a woman standing with a child in her arms in front of a group of farm buildings across the fields to the right, gradually grew into the familiar figure of my dear Blanquette. She came down the road to meet us, her broad homely face beaming with gladness and in her eyes a new light of welcome. Narcisse trotted at her heels. The rheumatism of advancing years gave him a distinguished gait.

We sprang from the cart. Bucéphale left to himself regarded the family meeting with a grandfatherly air, until an earth-coloured nondescript emerged from the ground and led him off towards the house. After our embraces, we followed, Paragot dancing the delighted infant, Blanquette with her great motherly arm around my shoulders, and Narcisse soberly sniffing for adventure, after the manner of elderly dogs.

"Do you remember, Asticot?" said Blanquette. "Four of us started for Chambéry. Now five of us come to La Haye. *C'est drôle, hein?*"

"*Tu es contente?*" I asked.

Her arm tightened, and her eyes grew moist.

"*Mais oui,*" she said in a low voice. Then she looked at Paragot and the child, a yard or two in front of us.

"He is the image of his father," she said almost reverentially.

I burst out laughing. Where the likeness lay between the chubby, snub-nosed, eighteen months old baby, and the hairy, battered Paragot, no human eye but Blanquette's could discover. I vowed he resembled a little Japanese idol.

"*Pauvre chéri,*" said Blanquette, motherwise.

The house of Paragot was not a palace. It stood, low and whitewashed, amid a medley of little tumble-down erections, and was guarded on one side by cowsheds and on the other by the haystack. You stepped across the threshold into the kitchen. A door on the right gave access to the bedroom. A ladder connected with a hole in the roof enabled you to reach the cockloft, the guest room of the establishment. That was all. What on earth could man want more? asked Paragot.

The old rep suite, the table with the American cloth, the coloured prints in gilt frames including the portrait of Garibaldi, the cheap deal bookcases holding Paragot's tattered classics, gave the place an air of familiar homeliness. A mattock, a gun and a cradle warred against old associations.

When we entered, the child began to whimper. Perhaps it did not approve of the gun. Like myself he may, in trembling fancy, have heard its owner cry: "I have an inspiration! Let us go out and shoot cows." Paragot found another reason.

"That infant's life is a perpetual rebellion against his name. I chose Triptolème. A beautiful name. If you look at him you see it written all over him. Blanquette was crazy for Thomas. In indignation I swore he should be christened Triptolème Onésime. Blanquette wept. I yielded. 'At least let him be called Didyme,' I pleaded. Didyme! There is something caressing about Didyme. Repeat it. 'Didyme.' But no. Blanquette wept louder. She wept so loud that all the ducks ran in to see whether I was murdering her——"

"It is not true!" protested Blanquette. "How can you say those things? You know they are not true."

"Her state was so terrible," continued my master, "that I sacrificed my son's destiny. Behold Thomas. I too would howl if I had such a name."

"He is hungry," said Blanquette, "and it is a very pretty name. He likes to hear it, *n'est-ce pas, mon petit Tho-Thom chéri?* There! He smiles."

"She is really convinced that he has heard her call him Thomas. Oh, woman!" said Paragot.

That evening, after we had feasted on cabbage-soup and the piece of beef which I had been too stuck-up to dandle on my knees, and clear brown cider, the three of us sat outside the house, in the warm August moonlight. Sinking into an infinitely far horizon stretched the fruitful plain of France, cornland and pasture, and near us the stacked sheaves of Paragot's corn stood quiet and pregnant symbols of the good earth's plenty. Here and there dark patches of orchard dreamed in a haze. Through one distant patch a farmhouse struck a muffled note of grey. On the left the ribbon of road glistened white between the sentinel poplars silhouetted against the sky. The hot smell of the earth filled the air like spice. A thousand elfin sounds, the vibration of leaves, the tiny crackling of cornstalks, the fairy whirr of ground insects, melted into a companionable stillness.

Blanquette half dozed, her head against Paragot's shoulder, as she had done that far-off evening of our return from Chambéry. The smoke from his porcelain pipe curled upwards through the still air. I was near enough to him on the other side, for him to lay his hand on my arm.

"My son," he whispered in English, "I was right when I said I had come to the end of my journey. Eventually I am right in everything. I prophesied that I would make little Augustus Smith a scholar and a gentleman. *Te voilà.* I knew that my long pilgrimage would ultimately lead me to the Inner Shrine. Isn't all this," he waved his pipe in a circular gesture, "the Holy of Holies of the Real? Is there any illusion in the unutterable poetry of the night? Is there anything false in this promise of the fruitful earth? My God! Asticot, I am happy! When the soul laughs tears come into the eyes. I have all that the heart of man can desire—the love of this dear wife of mine—the child asleep within doors—the printed wisdom of the world in a dozen tongues of men, caught up hap-hazard in what I once, in a failing hour, thought was my wildgoose chase after Truth—the pride in you, my little Asticot, the son of my adoption—and the most overpowering sleepiness that ever sat upon mortal eyelid."

He yawned. I protested. It was barely nine o'clock.

"It is bedtime," said Paragot. "We have to get up at five."

"Good Heavens, Master," said I, "why these unearthly hours?"

He laughed and quoted Candide.

"*Il faut cultiver notre jardin.*"

"No," said the drowsy Blanquette at last understanding the conversation, "we have to cut the rest of the corn."

"It's all the same, my dear," said Paragot tenderly. "We were talking philosophy. Philosophy merely means the love of wisdom. And all that the wisdom of all the ages can tell us, is summed up in the last words of one of the wisest books that ever was written: 'We must cultivate our garden.'"

But how my dear erratic master has managed for years and years to cultivate the farm of La Haye and to bring up my godson in the fear of the Lord and the practice of land surveying is a proof that the late Mr. Matthew Arnold was hopelessly wrong in his categorical declaration that miracles do not happen.

THE END

Made in the USA
Columbia, SC
15 April 2019